Kristy-Lu,
Thanks for
in my book!
enjoy it!

WITHOUT A

King

JULIE CÔTÉ

 FriesenPress

Suite 300 - 990 Fort St
Victoria, BC, V8V 3K2
Canada

www.friesenpress.com

Copyright © 2018 by Julie Côté
First Edition — 2018

All rights reserved.

No part of this publication may be reproduced in any form, or by any means, electronic or mechanical, including photocopying, recording, or any information browsing, storage, or retrieval system, without permission in writing from FriesenPress.

ISBN
978-1-5255-2209-3 (Hardcover)
978-1-5255-2210-9 (Paperback)
978-1-5255-2211-6 (eBook)

1. YOUNG ADULT FICTION, FANTASY

Distributed to the trade by The Ingram Book Company

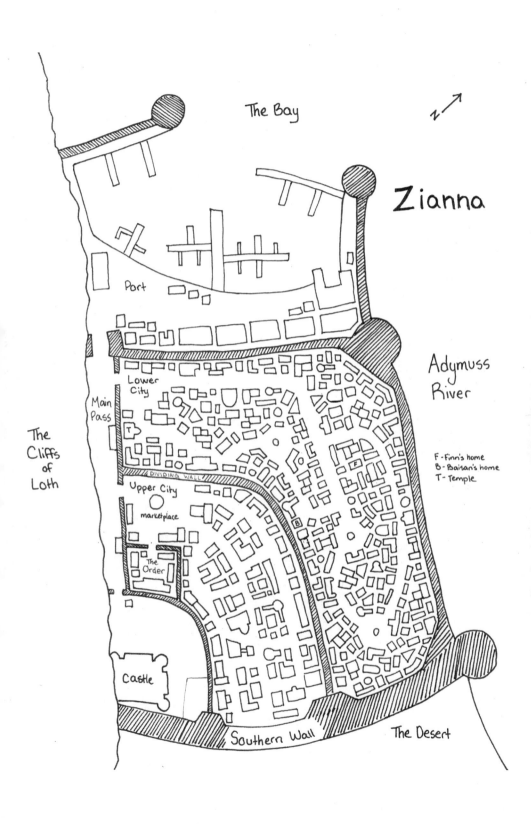

Part One

THE ORDER

CHAPTER
One

The sun was slipping behind the Cliffs of Loth, casting darkness upon the city of Zianna and making it seem much later in the day than it actually was. The citizens called this time the Lothian Dusk, the hours before real dusk settled across the winding streets of the ancient city. It affected the lower city more than the upper, due to narrower streets and the darker stones used to construct the buildings. Foreigners to the city never expected the shadows to arrive so early. They weren't wary of the darkness, as the citizens were. They never saw me coming.

I pressed myself into a thin crevice between two buildings. Holding my breath, I hoped the shadows were dark enough to conceal me as a couple of guards jogged past. I'd just slipped a hefty pouch of coins from a foreign trader. I wanted to pull out the pouch and count my treasure, but I knew better. The guards would be searching the upper city for me, and distracting myself was a poor approach. Instead, I waited until the guards' footsteps faded away before I made my move.

The upper city was a risky place for me, but the appeal of richer targets always lured me over the high wall that separated it from the lower city. I was one of the few of my kind in the city who dared venture its wide streets and smooth walls. The buildings were made of pristine white stone as opposed to the rough, sandy coloured stones I was used to. The walls were smooth and hard to climb. My crevice was no exception, so I had to take the risk and slip out into the street.

Normally, I couldn't even blend in with the people of the upper city. If my clothing didn't give me away, my physical appearance would. Like most of the poorer citizens of Zianna, I was a Native Zian. My skin, hair, and eyes were all darker than those of the fair-skinned people from Teltar, who made up most of the upper class. The Telts had taken over Zianna generations before I was born; the fair upper class was all I had ever known. Being used to them didn't stop me from hating them.

I pulled the hood of my cloak over my head, hoping that it would give me a little protection against the suspicious eyes of the people on the streets. My cloak wasn't quite high class, but I'd stolen it from a middle class trader so it appeared somewhat respectable. I had to make my way to the wall. Once I crossed over it, the guards would have no chance of finding me. The lower city was my domain; I knew every alley, street, and rooftop.

The shadows grew as I made my way through the cobbled streets. Even the streets in the upper city were made of white stone, designed to remain as light as possible in the Lothian Dusk. It wasn't long before I could see the dividing wall looming over the buildings in front of me. All I had to do was slip through the space between two buildings and climb over the top. I was close to freedom when someone caught my eye. I froze, half of me wanting to continue my escape, the other half needing to go after the man.

He acted like a local, but his dress made me think he was a foreigner, or maybe from one of the islands. He was wearing a dark green cloak with sliver embroidery. He was leading a light grey horse instead of riding it, which was unusual for the rich. What really caught my eye was the thick gold ring on his right hand. Jewellery was a favourite of mine. It was usually easy to take—and easy to sell. Merchants all over the lower city would pay good money for it.

I glanced quickly up and down the street. No guards were in sight, so I started trailing behind the strange man and his horse. My moment arrived when he paused in the middle of the street to speak to another man, who had been walking in the opposite direction. I slipped up beside them, using the man's horse to hide me from their view.

"It is good to see you back in Zianna, my friend," the second man was saying.

"It's been a long time," the first man agreed with a friendly nod.

I took my chance and lay my hand on the horse's side. "You've got a nice horse, sir."

The two men turned to me, looking startled. I grinned innocently at them; I was still young enough that that worked. "He's really friendly, sir."

The men exchanged a glance before the first man reached out to stroke the horse's nose. "She," he corrected.

"Oh, sorry, sir," I replied. I knew the two men were watching me, but they were focusing on my hands. With my foot, I carefully nudged one of the horse's legs, causing her to sidestep away from me. I pretended to stumble. The first man reached out to grab my shoulder to steady me. I ran my hand quickly over his as I regained my balance. "Thanks, sir. Sorry 'bout botherin' your horse, sir." I turned and jogged off, resisting the urge to go so fast that I would seem suspicious.

I finally made my way between two buildings and approached the dividing wall. I dropped the ring into a pocket in my cloak before reaching up, grasping a stone in the wall, and starting to haul myself up it. The wall was about three storeys on this side, but four on the lower city side, since Zianna was built on a sloping hill. Reaching the top was easier than going down the other side, but it wasn't long before I was safe within my own beloved lower city with its dirty and shabby buildings. It was perfect for a thief. It was perfect for me.

I walked down the narrow streets in the direction of the Adymuss River, where I lived near the lower city's main street. I didn't have a real home, but like most thieves, I had found a place to call my own. It was the abandoned upper floor of an old apartment building. Usually the lower streets were crowded with poor merchants or other people going about their daily business, but they were starting to empty due to the growing darkness. There was no one around to complain when I used a window ledge to climb up the wall. I slipped through a crack in the roof and entered my home.

It was a simple abode. In one corner, I had a pile of clothing I'd stolen, which is where I tossed my cloak after pulling it over my head. It also served as a mattress. I buried my hands into it, feeling for the wooden chest I knew was there. When my fingers brushed against the wood, I pulled it out. I reached under my shirt to pull out the key I wore on a sliver chain around my neck. The simple lock wasn't much protection, but it was better than nothing. I took the pouch from one of my cloak's pockets and dumped the coins on the floor. Even though the chest was full, I didn't have much money. Every coin was made of copper and only worth one siya—the lowest denomination of money. At my last count, I had about sixty siyas stashed away. I counted my new coins quickly before dropping them into the chest with the rest of my money. Then I turned my attention to the ring.

It was heavy, making it more valuable than I had thought. It had a dark stone embedded in it, which was surrounded by an engraving that I was sure was writing. Although I recognized it, I couldn't read. Once I'd gotten a better look at the ring, I wasn't sure if I wanted to sell it. It couldn't hurt to keep it. I slipped it over my right thumb. I already owned two pieces of jewellery, if the chain I wore my key on counted. The other was a gold bracelet I wore on my left wrist. It was adorned with red and white crystals. I'd kept it because it was from a foreign land and it intrigued me. I decided to add the ring to my collection. I could always sell it later, if the need arose.

My stomach grumbled, interrupting my thoughts. I needed to find some food. I shoved my money chest back under the clothing and replaced the key around my neck. Pulling my cloak back over my head, I stood up and made for the crack in the roof.

THE STREETS WERE MORE DESERTED THAN BEFORE, BUT THE VENDOR'S booths were still out. As I walked past a fruit stand, I casually reached out and grabbed an orange. Nobody noticed. It wasn't the prettiest fruit—those were reserved for the high-class merchants to sell in the marketplace—but it was food and it tasted good. I continued down the street, holding my orange with my left hand while admiring the ring on my right.

"Finn?"

I sighed and turned around. "Arow," I replied. Somehow, I had walked past him without noticing. He was the only threat posed to me in the lower city, because he believed he was in charge of all the thieves. He demanded cuts of our profit. Most of the thieves obliged, just to keep him away from them. I never had. I was more talented than he was, and I could usually avoid confrontation with him if I was paying attention.

"Nice ring," Arow commented. He was leaning against a wall with his arms crossed as he looked down at me. He was easily twice my size, but he didn't scare me. He could kill me with one hand if he wanted to, but he would have to catch me first. He never even got close.

"I agree," I said.

"So where's my cut?" Arow asked.

"What cut?" I started peeling my orange. Arow hated it if he didn't have people's full attention.

"My cut of the steal," Arow said.

"I don't pay you," I pointed out. "I never have."

"So you're in debt," he explained with a shrug. "That ring would pay it off."

"I'm not in debt."

His face flushed angrily. "Finn…"

I finished peeling my orange and pulled it in half. I stuck half of it in my mouth, chewed it slowly, and swallowed. "Yes?"

"Pay me, or you'll have to pay with your life."

I just grinned at him and ate the other half of my orange. "You'll have to catch me." I ducked under his arm as he lashed out to hit me. I jumped up the wall beside him and grasped the edge of a windowsill. Using the window like a step, I moved up the rest of the wall. Arow couldn't follow me up here; he was too big and bulky.

I traveled the rooftops for a while to ensure that Arow couldn't find me. Once I knew I was safely away from him, I sat down. From the rooftops, I could see the whole city, which was part of the reason I enjoyed being on them so much. A few streets away, yet another wall separated us from the port. I could see the tips of the ships' masts and the tops of some of the bigger warehouses.

The city was built on a hill right along the towering Cliffs of Loth. The castle was the highest point, and it pressed right against the wall of rock. A wall surrounded the castle and grounds, separating it from the marketplace and buildings of the upper city. The dividing wall then separated the upper and lower cities. In turn, the lower city was surrounded by another wall, protecting us from any attack from the river or bay. The port, flanked by large towers, provided the only way into the city. The main walkway ran down the cliffside, from the castle to the port. It was protected by walls and guards, and was only to be used by the higher class. The Southern side of the city had a large defensive wall, and beyond that was the desert. Not all of the kingdom's land was wasteland; it soon turned to lush terrain, where the lords of the kingdom owned large villas and farmlands.

Foreigners often wondered why the kingdom's capital city was in such barren territory. It was because Zianna was mostly a trading city. It had access to both the sea and river, making it easy to sail to other kingdoms and islands. The other good reason was the Cliffs of Loth, which provided protection. The cliffs and water meant that the only way to attack the city by land was to cross the desert. An attack from the sea was unlikely, since the large island of New Teltar guarded the entrance to the bay.

I'd heard that it was hard to watch proper sunsets from Zianna, since the cliffs blocked the best view. However, the skies around the cliffs still turned brilliant colours as the sun set. That was what I often lay back on the rooftops to watch. Satisfied with my day's work, I leaned back onto the tiles, rested my hands beneath my head, and watched the sky.

CHAPTER
Two

*I*t was hardly past noon, but the brothel was teeming with activity. I ignored the glances sent my way, slipped between the two girls standing near the entrance, and pushed open the doors. The building was old, its age evident in the worn-out carpet and cracking plaster on the walls. Ahead of me, a large staircase, which had once been elegant, led upstairs to all the bedrooms. Girls stood around the front room and the staircase, some already talking to customers with fake enthusiasm. I ignored it all, instead walking up to the front desk, where an older woman sat looking over a ledger.

She couldn't read, most Natives couldn't, but she understood numbers. I knew the system. Each girl had a symbol associated with her to put on the records, as well as a bedroom number and the amount of siyas this older woman thought she could charge. I'd been there often enough to understand everything in her ledger.

I reached the desk but stepped aside almost instantly so a drunk sailor could blunder past me. He paused to eye me, and I dropped my gaze. He looked vaguely familiar and I wondered if I'd stolen anything from him recently. After a moment he moved on, and dropped a pile of siyas on the table. He muttered the name of a girl he clearly saw often, and then started up the staircase. I watched him go before stepping up to the desk again. A cat was sprawled out upside down across the top of the desk. It blinked at me lazily with large yellow eyes.

The woman was counting the coins. After she wrote down a number in the ledger, she packed the money away and looked up at me. "Good afternoon, Finn."

I nodded. "Afternoon."

"We haven't seen you in weeks." She didn't like me. She tolerated me, as many of the other women did, but they didn't like me.

"It's been slow," I agreed. From a pocket on the inside of my cloak, I pulled out a long thin chain with a silver pendant hanging on the end. It was shaped like a bird in flight, with a green eye that I thought might be emerald. I watched the woman's eyes as she followed the pendant swing back and forth. The cat tried to paw at it but I moved it out of the way. "Fifty siyas." It was worth much more, but I had to be reasonable or I wouldn't get anything. Nobody in the lower city could afford to spend so much on a necklace.

She narrowed her eyes. We'd gone through this routine many times. "I'll give you ten."

"Forty-five," I said. In truth, I only expected to get about thirty siyas from her, but she'd try to haggle the price down if I asked for thirty right away.

"Fifteen."

We were interrupted as a young girl appeared and leaned against the desk. She was wearing a green dress that showed off far too much of her chest. I saw my chance. "This necklace would match your dress perfectly, miss. Only forty siyas, for someone as beautiful as you." Young as I was, these girls loved compliments.

She smiled. "Oh, how sweet. It is very pretty." She glanced at the older woman. "He's the good thief, isn't he?"

"Yes. All right, Finn. I know what you want. Thirty siyas." The older woman reached into her desk and pulled out three brass siyas.

I grinned and took them from her hand while putting the necklace down on the table. "Thank you, ma'am."

The older woman gestured lazily and the younger picked it up with glee. "Is that all you have?"

I glanced down at my ring quickly, but changed my mind. The thirty siyas was good enough for one day. "For now, yes. I'll be back as soon as I can." I tucked the coins safely within my cloak and left briskly. Selling my finds to the brothel was one thing, but I didn't like hanging around if I didn't have to.

IT HAD STARTED TO DRIZZLE LIGHTLY, SO I PULLED UP MY HOOD AND buried my hands in my pockets. All thoughts of going to the upper city flew from my head. Rain was rare in Zianna, and I wasn't going to go up there and risk slipping on the dividing wall. Instead, I wandered down the main street and eyed the stalls set up on either side of it. With money in my pocket, I felt like doing the proper thing and actually buying some food.

I stopped briefly at a small stand selling fresh bread and paid five siyas for a few slices. I ate them quickly so they wouldn't get soggy. Many of the other thieves around the lower city would never pay for something they could easily steal, but I thought differently. Life was just as hard for the vendors as it was for me. They deserved my money if I could afford to give it. I could afford it for now, with the sixty siyas I still had stashed away at home. Besides, what was the point of getting money if I never used it?

I continued walking down the street, looking at the stalls curiously. Most had food or other essential items—clothing, blankets, pots and pans. It was nothing like the luxuries in the upper city markets that came from different kingdoms and far off islands. I'd admired the marketplace many times, but never had enough money to buy anything there. It was well guarded, too, making it hard to steal things. Self-preservation came before greed; I didn't get caught because I was careful.

Occasionally, people would call out asking for any spare siyas. I ignored them, though I felt horrible doing it. Many of them were like me, hungry children who hadn't learned how to pickpocket. Some were older, the poorest Natives who had misfortune drive them into the streets. I couldn't help them. Self-preservation—I had to keep my money to myself, use it on myself.

I was about to turn around and go back home when a leather stand caught my eye. Usually I would ignore it, but there was a pair of dark brown boots sitting there. I walked over. The owner was talking to another man, but I could tell his full attention was on me as I picked up one of the boots to inspect it. It was simple but sturdy, with a good sole. I glanced down at my own worn out boots.

"You've got money?" the owner asked.

I realized then that the other customer had walked away, and I nodded. "Yes. How much for the boots?"

"Forty siyas."

He was doing the exact same thing I had done in the brothel. Everyone did it. "I can give you ten."

He leaned across the table slightly, probably so that he could grab me if I started to run off with the boots. "Thirty."

I paused. "Twenty siyas."

"Hmm…" He looked me over and glanced down at the boots I was wearing. "Give me the old ones. Some of that leather can be reworked."

"Deal." I handed over the rest of my money, and then quickly changed into the new boots before my feet could get wet. I left the man inspecting my old boots, trying to figure out how much of the leather he could save.

I began to go home. It had been a successful day, and I really didn't like the rain. I'd hide away until it cleared, and maybe go out for some more food. I'd decide later.

CHAPTER
Three

The allure of the upper city was too great, and a few days later, just as the Lothian Dusk was falling, I was back amid the white streets and buildings. I lurked in the shadows between two buildings that faced onto the largest courtyard in the city. This was where richer merchants and foreigners from the port could come to sell their goods. Colourful tents and wooden booths lined the edges of the courtyard and spread across the cobbled ground, each one decorated with signs or flags indicating what they were selling and where they were from. Around the courtyard, the large buildings held permanent shops and workplaces for people of the city. This was a highly dangerous spot for me to be, but also profitable if I was cautious. The chaos of the booths and tents gave me many places to hide. At the same time, the courtyard was filled with guards, who stood out easily in their armour and gold cloaks. They were mostly there to keep the merchants in line, but wouldn't hesitate to arrest a thief foolish enough to wander into the market.

After a long period of deliberation, I slipped into the crowds. I let the flow of people guide me into the middle of the courtyard, and only then did I start looking around at what the market had to offer. I was almost overwhelmed by the variety of goods. In one booth, a man was selling fine cloth, in another a woman had laid out a display of foreign jewellery. Beside her booth was a tent, inside which were baskets of fresh fruit, probably just transported by ship that morning. The next wooden booth had rows of shining blades; swords, knives, and daggers with fancy hilts. I had no weapons of my own, since I was nearly useless with any kind of blade—I was more likely to hurt myself than my enemy. Still, they drew my attention. I longed to slip one from the table and hide it in my cloak.

I tore myself away from the knife display to continue exploring the market. I first stole something at a bread booth. I hadn't eaten much yet that day, so while the baker's back was turned, I plucked a small bun from a basket. I turned away from the booth and let myself get lost in the crowd before tearing a piece off the bun and sticking it into my mouth. I ate while wandering past a few more displays.

Another jewellery stand caught my attention next. I paused in front of it, letting my eyes drift over fancy necklaces, rings, and brooches. They would be so easy to sell. There was always a poor wife or prostitute hoping to make herself look richer with the help of some gold or jewels. I was so distracted that I reached out to run my fingers over the large red jewel in one of the necklaces. My hand was slapped and I was suddenly brought back to my senses. I glanced up in alarm and met the angry eyes of the woman in charge of the booth.

"What are you doing, boy?" she demanded.

"My mother," I replied vaguely, feigning shyness. "I was hoping to maybe buy her something."

"You got money on you?" The women looked me over. I could almost feel her scrutinizing gaze. Thank Zianesa the market was always so full of foreigners. My darker skin didn't automatically mark me out as one of the poor.

I nodded. "Yes, miss."

She instantly changed her attitude toward me with those two simple words. "Well, boy, what exactly are you looking for?" She leaned across the counter towards me.

I shrugged. "Gold. She likes red." I reached out towards the necklace again and this time the women let my fingers lift it from the table. I lay the pendant in my hand and stared down at the large red jewel. It sparkled in the sunlight, almost making it look like it was on fire.

"Interesting ring you've got," the women commented.

"Oh, thank you," I replied.

"What's the inscription say?"

"I—" I couldn't tell her that I couldn't read the inscription; she'd realize I was of the lower class. "My family's motto," I lied. I handed the necklace back to her. As much as I wanted to take it, I couldn't now that she'd paid such close attention to me. I made my excuses and walked off.

I was still hungry, so I went back to the foreign fruit tent I'd seen earlier. Foreign fruit was always interesting to try. Luckily for me, the booth was crowded and it was easy to go unseen. I reached into the basket farthest away from the owner so that he would be less likely to see me. What I pulled out didn't really look like food. They were small, red, spiky balls. I doubted the outside was meant to be eaten, so as I walked away from the tent I carefully peeled the skin off one of them. Inside, the fruit was white and juicy. I popped it into my mouth cautiously. There was a pit in the centre and I spat it out. I'd taken four of the strange little fruit, so I reached into my pocket to pull out another. By the time I'd eaten all four, I'd made up my mind. They were delicious.

I still hadn't taken anything of value, and I was starting to get a little anxious. I wanted something to show for my trip to the market. Among the precarious ranking of the thieves in the lower city, I enjoyed my place at the top because I made these riskier trips. If I didn't take anything I could show off, the other thieves would start to look down on me. There were rules among the thieves. We were all trying to survive and for the most part had no reason to fight each other, but the lower one was in the ranking, the less the rules applied. To keep myself safe, I had to stay on top, and I couldn't claim to be the greatest thief in Zianna without consistently providing proof.

Two young boys ran past me, and of course they didn't notice when my hand slipped out and snatched the coin bag from one of their pockets. Normally I wouldn't take from children, but these two were obviously the sons of the rich, and could afford to lose a few coins. I emptied the bag into my hand, dropped it, and carefully placed the coins in my pocket.

Suddenly, yelling broke out near me and I flinched, thinking that the boys must have noticed their missing money. I looked for the source and found a large man yelling at a boy. After a moment, I realized that I recognized him. I groaned and made my way through the crowd towards them, stepping up beside him. They both looked at me. The man had a tight grip on the boy's arm, preventing him from running off. The boy was a couple of years younger than I was, and he knew me.

"Finn?" he asked. He wasn't questioning my name, but my actions. He'd made a mistake and been caught. We tended to not help fellow thieves; it was always too risky.

"Be quiet, Baisan," I replied sharply before looking at the man. "Sir? Excuse me, what did my brother do?" It was a lie, but we were both Natives and the man would have no reason to suspect that we weren't related.

"He stole food from my booth," the man growled.

I widened my eyes, pretending to be surprised, and then glared at Baisan. "Why would you do such a thing?"

"I... I'm sorry, Finn," Baisan mumbled, getting over his confusion and going along with the act.

"What did he take?" I reached into my pocket and pulled out the coins I had just taken from the little rich boy. "Will this cover it?" I dropped the coins into the man's hand. He released Baisan's arm to poke through the little pile. After a moment, he grunted in satisfaction and waved us away. I had counted them too, and I regretted handing over the whole pile. I'd given up ten whole siyas, much more than Baisan was worth. I grabbed his hood and used it to drag him out of the crowds to the edge of the marketplace, not bothering to be gentle.

"For the love of Zianesa, Finn, let go of me," he complained.

I did, and gave him a push into a little side alley. I stepped into it after him and stood in the way so he couldn't get out. "What are you doing?"

Baisan rubbed his wrist where the merchant had been holding him. "Trying to steal something good from the market, of course. You don't have claim to it, you know."

"You almost got arrested."

"Since when do you care? We aren't in the business of helping each other. I would have been out of your way."

"You would have been dead," I pointed out.

"Well," Baisan shrugged. "Thank you. You didn't need to be so rough, though." He rubbed his neck.

"Of course I did. I was being an angry older brother," I said. "Go home, before you get yourself caught again."

"So you are trying to get rid of competition, huh?" Baisan asked. "If you scare me away from the upper city, you get it almost entirely to yourself. Is that your plan?"

I sighed. "Fine, stay here. But if you get caught again, I'm not going to help you." I turned to walk away, but Baisan stopped me with a hand on my shoulder.

"Arow's out for your blood. Be careful when you go back down. I'll tell him I saw you out near the southern wall, so hopefully he'll be out of your way."

I nodded. We often traded favours; it was all we had to give. "Thank you." He let go of my shoulder and I left the alley. It was tempting to go back into the market, but it was getting darker as real dusk started to fall. I heard Baisan leave the alley behind me, and didn't bother looking to see where he was headed. Instead, I began walking down the road. I decided that I would head home and try again tomorrow, when I hopefully wouldn't have to use up my winnings saving another thief's life.

I HAD BEEN WALKING FOR ABOUT FIFTEEN MINUTES, HAVING NOT GONE straight back home, when Baisan appeared at my side, out of breath. "Finn, the guards…" He cut himself off as shouts rang out behind us. "Run," he said, before bolting down the street in front of me. I didn't hesitate to follow him. If the guards had seen him talking to me, I'd be arrested too. I quickly caught up.

"What did you do?"

"Nothing," Baisan protested. "It was just a couple of coins. They didn't need it."

"I told you to go home."

"It was on the way. I didn't expect—" he paused to duck under the arm of a passerby probably hoping to get a reward for catching him, "—them to notice."

I stopped running suddenly, and Baisan stopped a few steps later. "What are you doing?"

"Go home," I told him.

Baisan looked at me, then his gaze went over my shoulder to the men running up the street after us. He turned and ran.

I waited just long enough that Baisan was out of sight, and then ran to the edge of the street. I jumped on top of an abandoned cart and from there started up the wall. I wasn't sure what it was guarding, but it had to be something important to be this close to the castle. Just as I'd hoped, the guards chasing us didn't bother following Baisan. None of them could climb the wall, so they did the next best thing and started throwing things at me. Just small rocks, to try to startle me into falling. If I fell, I'd probably die, but even if I survived, I'd be arrested.

I ignored the rocks as best I could and continued steadily up the wall. Many hit me directly, mostly on my back or legs. One hit the back of my right hand and I almost lost my grip on the wall. When I reached the top, my arms were aching. I sat on the top for a moment to regain my strength. I was too high up by then for the guards' rocks to hit me, and there didn't seem to be anyone on the other side. I was confused by what I saw. I had walked past this section of wall a hundred times, and I'd always assumed it was surrounding part of the castle grounds. What I found instead was a handful of buildings separated from both the upper city and the castle.

I started descending the other side of the wall. Like with the dividing wall, the ground on this side was much closer than the ground on the other. I was grateful when I reached the cobbled walkway. I warily started walking down the path. I needed to get out of this place, but my curiosity drove me to explore it a little bit first. When I reached the end of the building beside me, I peeked around the corner. Past the building, I could see a wide courtyard. It looked deserted. I walked out to it, still wary but starting to relax. There seemed to be no one else around.

I rounded the next corner and was suddenly pinned to the ground.

CHAPTER
Four

My flight instincts kicked in and I struggled to roll out from under the person who had attacked me. He was just a boy, not much bigger than I was, which was why I thought I might have a chance getting away. He was trying to hit me, so I grabbed his wrists to keep them still. I tried to throw him off so I could slip out of his grasp. My talent was running and hiding, not fighting.

A sharp whistle pierced the air. Suspecting the guards to appear around the corner at any moment, I renewed my struggles. It came as a shock when the boy scrambled off me and took a step back. I jumped to my feet, my gaze instantly flicking around the courtyard, looking for a way out. What I saw made me forget about an escape. Dotted around the courtyard were pairs of other boys who looked like they had just separated from their own wrestling matches.

I returned my gaze to the boy in front of me. He was a Telt, but his light brown hair gave away some Native blood. He seemed older than me, maybe fourteen or fifteen. He was looking over my clothing quizzically, his blue eyes drifting over the old cloak, the silver chain that had escaped from under my shirt, and finally resting on the gold ring. He grinned. "You're pretty good."

He stepped forward and held out his hand. "My name's Tandrix, though I go by Tannix. Who are you?"

I cautiously took his hand and shook it, half expecting a trap. "Finagale," I replied, using my full name for the first time in years. I withdrew my hand as soon as I felt his grip loosen.

"What level are you?" he asked. "I'm in my first year, just got here a couple of weeks ago, actually."

I nodded. "I did too," I lied, though I had no idea what he was talking about. I reached up to brush some of my dark hair away from my eyes. If his skin hadn't already given it away, I'd be able to tell he was rich due to his fancy clothing, and the vivid blue of his tunic. In contrast, I knew that I must look like the lowest possible class, which admittedly I was. My dirty cloak and clothing, my darker skin and messy hair—the only thing we had in common was the ring. He had an identical one resting on his right thumb.

"You're a first year?" Tannix asked. "Why are you dressed like that? Were you on a training trip to the lower city?"

I nodded again, grateful that this boy seemed to keep giving me the answers to his questions.

"You must have blended in. You look Native."

"My mother is a Native. Is there something wrong with that?" I asked haughtily, hoping that I sounded like an insulted rich boy. My skin was slightly lighter than the pure-blooded Native Zians, so I hoped he'd believe me.

Tannix held up his hands in mock surrender. "Of course not. My mother is half Native herself." The sharp whistle sounded again, and he glanced over towards a double wooden doorway at the other end of the courtyard. "We'd better go in. You know how they are about people being late."

Against my better instinct, I followed him. We walked across the courtyard to the doorway. There was a large man standing beside it with his arms crossed, and he stared at each boy as they walked past. I tried not to flinch when his gaze rested on me. The doors opened into a long, dark hallway made with shiny rock. I hoped my amazement wasn't obvious as I gazed around the building. Huge pillars held up the vaulted ceiling. When I looked up, I could see at least two other floors opening into the atrium. Men were everywhere, either dressed in uniform like the large man by the door had been, or dressed in fancy rich clothing like Tannix. I felt entirely out of place and ran my hand through my hair nervously.

Beside me, Tannix smiled. "Did you lose your hair tie while we were training?"

I nodded. "Yes." My hair wasn't really long enough to tie back, I'd tried before but I hadn't liked it. I knew enough to agree with him, though. It was the style among the higher-class men to tie back long hair.

We followed the stream of boys across the atrium, past many large door-ways. Through one open doorway, I saw people clearing a long table of what looked like the largest feast in the world. My stomach grumbled, the strange fruit from the marketplace forgotten. I'd given nearly anything to get that much food.

I shook the feast from my mind as we passed the doorway and started up a staircase. It was made of the same black stone as the rest of the building. It looked so unusual to me to see something constructed out of black stone, as opposed to the sandy coloured or white stones used in the main parts of the city. The black stone must have been expensive, and it increased my curiosity about the whole place. I was still instinctively finding escape routes just in case someone noticed that I didn't belong. I was surprised that no one had said anything yet.

We ended up in a long thin corridor. There were doors along both sides, and at the far end I could see the fading daylight, which indicated a window. The boys around us started filing through different doors. Tannix paused outside one of the first ones we passed.

"Where's your room?" he asked.

I nodded down the hall. "Down there," I replied vaguely, hoping he wouldn't ask to see it.

"Well, see you tomorrow at breakfast. Maybe we can train together again?"

"Yes, maybe." He smiled and walked into his room. When his door closed, I should have taken my chance and escaped, but a different idea had crept up on me. If no one suspected me yet, I could sneak into breakfast. Even if it was only half as large as the feast I'd see, it would be worth the risk. Maybe I'd learn more about the interesting place while I was at it.

I walked down the hall, trying to look like I knew exactly where I was going, and only stopped when I reached the window. It overlooked the courtyard. Off to my right, I could see the huge defense walls that protected the city. Beyond that, there was the desert. I'd never had such a good view of the desert before. It seemed to run on forever, until it met faint mountains in the distance. They were the Adymuss Mountains, I knew that much even though I'd never seen them. The river cut through the desert and seemed to create a winding trail straight to the mountains.

I glanced behind me, and seeing that the hallway was now empty, knew I'd be safe to do as I planned. I climbed onto the windowsill and carefully leaned out. The wall above me looked easy to climb. I grasped the edge of a rock and pulled myself out onto the wall. Swiftly, I made my way up to the roof. It was perfect to sleep on, nice and flat. I found a little nook to huddle into and drew my cloak closer. The sky was starry and clear, and it looked like there was little risk of it raining overnight. I closed my eyes.

THE NEXT MORNING, IT TOOK ME A MOMENT TO REMEMBER WHERE I WAS. Clouds had rolled in overnight, which was good because it kept the sun from waking me up. Instead, I was woken by a gonging sound coming from the courtyard below me. I scrambled to the edge of the roof to glance down. The boys I'd seen the day before were standing in neat lines, and the large man from the door was pacing back and forth in front of them. I could faintly hear what he was telling the boys, something about breakfast and then training.

The training part didn't seem interesting to me, but the breakfast did, so I moved over to the wall I had climbed up the day before and descended until I found the window to the boys' corridor. I slipped into the deserted hallway. An idea came to me. I walked over to the closest doorway and carefully tried to open it. It didn't look like it had a lock, and I was right. The door swung open and I stepped in.

The room was simple. There was a bed on one end, a desk with a few books, and a wardrobe. That was what I went for. I opened up the wardrobe's door to see a number of different cloaks hung up. They were all the same deep, rich red. I assumed that it was the colour of the city the boy came from.

One of the cloaks had fallen from its hook and was shoved into the corner of the wardrobe. I gingerly pulled it out and looked it over, then tried it on. It fit me well, and it made me look much nobler than my old dirty cloak had. The boy probably wouldn't even notice that it was gone. I opened one of the smaller drawers of the wardrobe to find some thin red ribbons, one of which I took. The next problem was what to do with my old cloak. I didn't want to replace it, since it blended it so well with the stones in the lower city, and it had many useful pockets for me to keep things. I finally decided to return to the roof, shove it into the corner I had slept in, and hope it would stay there.

Donning my new red cloak and tying my hair back with the red ribbon, I walked down the boys' corridor to the black stairs. I started down them cautiously. Even though I now looked the part, I was still worried about being caught. Upon reaching the main floor, I saw that my timing was perfect, as the boys had just started trickling in from the courtyard. I ducked behind a pillar so they wouldn't notice me, and then when I had a chance, I slipped into the crowd so they would think I had always been there.

I looked through the crowd of boys until I saw Tannix near the back. I slid between the others until I ended up beside him. He was wearing a fancy blue cloak and a new ring on his right hand that I was sure he hadn't been wearing the day before. Caught up staring at it, I didn't notice when he saw me.

"Finagale." He sounded pleased. "I didn't see you out on the courtyard."

"I was off to the other side of the group..." I trailed off. "You weren't wearing that yesterday." I glanced away from the ring and met his gaze. "Sorry, I just... noticed."

Tannix sighed. "Yes. I don't always wear it while training." He raised his hand to look at the ring. "It's my family's crest ring. I know most families don't bother with them anymore, but my father likes tradition."

A crest ring. I'd stolen some of those over the years. "I thought only the richest families continued using them."

Tannix rolled his eyes. "Yes," he agreed. "I don't exactly want people knowing how high ranking I am. You understand, surely? I want to be treated as an equal here, that's the point in coming. But my father insists I wear it."

"Do you mind if I take a look?" I asked hopefully.

Tannix slipped the ring from his index finger and dropped it into my hands. "Just keep quiet about it, will you? If I don't mention it, people don't tend to notice."

I gazed appreciatively at the ring while we followed the herd of boys into the feast room. Two long tables ran down the length of it, and both were covered with food. Older boys and men had already settled around the room when we entered. I took that all in with a single glance, since the ring was much more interesting to me. It was one of the few things that could interest me more than food. It was made of gold with a flat piece of blue stone. Intricately carved into the stone was a miniature coat of arms—a shield with some sort of spiked circle in the middle of it, and two crossed swords above it. I had no idea where he came from; the crest wasn't one I'd ever seen before.

Tannix took a seat on one of the long benches and I sat down beside him. Reluctantly, I handed over the ring. "Where do you come from?"

Tannix glanced around, as if nervous of people overhearing him. "New Teltar. West Draulin."

I understood his discomfort. West Draulin was the second most important city in the kingdom, beneath only Zianna. It was in charge of governing the whole island of New Teltar, as well as being important in the protection of the Straights of Draulin. Going through the straights was the only way to get past the island into the bay. If Tannix wanted to be treated like an equal among these boys, coming from West Draulin was not going to help.

"Are you inheriting it?"

"Of course not," Tannix replied, giving me a confused glance. I realized that I had said something wrong. "My elder brother is. I wouldn't be here if I were the heir."

"Of course." I shook my head, pretending to be ashamed of myself. "My apologies. I wasn't thinking." I made note of the new information. Heirs didn't come to this mysterious place.

"Tandrin's going to get the city, and I don't envy him the responsibility. How about you? Older brother or sister?

I hesitated before replying. Tannix's comment had reminded me of the Telt habit of giving all their children similar names. "A brother. Finagan," I replied, hoping the name sounded believable.

"So you must shorten your name for everyday use."

"Oh, yes, Finn," I replied haltingly. "People call me Finn."

"And where do you come from?" Tannix asked.

"A small farm villa near Kitsi." I felt I had recovered smoothly. "It isn't much, but Finagan is a couple of years older than me so he's going to get it."

"Boys," a deep voice suddenly boomed from behind us. I flinched, but Tannix turned to face the man who had spoken. I hesitantly copied him and glanced over my shoulder. It was the large doorman, wearing the same uniform as the day before. It looked a lot like the gold and black uniforms the guards wore, but the colours all seemed to be a shade darker. On his right thumb was the ring.

"Would you two like to eat instead of talking like old women?" the man asked.

"Oh yes, Malte, sir, of course," Tannix replied. He sounded respectful, but I noticed the deliberate moving of his right hand that put his crest ring into the huge man's line of sight.

Malte's eyes flickered over the ring, and he nodded. "Then eat before we head out for training, Lord Tandrix," he grumbled. He didn't seem particularly fazed by Tannix's ring, but it was clear that he knew better than to upset the son of West Draulin. The man turned and walked down the length of the room, occasionally stopping to talk to other boys along the way.

"I thought you didn't want people knowing who you are," I said.

"Malte already knows. He did the paperwork admitting me to the Order, after all. He doesn't like me being here because I'm the only one of his students who outranks him. It must make him a little uncomfortable, but I try not to flaunt it too much. I want to be trained just like the rest of you."

"Of course."

Tannix sighed. "Oh well, he'll leave me alone for a while now." He reached across his plate to grab a bun, and then ladled some porridge into his bowl. "He's right, though. We don't want to train without breakfast."

"Of course not," I agreed again, but this time with real enthusiasm. I followed Tannix's example and began to eat. It was the first time I could remember having enough food in one sitting.

SOON, MALTE BLEW HIS ANNOYING WHISTLE AND THE BOYS STOPPED eating. I only stopped after a sharp nudge from Tannix. The older boys and men who were still in the dining room didn't bother to stop, so I realized Malte's authority must only be over the younger ones around our age. Malte didn't give any instructions, but he stalked out of the room and the boys got up to follow him. I grabbed an apple before getting to my feet.

"You're not supposed to bring food into the courtyard," Tannix said.

"I know," I replied. "But I'm really hungry." I took a large bite out of the apple as Tannix and I joined the flow of boys. "Besides, if I stick around you, Malte might not bother to do anything about me bending the rules, in case you pull out your hierarchy again."

"I told you I try not to do it very often," Tannix said.

I shrugged and smiled. "So you said."

"It's true," Tannix said, but he was smiling too.

When we reached the courtyard, I had finished with the apple. I tossed the core into the bushes and ignored Tannix's look of disproval. We joined the rest of the boys standing in the straight lines I had seen from the roof. I was uncomfortable, but feeling confident in my stolen cloak and with my filled stomach. Malte announced that we were to practice fighting, and then he dismissed us.

Tannix stepped up beside me. "So, what shall we practice with first? Swords or daggers?"

I tried not to look too horrified at the thought of either of the weapons. "Daggers," I finally mumbled. They seemed less intimidating than swords.

Tannix grinned. "Good idea." He took a couple steps away from me and reached under his cloak to draw out an expensive looking dagger. The carved hilt was adorned with blue jewels. He gazed at it for a moment before looking up and to see my stare. Luckily, he must have misunderstood my expression of awe over the expensive weapon, because he simply said, "Where's yours?"

"I… forgot it in my room," I answered. "I just realized."

"Oh. Swords, then?" he asked. "I could use some practice with my left hand."

"What?" I mumbled. Somewhere in my mind, I knew that I was at risk of ruining my persona, but I was still shaken from both the idea of fighting with a weapon, and also the absolute richness of the blade Tannix was holding. It fascinated me. It was beautiful, and I'd never seen such an expensive weapon.

"Well, I've been training with my right since I knew how to walk," Tannix said. He walked over to a weapons stand and drew two wooden practice swords. "I can even beat my father in a fight. Sometimes I like to practice with my left hand." He offered the second sword to me. "Do you mind if we use our lefts?"

I shook my head numbly and took the sword in my left hand. Thank Zianesa my left hand was my good one. I could simply pretend I had never practiced with my left, and maybe he would believe it. Maybe he wouldn't think my lack of fighting skills was suspicious.

Tannix grinned. "Excellent." He moved to stand in what I assumed was a fighting stance, and held up his sword. "Come on, Lord Finagale, let's fight."

"Let's," I replied, shaking myself out of my stupor. I mimicked Tannix's posture and held up my sword. "I must warn you, I've never fought with my left hand."

"I'll go easy on you," Tannix promised. Then he attacked.

CHAPTER
Five

"Today you will be practicing your climbing skills," Malte announced the next morning. Like the day before, we were standing in our neat rows in the courtyard. I hated living by such a strict structure, but the food I'd just eaten more than made up for it. Malte continued talking, reminding the boys of things I already knew. "Pair off and remember to always have someone on the ground watching you," he explained. "This is not like practicing with your swords; if you fall, you will be hurt. Go."

I groaned and rolled my shoulders as the boys around us started pairing off. Tannix moved closer to me. "Do you not like climbing?" he asked.

I almost laughed. "Climbing's easy, but my arms are still sore from that beating yesterday." Not to mention sleeping on the roof. I wasn't used to luxury but at least at home I had clothing to cushion me.

Tannix smiled sheepishly. "Sorry. I thought you'd be a better fighter than that."

"Yes, well… Let's climb." I noticed that the other groups of boys were heading towards the different buildings that bordered the courtyard. The walls, I could tell, had been designed to be easy to climb. The stones had been put together so that there were often pieces sticking out, which created perfect handholds. There were also many windows facing the courtyard. For the first time, I felt confident about a task the place had given me.

I led Tannix over to one of the buildings that the other boys had decided not to use. It was taller than some of the others, but of course that didn't bother me. "You stay here and watch me, in case I fall," I told Tannix, even though it was unnecessary. I never fell.

"That is the way we do it," Tannix pointed out dully. "Apparently a couple of years ago a boy fell to his death while practicing, because his partner wasn't watching him."

"How would his partner have helped?" I asked. I had my back to Tannix and was staring up at the wall thoughtfully, planning my route as best I could.

"He could have seen that he was having trouble," Tannix replied.

"And then what? Climbed up and helped?" I couldn't help but let a hint of sarcasm creep into my voice. "Or maybe he would have caught him?"

Tannix didn't answer.

I turned around. He had his arms crossed, and he was looking at the wall like it was some sort of enemy. "You don't like climbing," I guessed.

He nodded.

"This wall will be simple." I tried to sound comforting, but I really wasn't good at it. "Just watch me when I go up, and then when it's your turn, follow the same path." My words clearly did not have the right effect. "Maybe you can tell Malte that you…"

"No, I can't," Tannix said. "Everyone needs to practice this, though I don't see why. I'm not going to become a spy, or assassin, or whoever would do this. Soldiers don't climb walls."

"Spies?" I asked, wondering if I'd just solved the mystery of who these people were.

"I've always known I was going to be a soldier." Tannix continued as if I hadn't said anything. "Give me a sword, or a knife, and I can beat anyone here. Those are the kinds of skills I'll need, not climbing walls."

"Why would you want to be a soldier?" I asked carefully. I realized that I was heading into dangerous territory. It sounded like something I would know if I had actually been part of the group. I hoped that I had formed my question well enough, and that Tannix wouldn't notice that I had no idea what he was talking about. "Sounds boring to me. I mean, you should be helping to run your city. Right?"

"I want to go into the army, become a general. That's what my father's plan has always been. Tandrin gets West Draulin, I become a high-ranking soldier. Your father must have plans for you."

"Of course he does." I nodded.

"Does he want you to become a spy?" Tannix asked curiously.

"He believes I should do whatever it is that my skills are suited for," I lied. "I happen to be very good at climbing walls."

"A spy, then."

"Yes. I'm sure he'll be pleased, as long as I work my way up the ranks." I hoped that spies worked that way, with ranks. I turned my back on Tannix once again and shrugged off my stolen cloak. "Just watch me," I told him. Without looking back to see if he was watching, I walked up to the base of the wall. I reached as high as I could and let my fingers grip the edge of a jutting stone, then I began to climb.

It was easy. There was always a stone or window ledge I could grab or stand on. Not once did I have to pause to think about my next move. My sore arms seemed to forget about their bruises as I carried out something they were used to. I made swift progress, and almost before I knew it, I was perched on the roof of the building. I stood up and took in my surroundings. My favourite part about climbing was how far I could see. On the other side of the building was the huge wall I had scaled days before. Looking past that, I could see my lower city, and beyond it, the Adymuss River filled with ships.

After a moment, I leaned over the edge of the roof to look down at Tannix. "Easy!" I called before I noticed the large body standing next to him. Malte was staring up at me.

"Come down," he ordered. His voice easily carried up to me, even though he seemed to be speaking in a normal tone.

My mind switched to flight. I briefly considered rushing down the far side of the building and up over the wall to freedom, but I knew I wouldn't make it. Malte would simply have to run around the base of the building to meet me on the other side. My other option was to try to leap the gap between my building and the wall, but it was further then I'd ever jumped before, and even with a running start, I doubted I would reach it. The only option was to do what I had been told, and hope that Tannix might try to help me.

I carefully lowered myself back onto the wall. My descent was slow. It was usually harder to go down than up, since my own body blocked my view, but this time was slower than most. I dreaded reaching the bottom and facing Malte. Once I got close enough to the ground, I let myself drop and landed lightly on my feet. As I turned around, I tensed, ready to flee if I got the chance.

I was taken by surprise to see Malte holding my cloak out to me. I took it gingerly and draped it back over my shoulders. A quick glance at Tannix told me that he was just as confused, though I knew it was for different reasons.

"You climb well," Malte commented. "Very quick, instinctual. You have a lot of practice."

"Yes. There's a building back home I enjoy climbing to watch the sunset," I replied calmly. I almost amazed myself at my ability to lie so quickly.

Malte nodded, as if he'd once done the same thing. "Maybe you can teach Lord Tandrix how to do it. Climbing is his weak point."

"Of course I'll try," I promised, silently willing him to walk away. I wasn't worth talking to, unless he was on to me, but then would he bother telling me to teach Tannix?

Malte smiled briefly, so brief I thought I had imagined it. He looked like he was about to say something when a boy across the courtyard called for help. I gratefully watched as Malte turned and quickly walked over to him. I could see that his partner was about halfway up their wall, and it looked like he was having difficulties.

"You're going to teach me to climb?" Tannix asked, clearly unimpressed. "Why would you agree to that?"

I shook away thoughts about the other boy's wall, and turned to glance at Tannix. "I don't want attention any more than you do," I said. "I didn't want him to stay here and keep asking me questions."

"Why not? He was praising you."

"I don't like attention," I replied with a shrug. "Shall we?"

Tannix shook his head. "No."

"Then you'll be the one explaining to Malte why you can't climb such a simple wall." I strolled back over to the wall, this time not bothering to take off the cloak. After all, I was used to climbing with my old cloak. I used the same stone to start off, and climbed up a few steps before moving off to the side, so that the simplest path I had used the first time was clear. "Come here, Tannix. I'll tell you where to put your hands and feet."

I could almost see him thinking it over. It took a moment, but then he suddenly dropped his cloak to the ground and approached the wall. I grinned down at him. "Here, this one." I tapped the first protruding stone with my foot.

Tannix took a deep breath. Reaching the stone was easier for him because of his slight advantage in height. I noticed that and quickly adjusted the path for him in my mind. He would have an easier time reaching things I had ignored my first time up. After grasping that first stone, he managed to work his way up to be level with me quite easily.

"You're not as bad as you think," I commented.

Tannix narrowed his eyes. "Just tell me what to do."

We worked our way up the wall at a slow but steady pace. Sometimes I told him where to go next, but sometimes I didn't have to. We reached the top sooner than either of us expected. I pulled myself over the edge onto the roof first, and leaned over to help him up the last bit. When he was up, we sat together and let our legs dangle over the side.

After a moment had passed, Tannix broke the silence. "Thank you."

LUNCH FOLLOWED. LIKE WITH THE OTHER MEALS, WE WENT TO THE ROOM with the two long tables. This time there were pots of soup as well as various platters of cooked meats and vegetables. Once again, I had to monitor how much I took to eat, because a rich Telt would never try to hoard food the way I was used to doing. I followed Tannix's example, for the most part, taking the same amount of food he did and eating at the same pace.

I also took the time to look more closely at the other boys. At the other table there was a boy wearing a red cloak similar in colour to the one I had stolen, so I assumed I'd taken it from him. I decided to avoid him. Sitting near that boy was the one who had been stuck on his wall earlier. None of the others caught my attention. They all looked similar to me, same age, same arrogant actions that came with being a rich Telt. Tannix didn't act like that. Maybe it was because he was part Native. The thought left my mouth almost before I'd realized it.

"Why don't you act like the other Telts?"

"Telts?" Tannix replied.

I froze with my spoon halfway to my mouth. I suddenly realized my mistake. They didn't call themselves Telts. "Teltans, I mean," I said hastily. I glanced around furtively, wondering if any of the nearby boys or men had heard me.

"Why would you say Telt?" Tannix asked.

"I'm half Native Zian," I pointed out, trying my best to sound casual. "I picked up some things from my mother. She says Telts."

"High class Zians don't usually use that term."

"No, I know. She isn't. Wasn't," I faltered, but recovered quickly. "She was a maid, working for my father's family. They fell in love. It was quite scandalous, apparently. She's put a lot of Zian habits behind her, but some stick. I'm sorry if I insulted you, I'm just used to the term."

Tannix shrugged. "Oh well, it doesn't bother me as much as it does others. As for your question, I don't act like them because I have nothing to prove. I have money, I have rank, and if I wanted to, I could let them all know and instantly be in charge. You see, they're all trying to size each other up and figure out who is the most important or powerful. All I'd have to do is tell them my name, and they'd know it's me. I could ask you the same question, Finn. A boy from a farm villa near Kitsi must feel like he has a lot to prove."

"Either that or a boy from a farm villa near Kitsi knows he can't compete with the rest of them and has decided it isn't worth the attempt," I replied. "Not only that, but my mother taught me the values of the Natives. They're different than the Teltish ones."

"I'm not surprised," Tannix replied. "I suppose this is why we get along so well, isn't it? We don't need to compete for power."

I grinned. "You're way more powerful than I'll ever be, why fight you for it?"

"That's not what I meant."

"But it's true, and it doesn't bother me. I'm used to my place in the world." I finished my soup and started to work on the slab of meat. The fork and knife felt odd in my hands but luckily, years of carefully watching people meant that I knew how to use them. I began to slice off a bite-sized piece.

"You're left handed, aren't you?" Tannix asked.

I was startled and stared at my hands for a moment, trying to figure out what had prompted his comment. "Why…"

"People tend to hold the knife in their right, not their left. There's nothing wrong with that, it was just an observation. So when we were fighting with our left hands, was that your better hand?"

"What do you think we'll be doing this afternoon?" I asked, uncomfortable with the subject. The fact that I favoured my left hand had hidden my ignorance, at least involving the knife and fork, but I didn't want to let Tannix's mind linger on it.

"I believe Malte said something about the library."

"Yes," I muttered, remembering now that Tannix had mentioned it. I just had to figure out how to hide my inability to read.

THE LIBRARY WAS A HUGE ROUND ROOM WITH A TOWERING CEILING. Bookshelves lined the walls all the way up to the top, and there were walkways and ladders built in so people could get to the higher shelves. In the middle was a well-tended fire, and around that sat chairs and tables of different sizes. Some were meant for just one person, and some were longer so that many people could sit together.

I trailed after Tannix as he walked to a section of shelf that was obviously familiar to him. "So, what are you going to read?" I asked.

Tannix shrugged as he looked over the shelf. "I usually just look for a title that seems interesting."

I nodded like I did the same. "Anything you can suggest?"

"This one is good." Tannix pulled a book from the shelf and handed it to me. "Some of the chapters are, at least."

I flipped the book open and let my eyes run over the front page as if I were reading it.

"What do you think?"

"I'll give it a chance," I decided.

"Just skip to the chapter about warfare," Tannix suggested, pulling another book from the shelf. "That part is the most interesting." He led me to a nearby, empty table, where we settled into our chairs. The library quieted down as people got set up with their different books or pieces of parchment to write on.

I decided to follow Tannix's example once again. I pretended to be reading my book, while watching him out of the corner of my eye. Every time he flipped a page, I waited a moment before flipping my own. I wanted to make it look like I was reading at a normal pace, but at the same time not make it obvious I was copying him.

I was surprised when, about ten pages in, I found myself looking at a colourful map. It showed our kingdom, as well as our two neighbours, Deorun and Navire. I understood that much without needing to be able to read the labels. I recognized Zianna's location by the bay and the river, and the Cliffs of Loth. The shaky geography I'd learned over the years from listening in on conversations helped me understand the rest of the map. The Adymuss Mountains were to the right, Deorun was above them, Navire was beneath. Above the Cliffs of Loth was a huge island I knew to be New Teltar.

"There's West Draulin." Tannix interrupted my thoughts by reaching over and tapping the highest point of the island. Meaning the section of water between that point and the mainland were the Straights of Draulin, and the dot on the mainland must have been East Draulin.

"It looks far away, doesn't it?" Tannix asked. "It's amazing how much faster travel is over water."

"I don't like water," I muttered, without first thinking about whether or not it was a strange thing for a rich Telt to say.

"Why not?"

"I never learned to swim."

"But Kitsi's beside a lake."

"But my villa isn't," I told him. "It just never came up."

"So you didn't travel to Zianna by boat?" Tannix asked. "The trip must have taken days on horseback."

"Yes, it did, but I'm used to horses. After all, I live on a farm," I lied. Horses didn't scare me the way water did, but that didn't mean I liked them. I had never been on a horse's back before, and I could only pray to Zianesa that riding wasn't something these boys learned. There would be no way to fake that.

My words seemed to make sense to Tannix. After a moment he nodded. "Well, that is understandable. Ships and the ocean are important to my city. I've been on boats my whole life. I love them. There's a sense of freedom you get while sailing."

"There's a sense of freedom you get while galloping through empty fields on the back of a horse." Or at least I hoped there was.

"I know, I know. I ride too," Tannix said. "How do you think we get to smaller cities and towns in the centre of the island?"

"I thought you had flying ships," I replied, feigning seriousness. When Tannix started laughing, I couldn't help but join in, and we were quickly shushed.

AFTER DINNER, WE WERE ONCE AGAIN INSTRUCTED TO PRACTICE FIGHT-ing with either swords or daggers. Since Tannix knew I favoured my left hand, there was no reason to pretend I could do better with my right, so I insisted we stick with our lefts. I hoped he wouldn't judge me on not being able to fight, just as I hadn't judged him on not being able to climb walls. Unfortunately, Tannix didn't agree. He wanted to use our right hands, and I had to go along with it. The wooden sword felt even more foreign in my right hand than it had in my left. It was clear, as soon as we started, that I had no idea what I was doing.

Tannix and I stood facing each other. I wasn't sure how much time had passed since we started practicing. We were both still holding our wooden swords, but limply, and not with the intention to strike at each other.

His eyes were running up and down my body thoughtfully. "You've never fought before."

"No," I admitted. There was no point denying that.

Tannix glanced over my head, at the wall we had climbed that morning. "You helped me, so I'll help you. I don't know why you haven't had training yet, but I won't ask questions, agreed?"

I thanked Zianesa. "Yes."

He spun his sword at his side and held it up. "Then I'll teach you."

Tannix easily ducked under the wild swing of my wooden sword. He knocked it out of my hand with a simple flick of his wrist. I watched it fall. I didn't think I could ever be good at sword fighting. Confrontation felt wrong to me, unnatural. My eyes were drawn back to Tannix when he gestured at my wooden sword with his own.

"Pick it up," he told me. We'd been at this for hours, and I could tell he was starting to get frustrated with me. The other boys had gone inside when the sun started setting. It was only the two of us still out in the courtyard. "Really, Finn, I don't understand why you have so much trouble with this."

"Different people have different skills," I muttered as I leaned over to pick up my sword.

"Yes, I've noticed," Tannix said. "And I thought you were bad with your left hand."

I glared at him. "My left hand is stronger."

"But everyone else is better with their right, so when fighting us, it'll be easier for you to use the same hand."

"Then don't complain about my form."

Tannix sighed and held up his sword again. "Come on, then. Attack me."

I lunged at him and swung the sword at his. They clashed together and once again, he did some apparently simple motion with his wrist that flung my sword from my hand. It thudded against the cobblestones of the courtyard. He drew his sword back and swung it toward me for a blow that would have killed me had the sword been real. I forgot about form and dove at the ground to his left. I rolled to my feet behind him. Tannix spun around, and his wooden sword met a metal blade.

For a moment, we were both frozen. Tannix stared in shock at his jew-elled dagger, the blade of which had bitten into the wooden sword. I held the knife upside-down, the way I had grabbed it as I rolled past. I'd held it up just in time to block Tannix's strike. While I jerked the dagger free, I met his eyes. I passed it into my right hand before offering it to him, knowing enough to give him the handle instead of the blade. He lowered his sword and took the knife.

"When?"

"Now, when I rolled past you," I said.

"I didn't notice," he said.

"Of course not, you weren't supposed to." I shrugged.

"That wasn't proper fighting," Tannix complained, finally coming out of the stupor my trick had caused. "That was cheating."

"Would keep me alive though, wouldn't it?" I asked.

He nodded. "Yes, it would." He slipped the dagger back under his belt. "Very well then, you may have not won the fight, but you're alive." Tannix moved his sword into his left hand and held out his right for a handshake.

I let myself be drawn into it. His grip was firm and warm, and it lasted longer than I expected. Usually, when I shook someone's hand, it was quick and light and with the intent of slipping off a ring or bracelet. When Tannix released my hand, he was grinning.

"Looks like I've found another one of your skills, besides climbing walls," he teased. "Fighting dirty." He walked past me, toward the rack for the swords, and as he passed, he clapped my shoulder briefly. I hesitated before picking my sword up from the cobblestones and following him. We placed our swords back on the rack and walked slowly towards the doors.

"You were getting better. A little."

I mumbled something incoherent in reply. Holding Tannix's beautiful dagger had distracted me, the way fancy things tended to. I knew I needed to own one, and it was quite obvious how I would have to get it.

CHAPTER
Six

I waited a few days before I began my search for a dagger, and I decided not to go back to where I'd taken the cloak. I'd been lucky in that the theft had not yet been discovered; I wasn't willing to risk taking a dagger from the same person. I had noticed, though, that the decorative jewels on the handle of Tannix's knife were blue, the colour of his city, and I knew that I had to find a red one to use as my own.

That night, after all the boys were asleep, I crept back down into their hallway. I was wearing my old cloak because it blended into the shadows, and if I were seen, it would be less recognizable. I had noticed that there were multiple boys with red coloured cloaks, but not enough to make me anonymous if I was seen. Earlier that evening, I had paid close attention to which rooms belonged to everyone who wore red, so I would know where to check.

It was dark in the hallway, but I was used to working in such conditions. Daylight raids to the upper city were fun, but I didn't do it often enough to sustain myself. It was sneaking around at night that really kept me going. I paused at the first room and stood silently in front of it for a moment. Inside, I could hear the boy tossing and turning on his bed. It could mean that he was still awake, and I decided to move on. At the second room, a few doors down and across the hall, I heard nothing. I put my hand on the knob and slowly turned it.

The door creaked a little and I froze. When I heard no sounds from inside the room, or anywhere else nearby, I carefully pushed it open enough so that I could slip through, then gently closed it behind me. Moonlight was shining in through the window, so I had enough light to work. The room looked nearly identical to the one where I'd stolen my cloak. The only difference was the boy lying asleep in his bed, and the slightly darker colour of the cloaks hanging in the wardrobe.

I decided to check the desk, so I crept around the boy's bed. The first drawer I opened held normal things, some pieces of parchment and paper, two quills, and bottles of ink. The second drawer held what I was looking for. The boy had many different daggers and small knives, and I forced myself to ignore the fancier ones. Not only would their absence be noticed, but I didn't want to draw too much attention to myself.

Instead, I picked out one that looked quite plain. It was slightly heavier than Tannix's, though it looked to be about the same size. The sheath was black leather, decorated with dark, beaten gold—some at the tip, and some running around the top of the sheath, which had an imprinted design. The handle was black as well, with the same dark gold for decoration. Gold also made up the knife's guard. I slipped the dagger from the sheath to look at the blade and saw that it, too, was made of the dark metal. The dagger wasn't nearly as rich looking as Tannix's was, but I knew it would serve my purposes just fine. I slid the blade back into the sheath, and hooked it onto my belt. I quietly closed the drawer, and then, instead of taking the door, I left through the window.

I MET TANNIX THE NEXT MORNING BY THE DOOR TO HIS BEDROOM. I HAD my new dagger with me, but I didn't flaunt it like I wanted to; I let it stay under my cloak where it was meant to be. It was comforting to feel the weight of the weapon on my hip, even though I wasn't used to carrying one around.

When I knocked, Tannix opened the door and glanced over me sleepily. "Why do you look so proud of yourself?" He'd opened the door before he was finished getting ready for the day, so he walked back into his room and I followed him. I leaned against the wall near his door and crossed my arms.

"Good dreams," I replied vaguely.

"About a girl?" Tannix pulled on his cloak.

"Maybe."

"A servant back at your villa?"

I shrugged. "Maybe." He had picked up his dagger from his desk and was fitting it to his belt. I couldn't help but stare at it until it was hidden from sight by his cloak.

"Does she have a name?" Tannix asked.

"You seem to assume it was only one servant girl," I replied seriously.

Tannix laughed. "My mistake. Do *they* have names, then?"

"Of course, everyone has a name. That doesn't mean I knew them all," I said. "My favourite girl was named Ninavi." She was actually a girl from the streets, a girl I knew who lived with Baisan, but Tannix didn't need to know that. "And who do you dream about, Lord Tandrix?"

"I don't think I want to tell you."

"You can't—" I started to protest, but Tannix held up his hand to silence me.

"Yes, I can," he taunted playfully, "because I outrank you, Lord Finagale." He walked by me to leave his room, and nudged me on his way past. "Come on, most of the others have left."

My annoyance was quickly overtaken by the fact that he'd once again called me Lord Finagale, and I loved it when he said my name like that. It sounded amazing, and almost real. I felt as if I was actually a lord and my life on the streets was the lie. With my new dagger, I even felt more like one of the elite.

"Finn, come on," Tannix repeated. I realized that a moment had passed while I basked in the idea of being a lord.

"Sorry," I muttered, and followed him from the room. We joined the rest of the boys in the dining room, and I was dismayed when a couple of them shuffled closer to speak to Tannix. They talked about training and ignored me, so I quickly lost interest and concentrate on my food.

After breakfast, we went out to the courtyard again. We stood in our lines and Malte told us all what we'd be doing for the morning. It was sword fighting again, and I groaned inwardly. Tannix nudged me with his elbow.

"Hey, you are getting better."

"That doesn't mean I want to do it again," I grumbled. "Can't we climb walls instead? I like doing that."

"We don't get to decide what we practice, unfortunately." Tannix led the way over to the sword rack. "Although, I will let you try with your left hand today."

"Thank Zianesa," I muttered. I took the wooden sword he was offering with my left hand. "This is better."

"Wait."

I jumped, startled. Malte had come up behind me without warning and placed his hand on my shoulder.

"Put the swords back. You two are coming with me today," he said. "We're going on a training trip to the lower city." He walked away without another word, expecting us to follow.

"Excellent." Tannix did not sound pleased at all, and I wondered why He could have been nervous about going into the lower city, or maybe it was the task we'd be doing that he disliked. I wondered what that could be, while Tannix took the sword back from me and hung them both up. We started to follow Malte. "It seems like you'll be climbing walls after all. Why do you look so scared?"

"I don't like it when people come up behind me," I said a little shakily. I'd also for a moment thought Malte had caught on and was going to arrest me, but of course, there was no way to tell Tannix that. "I was startled, is all."

He nodded. "He is a little intimidating, I agree."

"A little," I muttered under my breath. Tannix clearly heard me, since he reached out to punch my shoulder lightly, but he said nothing about it.

Malte led us into the building. He walked past all the doors and staircases I'd become familiar with, and instead took us to a small, insignificant looking door down near the end of the atrium. He stood in front of it, arms crossed over his huge chest, and nodded at the door. We were clearly meant to go in by ourselves.

Tannix stepped forward, but Malte dropped a hand on his shoulder to stop him. "Make sure you leave your crest ring behind, Lord Tandrix. It will draw thieves to us, and we do not want to be attracting any attention."

Tannix nodded and shrugged off Malte's hand. He pushed the door open and I hurried to follow him, afraid that Malte might grab me as I passed. As was becoming common with me, I had to act unsurprised when I took in the room we had entered. It was small, with a continuous bench running along the walls. There were hooks, on which various sizes of cloaks were hung. They were all dull colours, brown, grey, or sandy like mine. Above the hooks was a shelf, which like the bench, ran around the whole room.

The cloaks seemed to be arranged in order of size, so I went to a group slightly smaller than the ones Tannix had approached. He tugged off his crest ring and placed it on the shelf before taking off his cloak. I imitated him carefully, trying to make it seem like I actually knew what was going on. He took a grey cloak from a hook and hung his own blue one in its place. As he draped it over his shoulders, he glanced at me.

"I know most people dislike the grey ones, but they seem more stone coloured to me," he offered, as if I'd asked him about his colour choice.

I grabbed a sandy one for myself. "This matches the buildings in the lower city better," I pointed out. As I put it on, I marveled at how similar it was to my own cloak. Mine was more worn, of course, and dirtier. I still preferred mine; it had more pockets. Tannix looked at me quizzically, so I paused nervously just as I was tying the cloak in place. "What?"

"You actually remembered your dagger for once," Tannix said.

"Oh, yes." I'd forgotten the knife was there, hanging at my side.

"Well, if you're done, let's go see Malte." He sighed.

"Wait," I said suddenly. "If we want to blend in down there, we need to do this." I pulled the ribbon from my hair and let it fall free. I'd been making sure to wear my hair tied back, but it still felt strange and uncomfortable. I shook my head, much like a dog would, to let my hair fall into a more natural looking state. "Natives don't tie back their hair."

"You know a lot about Natives."

"I've told you, my mother's a Native," I replied. "And their hair never looks like that." I gestured at Tannix's head. His light brown hair looked perfect, as it always did, and even though it wasn't long enough to tie back, it was still cut in a distinctly Teltish style. Without warning, I reached up and ruffled it. "Much better." I grinned at his displeased expression and led the way from the change room.

I SHOULD HAVE EXPECTED WE WOULD NOT BE CLIMBING OVER THE DIVID-ing wall for our descent into the lower city, but taking the main walkway down had not even crossed my mind. It had always seemed so high class, surrounded by guards and almost only used by the rich to get from the upper city to the port. To my left, the Cliffs of Loth towered into the sky. To my right was a wall patrolled by guards. I felt small and insignificant. People, some walking, some riding horses, and some being pulled in carts, were moving up and down the wide walkway. There seemed to be some sort of order. People going down to the port stayed on the right, whereas people heading towards the palace walked on the left. People on foot stayed off to the edges of the walkway, leaving the middle for the faster moving riders and carts. I'd been on the walkway a few times, when I was very young, while I accompanied my mother on trips to the upper city.

We were near the end of the walkway when Malte stopped in front of a large gate. It was the only gate that led to the lower city. It was, in fact, the only way to get into the lower city from the upper, aside from climbing over the wall. He spoke briefly to the guards standing by the gate, and I noticed him display the ring on his thumb. I wondered briefly why we hadn't been told to take them off. Tannix's crest ring would have drawn attention, but so would three gold rings.

The gate was opened and Malte led us through it. Suddenly I was home. I knew that this would be my best chance at escaping, because there was no way either of them would be able to keep up with me. I was almost tempted, but then I remembered the delicious food I'd eaten that morning. Malte walked straight down the street, and the crowds almost parted before him. Tannix looked around nervously, as if he expected to be attacked, but he still followed our huge companion. I paused, taking in the sight of the thin, crowded streets, and sandy buildings that were so familiar. I pulled my hood up over my head, letting it hang down just enough for it to obscure my face. The hood of my real cloak, I couldn't help but note, was better because it was slightly larger. Once I was satisfied that I was disguised as best as I could be, I hurried after the other two.

I caught up with them just as Malte stopped and stepped off into a little side alley. After exchanging a confused glance, Tannix and I followed him. He looked us both over for a moment. "Boys, this is a training exercise and an assessment of your skills. You will each have a chance to lead us through the lower city by means of climbing walls and traveling the rooftops. Your goal is to get us from here to the dividing wall without having to step on the streets. Then, whoever has not led will bring us back. Understood?"

Tannix and I nodded. He looked nervous, but I was delighted. It was so simple I could do it with my eyes closed.

"Lord Tandrix, you will begin," Malte said.

Tannix sighed and walked towards the wall beside us. He paused for a moment, probably to build up his resolve, and then reached up to grab a protruding brick. He started climbing well, going quickly by his standards. When he was high enough that he was out of the way, Malte began to follow him. I grew impatient, I couldn't help it, so I made my way swiftly up the wall opposite the one they were climbing. Once getting to the top, I easily jumped the gap between my building and theirs, landing just as Malte was pulling himself onto the roof.

He got to his feet, and while brushing his hands off on his pants, looked at me. "You said you used to climb a building to watch the sunset, I recall? Where was that?" I struggled to hide my growing worry. "At home. A small farm villa, sir. Near Kitsi."

Malte nodded slowly. "What is your name, again?"

"Finagale, sir."

"Malte," Tannix interrupted. "Am I supposed to take us directly to the dividing wall, or would you like a longer route?"

Malte turned his attention away from me. "As direct as you can make it, without taking to the streets."

Tannix nodded. "Good, thank you." He walked over to the edge of the roof to look down into the street we had been on earlier. "And, sir, are we supposed to be subtle?"

"Yes," Malte replied. "The less the Natives notice, the better."

They had already noticed us, but I didn't dare speak up. I had decided, as soon as Malte's attention had gone to Tannix, to keep my head down and stop showing off. I didn't want to seem too familiar with the place.

Tannix nodded again. He crossed to the other side of the roof. He had picked a good building to climb, though he hadn't done it on purpose. It was long and ran alongside a smaller side street. There were different levels of roofs, meaning that we would need to climb sometimes, but there were no alleyways to jump for a while. Tannix hopped from our roof onto the slightly lower one beside it and began leading the way to the dividing wall. Malte hurried to catch up, and I realized that he was trying to stay close to Tannix to protect him from thieves. Tannix was important enough to merit that, but it would hardly matter if I got hurt. I trailed after them.

When we reached the first gap, Tannix jumped over it after a slight hesitation. I jumped across after him, landing lightly on my feet. Malte followed, much less gracefully. It comforted me to know that jumping was not a talent of his. If I had to run, I could get away.

It was about five minutes after that when Tannix, who had gotten a little further ahead, was attacked. Two thieves jumped on him, easily knocking him to the ground. Malte yelled at them before rushing forward to help, but was halted by two more thieves. One jumped onto his back, and the second ran around, ducking and jumping away from Malte's arms when he tried to grab her.

I felt a hand on my ankle and I was pulled over the edge of the roof onto a slightly lower one. I landed in an awkward crouch, but at least avoided injury. Baisan was there, grinning at me.

"Thought my gang would give you a hand, Finn." He offered me his hand and I used it to get to my feet. "The big one looked a little difficult. You get first pick of the winnings, of course. Where have you been, anyway? I thought you had been arrested."

He looked proud of himself, and I almost felt bad as I leaned closer to him and hissed, "They're both mine, do you understand? Call off your friends." I counted upon my higher status among the thieves to make him listen to me.

Baisan looked confused. "I know you like to work alone, but I thought you'd appreciate some help."

"Call them off."

Baisan met my gaze defiantly for a moment, and then whistled loudly. I could hear the thieves scampering away from Tannix and Malte. One of them, a girl about Baisan's age, landed on the small roof beside us.

"Baisan, the big one hurt Ninavi. Castin had to carry her away."

"How badly?" I asked. I rarely associated with any of this group, besides Baisan, but I knew Ninavi. We'd grown up together. She was young and quite pretty.

The girl looked at me. "He pulled out his knife and cut her leg. She fell over when she tried to run away."

"Take me to her," Baisan said. "Good luck, Finn."

We exchanged a nod. He and the girl swung over the side of the roof to climb down the wall. I turned to pull myself back up onto the higher roof. Malte was on his feet, holding his short dagger and looking furious. Tannix had his dagger out as well. His face lit up when he saw me get back up.

"Finn, you're all right!"

I nodded. "One of them pulled me over the side, but yes, I'm all right."

Malte grumbled something under his breath. "Well, Tandrix, carry on. From now on, however, we will stay closer together, in case those children decide to attack us again."

It was hardly an attack. Baisan's group had simply been keeping the two of them from getting away until they had been given the signal to actually steal from them. I wondered if Malte would be grateful if he knew that I had been the reason the thieves had left, but I doubted it.

THE REST OF THE WAY TO THE DIVIDING WALL PASSED WITH NO INCIDENT. I got the feeling that Baisan's group had spread the word that I'd claimed these two for myself, because we certainly weren't blending in with the locals. I knew we had been attracting the attention of every thief who saw us. Tannix and Malte, despite their disguised cloaks, were still clearly Telts. The lower city was a dangerous place for them because they stood out and everyone knew they had money.

My mind lingered on Ninavi and I hoped Malte hadn't hurt her too badly. It comforted me to know that she was with Baisan, though. He was ambitious, and often got into trouble trying to do things he wasn't capable of, but he did take good care of his little group of street children.

When we reached the dividing wall, we turned around. It was my turn to lead. True to my earlier promise to myself, I did not try to show off. I took a simple route back to the building where we had started. Malte congratulated us both and led us through the thin street back to the gate. A couple of words exchanged with the guards and the gate was opened. We were on our way back to the Order.

THAT EVENING, AFTER EATING DINNER, WE HAD FREE TIME. SOME BOYS went to the library to study, some decided to practice more before going to bed. I had a different idea, and convinced Tannix to come with me. I led him into the courtyard before explaining what I wanted to do.

We were once again dressed in our fancy cloaks. Tannix's crest ring was safely back on his finger, and my hair was protesting being tied back again. I took him up to the building we had climbed together days before.

"Finn," Tannix groaned, as he understood what I was going to make him do. "I'm sore from climbing around the lower city and being attacked by children."

"They were just children." I sighed. "And they didn't hurt you." I started up the wall, taking the same route I had last time. "Tannix, please come with me."

"You'll have to help me again," he said.

"I know what I'm doing, trust me."

He didn't enjoy it, but he followed me up the wall. When we were both safely on the roof, I lay down and put my hands under my head. Tannix, after a moment, lay down next to me.

"What are we doing?"

"Watching the sunset," I replied. "The Cliffs are in the way of the best of it, of course, but if you just stare at the sky it still turns pink and orange. It's easier to see from the roofs."

"Is this what you do at home?"

"Yes," I replied, and for once, I was telling him something about my life that wasn't a lie. "Today, when you distracted Malte… thank you."

"If I asked you to tell me why you hate his attention so much, would you?"

"No," I said truthfully.

"So there is something going on, then?"

"There always is, isn't there?" I said quietly. "You didn't hurt any of the children, did you? I feel sorry for them."

"No." Tannix allowed the change of subject. "Malte did, though. One of the girls. She seemed to have trouble walking, but I don't think she was hurt badly."

"Oh, good. They must have been desperate to attack someone like Malte."

"Must have been," Tannix agreed. We fell into a companionable silence as we watched the sky. The blue gradually turned into the beautiful oranges and reds that I loved so much. I wished, not for the first time, that I could move the Cliffs of Loth and see the sun setting properly. It was only when darkness was starting to creep in the corners of the sky that Tannix broke the silence.

"It's beautiful," he said.

CHAPTER
Seven

"I was thinking we could go over close combat fighting with the daggers, now that you finally have yours with you." Tannix nudged me. "What do you think?"

"Yes, sure," I agreed distractedly. "You're in charge when it comes to the fighting. I thought we had established that by now. Wait... what?" I paused, breaking out of my thoughts to glance at him. "The daggers are sharp."

Tannix nodded. "Yes."

"The practice swords aren't sharp."

"Of course not." He took a couple steps away from me and drew his dagger. "They're made of wood."

"You want to attack me with something sharp?"

"I'm not going to hurt you. The point of training is not to hack each other to pieces. I'm sure you know that."

"Do you even notice how often you hit me with the swords? If they were real, I would be dead by now. Why should I believe that you won't hit me with the dagger?"

"Maybe because I'm not out to kill you," Tannix replied simply. "If I was, you'd be dead by now." He grinned, taunting me. "Let's see what you can do. That trick where you rolled past me won't work this time."

I grumbled under my breath and reached for my dagger. I wasn't sure if I really wanted to have the other boys see it. It had, after all, only been a few days since I'd stolen it. Then there was the part of me that wanted to show off that I owned it. It was pretty, maybe not as fancy as Tannix's, but still impressive. I drew it with my left hand so I would at least have a chance at defending myself.

Tannix rolled his eyes, but didn't complain. "So remember, Finn. Fighting with these is different from fighting with the swords. Not only because these are sharp," he added, before I could make the point myself. "But because we'll be closer together. When we're practicing, we'll just go slowly. I'll make a good fighter out of you eventually."

"I doubt that," I muttered, but I walked a little closer to him and resigned myself to the next few hours. For all my complaining, I knew that Tannix wouldn't hurt me. He was too skilled to do so by accident.

He was already unsatisfied with something. His eyes flickered over my left hand. "You're not even… Here." He cut himself off, apparently finding it easier to show me than to explain. He adjusted the way I was holding the dagger, and then nodded. "Much better, now I can teach you something."

I was distracted by movement nearby, and I glanced up to see that Malte was walking towards us. "Um… Tannix? Malte's coming."

"What?" He sounded a little startled, I think because he'd been concentrating on what he should teach me first. He looked up and followed my gaze. "Oh, he's just coming to see what we're practicing." I knew that wasn't true. Malte's facial expression, though usually grumpy and disdainful, had taken on a look of anger. I knew it was directed at me. Only Tannix's light grip on my left arm kept me from bolting, even though he wasn't trying to trap me. Instead I froze, without really meaning to. Tannix noticed. "Finn? What's wrong?"

I couldn't reply because Malte had reached us, and stood looming over us both. "Come with me," he ordered.

"Why?" Tannix asked. "Are we going to the lower city again?"

"Not you. Finagale," Malte replied dismissively. He grabbed my right forearm and tugged me away. I barely managed to slip my dagger back into its sheath, hoping that maybe it would be useful later.

"Lord Malte," Tannix argued. "I find this highly…"

"You may outrank me by birth, Lord Tandrix," Malte grumbled, "but within this Order, I am your superior. There are things that go on in this kingdom that you have yet to learn about." He left that as his only explanation before dragging me away across the courtyard. There was no point in putting up a fight, so I trailed along dejectedly. I hoped that the appearance of having lost hope would make him lower his guard, potentially let go of my arm, and then I could climb away.

IT DIDN'T HAPPEN, AND I SHORTLY FOUND MYSELF IN A SMALL OFFICE. I was placed in a chair facing a large desk, which Malte sat behind. The door was behind me, and I knew I wouldn't make it out if I just ran. On Malte's desk there were numerous piles of paper, one of which he pushed to the side so that he could rest his arms on the wood.

I realized, suddenly, the reason he hadn't arrested me. As suspicious as he was, he had no proof that I wasn't supposed to be there. He was going to interrogate me. The realization brought with it a flicker of hope. I put on my best offended nobility look and sharply said, "Is this how you treat all the boys you don't like?"

"I think you know exactly why you are here," Malte replied.

"Yes," I agreed. "Because I'm good at climbing walls and you don't trust me because of it. Lord Tandrix is good at fighting, do you not trust him?"

"That is not the reason," Malte said calmly. "Finagale… That's not a Teltish name, is it? Sounds quite Native to me."

"My mother is a Native. She insisted on the name."

"And the way you speak… You see, Finagale, I do not only teach young boys the basic skills they will need in the Order. I specialize in languages. A particular fascination of mine is dialects. Do you know what that means?"

"Of course I do," I replied, hoping that I sounded insulted at his assumption. Of course, I didn't know.

"Teltans, across the kingdom, tend to sound similar in the way they speak and the words they use," Malte continued. "And their accents are often indistinguishable. Natives, on the other hand, speak differently city to city. This is because they do not come in contact with each other very often, and because of that have developed different ways of saying things. Your pronunciation is distinctly Native, particularly the Zianna dialect."

"My mother is a Native," I repeated, slightly less sure of myself this time. "I picked up things from her."

"You claim to come from a farm villa near Kitsi, correct?"

I nodded.

"So tell me, how does a common Ziannan Native end up the wife of a lord, albeit a lesser lord, near Kitsi?"

"She was raised here, but her family moved to Kitsi when she was young. She ended up working in my father's household, and they fell in love," I said. "I can't explain love, sir. I know it's unusual for Teltans to fall in love with Natives, but it happens." I had to consciously make the effort to say Teltans. I knew that saying Telt would have given me away.

Malte narrowed his eyes. He picked up a piece of paper from the stack beside him and glanced over it casually, but I knew he had probably memorized everything it said. "Where is your farm villa?"

"North of Kitsi," I replied.

"North of Kitsi is Lord Paonne's land."

I nodded. "Yes, of course, most of it." I agreed quickly, before realizing that he might have made up the name to trick me. I hesitated, sure that I had made a mistake, but he didn't say anything. "Lord Paonne owns most of the land," I continued warily. "My father is just a lesser lord beneath him."

"So why is it that I can find no record of your family in this Order?"

"I'm the first one to come here, sir," I lied. "My father was the only son, and my grandfather is the one who earned the land from Lord Paonne. I've been the first son able to come."

"So you have an older sibling?"

"Yes, Finagan."

"What is your father's name?"

That question caught me off guard though I should have expected it. "Lord F—" Loud knocking at the door interrupted and saved me.

Malte groaned. "Enter!" he called.

I resisted the urge to glance back to see who had opened the door. I didn't need to, anyway, as it was Tannix, who spoke after the door creaked open.

"Sir, Lord Co is here. He wishes to speak to you immediately."

"When did he get here?"

"He just charged in on his horse, sir."

Malte looked thoughtful for a moment. "Tell him I can speak to him now." He looked at me and nodded towards the door. "Go."

"Thank you, sir," I said quietly. Hopefully, I didn't sound as scared as I felt. I got to my feet and walked past Tannix to leave the room. He let the door close and quickly caught up with me.

"What was that about?"

I shrugged, but my mind was racing. I had to get out. My lies might have been convincing enough this time, but I knew Malte wouldn't leave me alone. I was so distracted that I didn't notice the man standing in front of me until I had walked into him. "Sorry, sir, I…" but then I stopped, because I recognized him. He looked down at me quizzically, as though he was trying to remember where he'd seen me before.

"Lord Malte is ready to see you, sir," Tannix spoke up.

The man stopped looking at me to nod at Tannix. "Thank you." He walked off without another word.

"What's wrong with you?" Tannix whispered.

I was shaking, but I hadn't noticed it before he brought it up. "That man…"

"Lord Co?"

"He's… missing his ring, isn't he?"

"I didn't notice." Tannix sounded confused. "Finn, what's going on?"

"Can we go up to your room?" I asked.

Tannix nodded hesitantly. "Yes, come on."

I tried not to look the part of nervous criminal, but it was hard. Every noise startled me, and I expected Malte to leap from the shadows and grab me. Lord Co must have explained how his ring had been stolen, and Malte must have made the connection. The trip up to Tannix's room seemed to take twice as long as usual. The staircase seemed taller, the hallway longer. Everything was drawn out and every sound was a threat. When we did eventually reach Tannix's room, without having been stopped along the way, I thanked Zianesa.

Tannix closed his door and leaned back against it. He crossed his arms over his chest and stared across the room at me. I had gone straight for the window and opened it, but I didn't leave. I needed to leave when he wasn't watching me so carefully, so that I'd have a least a moment's head start.

"Tell me what's going on."

I took a deep breath. "I'm sorry. I lied to you."

"About what?"

I paused and met his gaze across the room. "Everything."

Tannix looked startled, but before my words really had time to sink in, a loud gonging sound echoed in from outside. I flinched, and glanced quickly at the window. It was different from the gong that woke me up every morning. It was an alarm.

"Finn, what did you do?" Tannix managed to ask.

"I'm sorry," I repeated, glancing quickly back over at him. He was still near the door, though now not leaning against it. I turned and pulled myself out of his window before he could even take a step in my direction. I wasn't used to this section of the wall, but I still hurried up it onto the roof. Hopefully, no one would know I had fled this way except for Tannix, and I desperately hoped that our friendship would keep him from coming after me. I first went to the corner were my cloak was stashed. The red of my stolen cloak would be nearly impossible to hide. I pulled my sandy cloak over the red one, unwilling to leave it behind.

I crept to the edge of the roof to look down into the courtyard. It was filled with people, both men and boys. Malte and Lord Nata of Co were standing in front of them all, explaining what the alarm was for. The whole place would be looking for me, so I knew I had to be quick. I picked the wall that was hidden from the courtyard and slowly started for it. I was about halfway down when the gong went again, and I assumed that meant people had started their search.

I was still out of sight from the courtyard when I reached the ground. A quick glance around confirmed that I was alone, so I hurried across the courtyard to the main wall. If I could get over it and into the upper city, I would stand a chance at getting away. If I could make it to the lower city, they would never be able to find me.

I grabbed the edge of a large brick and began to haul myself up, only to be pulled back down and have a hand clamped over my mouth. I began struggling furiously, until he spoke.

"Finagale, stop it."

I did. Despite the fact that Tannix could have been arresting me, I listened to him.

"Lord Tandrix?" a call came from further down the walkway. Whoever called was right behind one of the other buildings, if they just turned the corner, they would see us. I couldn't help it and started to struggle against Tannix again.

"He's not here!" Tannix yelled back. "I'll check around the next corner!"

I froze again. Tannix let me go and glared at me, while rubbing a spot on his arm I thought I had hit with my elbow.

"You're lucky I knew you'd come down over here," he said.

"You're not going to…"

Tannix shook his head. "No. Did you steal that ring from Lord Co?"

I nodded.

"So who are you?"

"I…" I hesitated. Telling him seemed harder than it should have been. Maybe it was because I valued his friendship, or maybe it was because the son of West Draulin deserved to be friends with better people than me. "I'm a thief from the streets."

Tannix looked disappointed, but he nodded. "I suppose that explains a lot." He jerked his head at the wall. "Go," he said, before he spun around and walked away.

"Thank you," I quietly called after him, but he ignored me.

CHAPTER
Eight

I went home. The lower city seemed both familiar and foreign. The streets and buildings I was used to were now boring compared to the Order's huge, black stoned building. I wondered if I would ever see the inside of it again. Distracted as I was, I still managed to get to my little home without being noticed by anyone who knew me. I climbed the wall to my room. It would be nice not to have to sleep on a roof anymore, I noted, trying to keep positive.

My room looked untouched. Baisan knew where it was, and it surprised me a little that he hadn't raided it during my absence. I knelt beside the pile of clothing and dug out my wooden chest. I ran my hand across the top of it thoughtfully, amazed at how old it looked. Before, I had simply been used to owning shabby things. Being at the Order had made me used to a higher standard of living, and I hadn't even realized it. I pulled my chain over my head and unlocked it. The pile of coins inside was pitiful compared to what someone like Tannix would own, but it was everything I had. I picked up a couple of the coppers and started fiddling with them while I tried to figure out what to do. I'd been gone for a about a week and a half, not long enough that I'd have been forgotten, but I would probably have to claw my way back up to the top of the thieves' shaky hierarchy. Everyone would expect me to have something impressive to show off after being gone.

While I dropped the coins back into the chest, the ring caught my eye and I stared at it for a moment. I had gotten so used to it being there, but now it didn't seem right. I pulled it off my thumb and held it in my palm like I had that first day. I still didn't want to sell it, but I knew it wouldn't be safe to wear it in plain view. I glanced at the key on its chain and suddenly realized what to do. After locking the chest, I slipped the ring onto the chain so that it hung down next to the key. I draped the chain back around my neck and tucked it under my tunic. I buried the chest back under its pile and left my room.

BAISAN AND HIS GROUP OF CHILDREN LIVED IN A RUINED, ABANDONED building pressed up against the dividing wall. They had moved a few times over the years, but I always paid attention to where they were. They lived closer to me than any other thieves did, so we often ran into each other.

When I reached their building, I noticed that Baisan had blocked off most of the entrances. It was a good idea, and would make it harder for another group to chase them out. It also meant that I couldn't simply sneak in as I had planned. I went for the door instead, and had hardly taken a step in when I was met by Baisan.

"Finn," he said my name simply, as a greeting.

"Baisan," I replied. "I'm back."

"You're not going to tell me where you've been," Baisan said. "So why are you here?" He leaned against the frame of the doorway, blocking my way in. I knew it would be easy for me to push him out of the way, but I was in his place and I decided to show a bit of respect.

"I want to see Ninavi," I explained.

"Why?"

"You know we grew up together," I said. "I'm not trying to take her from you." In the past, he had been suspicious of me trying to take over his group, but I had no desire to lead it.

Baisan narrowed his eyes. He turned his head to shout into the darkness of his ruined building. "Castin! Is Ninavi awake?"

"She is now," came the sarcastic reply.

Baisan sighed. "All right, Finn. You can come in and see her." He walked down the little hallway, and I trailed after him. The hallway windows had been blocked off, so it was dark—another one of Baisan's defenses, I assumed. The room we walked into had a small fire burning in the middle of it. Its window had been blocked too, but only with a piece of wood that they could move if needed. Sitting beside the fire was a boy who I assumed was Castin, and on a makeshift bed against the wall was Ninavi.

Baisan started explaining why I was there, as I walked across the room towards her. I knelt beside the bed. "Ninavi?"

"What?" she asked sleepily. She sat up slowly and looked at me in confusion. "Who're y— Finn?"

I nodded. It had been a few years since we'd last properly seen each other, and I understood her momentary confusion. "I heard you got hurt."

This time she nodded. "It isn't too bad. That huge man just got my leg with his knife. It hurts when I try to walk, but Baisan says it'll heal fine." She glanced over my shoulder at him for confirmation. "Did you come to check on me?" She turned her gaze back on me.

I smiled and nodded. "Of course. Why else would I want to put up with Baisan? I have something for you."

"You didn't…"

I ignored Baisan's protest and pulled off my sandy cloak. The red one was still underneath, and I took it off as well. Then I handed it to Ninavi. I hadn't planned it ahead of time, but it suddenly seemed like the proper thing to do. Her eyes widened as she took the cloak and felt the expensive material.

"Where did it come from?" she whispered in awe.

"That huge man," I explained. "After you left, I followed him to his home and I took this from inside. He had so many, I doubt he'll notice. And you deserve a good prize after getting hurt."

"It's beautiful, Finn," Ninavi murmured. "Are you sure you want to give it to me? Imagine what you could sell it for!"

I shrugged. "You can sell it, if you want to."

"No, I won't." Ninavi hugged the bundled cloak to her chest. "It's beautiful. I'm going to keep it forever. Thank you."

"You deserve it," I told her again. I picked up my own cloak and stood up while slipping it on. Baisan was still standing in the doorway, watching me warily. Castin was holding an old knife and a rock he had been using to sharpen it, but he had stopped and was staring at me.

"Did the dagger come from the huge man too?" he asked. "Because I think that should be a gift as well. Seeing as we helped you."

"Castin," Baisan said. "We don't beg from fellow thieves. No matter how important they might think they are."

"I wasn't begging," Castin protested, but he went back to sharpening his own knife.

"It didn't come from him, anyway," I replied. "Baisan, I actually have another reason for being here."

"Of course you do."

I hesitated. "Being away has made me realize how lonely my life used to be. I would like to, well, join your group. Not permanently, I just want to be allowed to come and go. While here, I'll respect your position of leader and follow your rules, and I will contribute to the group's wellbeing. But while on my own I would like to be left alone."

He stared at me blankly. "What?"

"I know it's unexpected, but I've been through a lot and I would feel safer with a group. I don't know how long this will last, but I promise I will be helpful while I'm here."

Baisan glanced at Castin. He seemed to be the second in command. The other children would be out looking for food or money to bring back to the group, but Castin had been trusted to stay and look after Ninavi. He was clearly important. They exchanged some sort of silent conversation, and Baisan looked at me again.

"A trial period," he said. "And if you make any move to take over, we'll chase you out."

I nodded. "Sounds fair."

Baisan visibly relaxed. "Would you mind going out now, then? Without Ninavi, the others might be having trouble getting enough food. People are more likely to give her things."

Girls always had an easier time of begging, people tended to pity them more. "Of course."

"Pickpocket or beg, I don't care what you do. Just try to get enough food for two people."

"Easy," I replied with a casual shrug. "I'll be back within the hour." I brushed past him to leave the room, and I heard him following me, probably to make sure I was actually leaving. I reached the door and was about to step out when a hand dropped onto my shoulder.

I yelped and flinched, expecting to see Malte looming over me, but it was a different large man. He started chuckling at my reaction.

"Finn, who knew you were so jumpy? And you're getting friendly with Baisan, are you?" Arow let go of me and turned to Baisan. "You haven't paid me yet, boy. Finn being here triples the price, because he owes me."

"I haven't joined him, Arow," I said. "I also don't owe you anything."

"Yes you do," Arow growled. "Everyone pays me."

"I don't pay you. Neither does Baisan," I said. "Maybe you should start to steal things for yourself instead of taking them from us. Or are you afraid you'll get caught and hanged?"

"Finn," Baisan pleaded quietly. "Stop it. We'll pay him."

"No, we won't."

Arow was glaring at me, furious. It would have scared me before, but it was nothing compared to the way Malte had looked at me. He lunged, just like I'd expected, and I ducked out of the way. I whipped out my pretty dagger and held it backwards in a way that would have made Tannix cringe.

Arow looked concerned. "Finn learned to fight, did he?"

"I did," I replied coldly. I hoped he would take me at my word and not test my abilities, because if it came to it, he would win. He apparently decided that it was too risky to attack me. It helped that Castin had heard our conversation and appeared holding his own little knife. It was small, but I didn't doubt that he would be the bigger threat. Arow glanced between us, and without a word, ambled off.

Once he was out of sight, I put my dagger away. Baisan was staring at me, wide eyed. "I thought you didn't like conflict. Where did you learn to fight?"

"I didn't," I replied. "I just know how to hold a knife and pretend I know how to fight."

Baisan and Castin exchanged another quick glance.

"Thanks, Finn," Baisan said. "Um... forget about the trial period, right? Welcome home."

Part Two

THE LETTER

FOUR YEARS LATER

CHAPTER
Nine

"Help me! Please help!" Ninavi's scream echoed across the market-place. I peeked cautiously around the edge of the wall I was hiding behind. I could see her running across the cobbled upper city street. The red cloak billowed out behind her as she ran. She'd started to grow into it, but it was still slightly too big on her. Her hair was messy and tangled, but despite that, she still managed to look like a little rich foreigner, though her skin was too dark to pass off as a Telt. However, the marketplace was filled with traders and merchants from different kingdoms, and she blended in.

Ninavi ran straight into two men who had been walking slowly side by side, deep in discussion. The one she hit lost his balance, but didn't fall over. She clung to his arm desperately. "Please help me." She started sobbing, quite convincingly. "I lost my brother and these two boys, they…" She cut herself off with a shriek as Baisan and Castin ran around the corner. Castin's knife glinted in the sunlight as he used it to gesture towards Ninavi and the two men.

The two of them ran closer to Ninavi, only stopping when they seemed to realize that she was with the men. Baisan stopped first and grabbed Castin's arm. "Stop." He was the better speaker of the two, so as planned, he took a tentative step closer to Ninavi and the men. "Excuse me, sirs. That's my little sister there."

"He's lying," Ninavi sobbed. She clung tighter to the man and tried to hide herself in his cloak. "They're chasing me. They tried to hurt me."

"You tried to hurt this girl?" the second man said. He drew a short dagger. "Go back to where you belong before we call the guards on you."

"No, no, sir… no need for that." Baisan held up his hands as if in surrender and walked backwards until he was next to Castin again. "We weren't trying to hurt her, were we, Cast?"

Castin shook his head and held his hand behind his back, like he was trying to hide the knife that had been so easy to see a moment before.

"No," Baisan continued. "No, sir. She took something from us, is what happened, sir."

"This little girl?" the man who was holding Ninavi asked. "She took something from you?"

"Yes sir, she did. That cloak is mine," Baisan explained.

"No, it isn't," Ninavi protested. "They tried to take it from me and…" she paused to widen her eyes and stare up at the man holding her. "And the ugly one with the knife said he'd cut me up if I didn't give it to them. But I ran away."

The three of them played their parts well. The two men didn't notice me when I snuck up behind them and slipped my hand into their pockets. The one holding Ninavi had a hefty little coin pouch, which I was more than glad to take from him.

"That was very brave," he told Ninavi gently. "You're safe now."

"She's lying, sir," Baisan said. "It doesn't fit her, see? It can't be hers."

"It's my brother's," Ninavi replied sharply. "Go away!"

I reached into the second man's pocket and was momentarily disappointed. My fingers only felt a piece of paper. I carefully pulled it out and slipped it under my own cloak along with the first man's coin pouch. A quick reach into his other pocket resulted in a small handful of coins. I made quick eye contact with Baisan and nodded so that he would know I was done before sneaking away and ducking back into the alley.

"Go away. Make them go away," she pleading, tugging on the first man's arm.

"Leave," the man told Baisan and Castin sternly. "Or we will call the guards and you'll be thrown back into the lower city."

Baisan said nothing to that. Instead, he just nudged Castin and the two of them ran off. Ninavi kept talking to the men while the boys ran into a nearby alley, and quickly ended up standing with me.

"Good?" Baisan asked.

"Not bad. Forty siyas." I handed him the coin pouch, to which I had added the second man's coins and the letter.

"Paper?" Baisan scoffed, turning it over in his hand. "Why did you take this?"

"I already had my hand on it." I shrugged. "It might be important." I handed my cloak to Castin and held out my arms. "How do I look?"

"Rich," Baisan replied distractedly. "Go get her."

I punched his shoulder lightly before walking out of the alley. I was wearing a dark tunic and pair of pants I had stolen recently, along with some new boots Baisan had found for me the day before. My dagger was attached to the belt I had bought about a year before. My hair was tied up with the old red ribbon to match Ninavi's cloak. My foreigner bracelet, the gold one with red and white jewels, also matched. I didn't look rich, but I easily looked like the child of some middle class merchant.

When Ninavi saw me, she tore herself from the man's grasp and threw herself into my arms. "You found me!" she cried, clinging to me so tightly I had trouble breathing for a moment.

The two men looked over me suspiciously. "Who are you?"

"He's my brother." Ninavi smiled at them brightly. "He'll protect me from those ugly boys."

"What boys?" I asked, doing my best to sound concerned. "What have you been doing?"

"Some street children tried to attack her," the first man explained.

"But they saved me," Ninavi said. "They scared the boys away."

"Thank you." I nodded to the men gratefully.

"Are you sure you'll be safe now?" the man asked, addressing Ninavi. She had obviously won them over with her act.

Ninavi nodded. She loosened her grip on me to take my hand. "My brother will protect me. He has a knife too. They'll be scared."

"We're going to go straight to father," I told her. "He should be done selling everything by now."

The two men seemed satisfied that she would be safe, once hearing that I would be taking her to an adult. "Be careful," the second man said. "Those thieves are everywhere."

"They usually stick to the lower city," the first man added. "But these ones must be desperate for something good."

I smiled and acted grateful for the man's information. "Thank you, we'll be careful. Come now, Ninavi." I turned and led her away.

WE GOT HOME BEFORE BAISAN AND CASTIN BECAUSE THEY HAD GONE out to buy some food with the money our trip had earned us. We entered the old building and found that the other three members of our little family were also home from their adventure. Ninavi went to sit by the fire, next to the other girl.

"Good trip?" the girl asked.

"Stria, you should have seen these men." Ninavi started giggling. "They believed every word I said! It was great!" She dramatically started telling the story, interrupted only by questions from Stria.

The two other boys in the room, half-brothers Orrun and Leker, both greeted me with a nod. They were the only two who had joined our group after I had four years before. They had shown up a few months after one of our own, a young boy named Drio, died of a sickness. Although they came to us without any skills, it hadn't taken long to teach them how to be good thieves. I liked them. They looked up to me, unlike Baisan and Castin.

I joined them at the fire. "The other two are buying food. How did you three do?"

"Stria got some bread from a stall owner," Orrun explained. "Leker and I stole four oranges." He gestured at the little pile of food. "We were noticed before we could get more."

"We'll each get half," I said. "And the bread can easily be sliced into seven pieces. Baisan and Castin will probably buy some meat. It'll be a good meal." I reached across them to pick up the loaf of bread and pulled out my knife to start cutting it into equal pieces.

There was a rustling from the door and we all froze until we heard Baisan's voice. He and Castin appeared in our room a moment later. Baisan was triumphantly holding a bundle wrapped in dirty cloth. "Another wonderful performance by our talented Ninavi. Look at what that money bought us." He knelt beside the fire and put down his bundle. We all stopped what we had been doing to watch as he slowly unwrapped it. Underneath the cloth was a whole cooked chicken, the smell of it filled the little room.

Baisan looked up and grinned at our expressions. "Amazing, isn't it? That plan was great, Finn."

"Ah well." I waved my hand dismissively. "Wouldn't have worked without your acting as well. We need conflict, after all."

Ninavi giggled. "I need some ugly boys to chase after me," she teased.

"Ugly?" Castin tossed my cloak at me. "You must be blind."

"I agree with her," Stria said. She laughed when Castin glared at her.

"None of us believe that, Stria," Baisan said. He took Castin's knife and began to cut up the chicken carefully. "We all saw you two together a few nights ago." His comment received more laugher from Ninavi, a blush from Stria, and another angry glare from Castin.

Baisan started handing out pieces of chicken, and so I handed out the bread. We fell silent as we ate our hard-earned food. It was one of the rare times we could eat more than one helping, and we relished it. Baisan kept cutting away at the chicken until there was no meat left, and then we ate the oranges the boys had stolen. By our standards, it was a feast.

After the meal, when we were all relaxing around the fire, Ninavi once again told the story of the two rich men. When she described Baisan's acting, the other boys all teased him, but he just grinned. Ninavi then moved on to me. "And then Finn walked out and they actually believed he was a Telt!"

"Maybe not a Telt," I protested.

Orrun tossed the chicken bone he had been chewing on at me. "And so Finn, the greatest thief, can pass as a Telt? What can't you do?"

"They didn't think I was a Telt," I said. "They thought I was some merchant's son."

Castin was sprawled out on the floor near me with his arms crossed under his head, so he resorted to nudging me with his foot. "Not going to protest the greatest thief part?"

"It's true, isn't it?" I replied with a cocky grin, even though my words were laced with sarcasm.

"Oh, that reminds me." Baisan reached under his cloak and held out the envelope I had stolen. "Here you are, *my Lord*. Don't know why you want to keep it."

"It might be important," I said, taking it from his hand. "Information can sell." I angled the letter so that the light from the fire would light it up, and I stared down at it. It was made of nice paper, but the part that interested me most was a blob of wax holding it closed. Only important letters had such seals.

"None of us can read," Baisan pointed out. "How will you know what it's about?"

I paused. I hadn't actually thought that far ahead when I'd taken the letter.

"So the greatest thief made a mistake that resulted in his downfall," Castin said with a grin.

I shook my head. "No, not yet. I know someone who can read."

Baisan took it from my hand and inspected the seal curiously. "Do you really think you can sell it? What if it's just a love letter?"

I shrugged. "I guess it could be. But it's worth figuring out, isn't it?"

"Sure, if you want to." He handed it back to me, already having lost interest. But I couldn't stop being curious, and besides, the letter seemed like a perfect push to do something I'd been meaning to do for ages.

CHAPTER
Ten

"**D**on't get yourself killed, right?"

"Baisan, I didn't know you enjoyed my company that much," I said. Most of the others were asleep. I had decided to leave that very night. I had also decided to leave my cloak behind. It was a warm enough night, and its colour did nothing to help me blend into the upper city. The black tunic and pants I was wearing would work much better, especially when I reached the black stone walls of the Order's building.

I hadn't told Baisan where I was going, because I had never told him where I'd disappeared to years ago. That part of my life had remained a mystery to our little family. At first, I'd been holding back from telling them, but later it was just never brought up. I had, over the years, gotten closer to them, to the point where I lived with them all the time. I understood why Baisan was worried about me disappearing again; I was family.

"I don't," he replied, though we both knew it wasn't true. "I'm worried about the girls, is all. They like you."

"I'll let you in on a bit of a secret, Baisan." I put my arm over his shoulders and lowered my voice. "I'm immortal. Besides, I know exactly where I'm going. I'll be fine."

Baisan rolled his eyes and pushed me away. "Go then. Be back tomorrow."

"Yes sir," I said. I had kept to the promise I'd made back then about letting him stay in charge. He just shook his head at my grin, and then turned to walk back into our building.

IT WAS EASY MOVING THROUGH THE UPPER CITY. I STILL LOOKED LIKE A middle class foreigner, and so I had no need to hide in the shadows and duck away from guards. I got nervous every time a set of guards walked near me, but they never gave me a second glance. I reached the Order's wall sooner than I expected, and hesitated before starting up it. It had been years since I had last been over that wall. I didn't know what to expect. I didn't know if he would remember me, or if he would want to help, or if he'd even still be there. I had to take the chance, though. I could hardly go to any other Telt without running the risk of being arrested on sight, and any Native who could read would want in on the prize. Assuming there was a prize.

I slipped into a corner while yet another pair of guards walked past. Once I could no longer hear their footsteps, I started climbing up the wall. It took less time than I had expected. Before I knew it, I had safely reached the top and was working my way down the other side. The courtyard was deserted and perfectly silent. I could see no lights from any of the smaller buildings. In the main building, some windows were still lit, no doubt because someone was reading old documents.

I remembered which window was his, so after making sure there was nobody around to see me, I began to climb up the side of the building. On the way up, I prayed quickly to Zianesa, hoping that he would still be in the same room. If it wasn't him and a stranger responded, I would have to be quick to get away.

I hesitated outside of the window that used to be his. I decided on an escape route, just in case. A quick drop to the windowsill below me, and then I would be far enough out of reach to climb down without being grabbed. Getting over the wall quickly would pose a problem, but I could deal with that if it came to it. I took a deep breath, muttered another prayer, and knocked on the window. I knocked again after a moment of nothing happening. The window opened suddenly and before I could make even the slightest move towards my escape, I was pulled into the room. I was pinned against the wall with one strong arm, and I could feel a blade edge against my neck. I froze, knowing that fighting would probably just earn me a slit throat.

"Finn?"

My eyes widened when I realized it was Tannix's voice. It was deeper than it had been the last time I'd seen him, but still his voice. He let go of me and without his support, I fell to the ground, where I landed on my hands and knees. I ran a hand across my neck, feeling for a cut.

"Sorry." He offered me his hand and I let him help me to my feet. My other hand was still at my neck, and I gave him one of my best unimpressed looks. That was when I noticed just how much he'd grown since we'd last seen each other. He had been taller than me before, but not by much. Now I just managed to reach his shoulder. Suddenly nervous, I dropped my gaze.

"You know I'm obliged to arrest you on sight," Tannix said. He had moved over to his desk and lit a small candle. The moonlight was enough that we had been able to see each other's shapes, but that didn't seem to be enough for him. He was dressed just like he used to in dark pants and a deep blue tunic. Telt clothing.

I nodded. "Yes."

"So?"

"I have something for you," I replied, faltering. I pulled the envelope from under my tunic and offered it to him.

He crossed his arms and leaned back against his desk. "What is it?"

"I don't know," I admitted. "It looked important."

"Why did you bring it to me?"

"Because we're… were once… friends," I said. "And I can't read."

"You read with me in the library."

"I stared at a book in the library."

He didn't reply for a moment, then sighed. "Where did you get it?"

"I stole it."

"Then I want nothing to do with it. Rich lords don't tend to associate with thieves."

I flinched. "I know, Tannix. I'm sorry I lied to you and…"

"Lord Tandrix."

I stared at the floor again and bit my lip. "Sorry, Lord Tandrix."

Tannix pulled the letter from my hand, but instead of looking at it, he just tossed it onto his desk. "Finn, sit down."

"Please don't call in the guards," I said quickly. "I'll leave, I'll never come back. I'm sorry I bothered you."

Tannix gestured at a comfortable looking armchair with his knife. I looked at him nervously, but then did what I was told. I pulled my legs up and huddled into the chair, as if it would protect me. He started to pace in front of me.

"Four years. Not a word until you need help with something?"

"I'm sorry." I muttered, but then his words sunk in and I looked up. "Wait, you wanted a word?"

"Yes!" Tannix exclaimed. "You lied to me, you broke the law, but you were my friend."

I didn't know what to make of that. "So you missed me?"

"I didn't say that."

"You know, in my defense, I didn't want to lie to you. I was running away from some guards and you tackled me to the ground."

"Probably should have turned you in then."

"Probably," I agreed. "So, that letter?"

Tannix shook his head. "I'll look at it after you tell me who you really are. It's hardly fair that you know so much about me."

"I don't think you want to know who I really am."

"Finn," he said sternly.

I swallowed. "Um, all right. My mother was a prostitute. My father was probably a Telt, but there's no way to know for sure." I warmed up to the story a bit, having the hardest part out of the way. "I grew up in the brothel. All the women there took care of me, and they all cared about me, but at the same time I was a burden to have around. Men don't want to walk into a brothel and see a child running around, after all. So I quickly learned how to fend for myself. I became a pretty good pickpocket, and the women noticed, so they encouraged me to steal things for them as well. Money, food, jewellery, new clothing, anything they could think of, really.

"I learned to climb walls because they didn't want me using the front door, so I had to climb up to one of the windows on the second floor. As I got older, I relied less and less on the women at the brothel and stopped going back to them as often as I should have. I started to spend nights out on my own, which led to weeks out on my own. A few years before you and I met, my mother was killed by a customer. A Telt."

Tannix had stopped pacing early on, and was just staring at me. "What?"

"I know lives like that seem impossible to you, but it's all true," I muttered. "I didn't lie this time."

"No, I believe you," Tannix said. "I just... I apologize for my people."

"It isn't your fault Telts like to ruin our lives," I said. I felt surprisingly good, having told him the true story about my life. "But thank you."

"So much has already happened to you," Tannix muttered. "How old are you?"

I shrugged. "I don't know, not really. My mother never remembered my birthday, so of course she could never tell me. Baisan's fifteen and I think I'm older than him..."

"You don't know how old you are?"

"It isn't that unusual. Not for a Native orphan. How old are you?"

"Eighteen," Tannix replied. "You're probably..." he paused thoughtfully. "Around sixteen, I think."

"Why do you think that?"

"Well, you're younger than me. I knew that when we first met. It's still just a guess, though."

"Oh, well, maybe I'll be sixteen," I decided. "The letter?"

Tannix sighed and walked over to his desk to pick it up. He slipped the blade of his knife under the wax to break it, and then pulled the letter from the envelope. He didn't put down the knife.

"Are you afraid I'll attack you?"

"A little," he replied, distracted because he had started reading.

"You know you could probably kill me with your bare hands if you wanted to."

"Of course I could," he agreed. "Be quiet."

I sighed grumpily and adjusted the way I was sitting. It seemed like I'd been forgiven for lying before, and I felt more comfortable being around him. There was no longer a need to huddle into the chair as if it could wrap around me and protect me.

"Finn?" Tannix looked at me. "Are you sure you haven't read this?"

"I can't read," I insisted.

"So you didn't make this up?" he asked.

"If I can't read, I assure you I can't write," I said. "Why? What does it say?"

He looked torn for a moment, probably wondering if he should tell me or not. Then he looked down at the paper and took a deep breath. "My dear Associate, I trust your trip was pleasant. As a method of transportation, the sea has always been a favourite of mine. Zianna is a city full of traders and goods; you will find it effortless to blend into the crowd. Be wary of men in yellow, for they are the city guards, and sometimes enjoy arresting people for offences that you would most likely find harmless.

"I have included a map of the city that I believe will be beneficial to your visit. The city is built in a style that will be familiar to you, but the Cliffs of Loth create minor alterations that can occasionally be confusing. Remember what I told you about the Lothian Dusk. The city darkens earlier than you are accustomed to. This is the time when the lowly thieves thrive. Always watch for them, for they are crafty.

"I hope you will find time to visit my old friend, M. He and I grew up together, trained together, and now he is my invaluable associate. He has a deeper knowledge of the city, and will be able to provide you with information that I, unfortunately, cannot. I am certain that you have remembered the address I gave you.

"Please remember, a king leads a country. Without a king, the war begins, and a country falls. Your Associate."

When it was clear that Tannix wasn't going to continue, I shrugged. "So is it important?"

"Finn! Did you listen to anything I just read?"

"Sounded like someone describing Zianna," I said, confused.

"It's supposed to sound like that," he said. "The last line is the important one. Without a king, the war begins, and a country falls. It sounds like an assassination."

"Really?" I felt more interested in the letter. "Isn't this good? You can go hand it in, and then the king will be saved. I saved the king! Do you think he'd give me a reward?" I imagined all the gold and jewels the king must have had stowed away somewhere.

"No." Tannix interrupted my wonderful vision. "No, Finn, he wouldn't. I can't even turn this in."

"What? Why not?"

"Because I'm not a spy," he explained. "I can't explain having this. They'll assume that I'm somehow involved and just got nervous and decided to turn the whole thing in. I'll be arrested, and probably tortured for information, which I wouldn't have to give up."

"The son of West Draulin?" I asked. "They wouldn't suspect you. They wouldn't torture you."

"For the sake of the king's life?" Tannix shook his head. "My position wouldn't save me."

"But they couldn't hurt you," I protested.

"Yes, they could."

"Maybe we can figure it out ourselves," I suggested. "They mentioned someone named M, right?"

"No, M is a letter, not a name. The person's name probably starts with it."

"Oh," I paused to think. "Probably Malte, that sounds like M, right? I could see him involved in something like this."

My suggestion got a smile from Tannix. "You just don't like him because he saw through your lies."

"I still think it's him," I insisted. "So what else do we know?"

Tannix glanced back down at the letter. "It has the stamp of Navire in the corner. We can't work off that; we need to give it to someone." He paused thoughtfully. "Do you know where the director's office is?"

I shook my head warily. "Why?"

"Because you could sneak up and drop it off on his desk," Tannix explained. "Anonymously. Then I won't be suspected for it."

"I don't know…"

"Come on, Finn. I think you can manage this. You snuck in here without anyone noticing."

"Yes…"

"So you can do this." He turned to his desk and started doing something I couldn't see. When he turned around and offered the letter to me, I saw that the wax had been re-melted and stuck back onto the envelope.

"Now?" I groaned.

"We should do it soon, but we can wait for a bit." He went back over to his desk and opened a large book. After flipping through a couple of pages, he motioned for me to join him. Reluctantly, I climbed from the comfortable chair to stand beside him. We were looking down at a layout of the building. "This is the director's office," Tannix said, pointing to a room on one of the drawings. "This is my room," he pointed to another drawing. "We're on the third floor, the director is on the fifth. Think you can find it?"

I studied the drawing a little longer before nodding. Memorizing maps was something I happened to be good at. "Yes, I can find it."

CHAPTER

Eleven

We decided to wait until the sun was starting to rise, having realized that I would have trouble finding a window I had never been to in the dark. We spent the time talking, partially, I thought, because he wasn't sure if he trusted me yet and didn't want to go to sleep. He even went down to the kitchens to get me some food. When he returned, he sat on his bed, and I had once again buried myself into the comfortable chair. He was asking me questions, but I didn't mind answering them, not after getting the hard topic of my parents out of the way.

"So, that dagger?" he started, after giving me a moment to start devouring the bread he had brought me. "Fairly soon after you left, one of the others started complaining about how he couldn't find one of his daggers. I assume that's it?"

I nodded.

"And the cloak too?"

"Someone else's," I explained. "I knew better than to take both things from the same person."

"And the ring is Lord Co's?"

I nodded again. This time I took the chain I wore around my neck and pulled it out from under my tunic. The ring still hung on it. The key I'd long ago given to Baisan so that he could use my little chest for our money. "I was thinking of selling it, but I got a little attached to it. I didn't know I was getting myself into anything important when I took it, I just thought it was another piece of jewellery." I tucked the chain back under my tunic and tore a piece off the bread.

"You like jewellery?"

"It's easy to hide and easy to sell," I told him. I was a little surprised at how open I was being about my life, but Tannix seemed fascinated by the way I lived. "There's always a prostitute who wants to make herself look nicer."

"Know a lot about prostitutes, don't you?"

I looked up from my bread. "For the love of Zianesa, Tannix, I grew up in a brothel. That doesn't mean I go visit them often. I couldn't afford them anyway, not like you could."

Tannix laughed. "I have been, more or less, locked up in this compound since I was fourteen," he pointed out. "When do you think I would have time to go to a brothel?"

I shrugged. "You're the son of West Draulin. I assumed you could make time."

He shook his head. "Why did you decide to stay here for as long as you did?"

I hesitated. "To be honest, it was for the food at first." He looked a little insulted. "You don't understand. You've spent your whole life being given enough to eat. I've had to fight for food. This," I waved the piece of bread, "is a day's worth of work for me. All you had to do was walk downstairs and ask for it. At the very beginning, when you tackled me, I went with you to avoid suspicion. Then the next morning I heard about food, and I couldn't help myself. I found you again because you'd been nice to me the day before. I was used to being on my own, but as soon as I started sticking with you and we became friends, I don't know. I didn't choose you because of your status; I didn't even know who you were until the second day."

"So we became friends because you were hungry?"

"I'm always hungry," I said. "After leaving, I didn't want to be on my own again, so I joined one of the groups of people my age. The one that attacked us when we were out with Malte, remember?"

"You joined someone who attacked you?"

"They didn't attack me." I paused to eat another piece of the bread. "They thought I was following you two because you had something good, so they decided to help out. The only reason they left is because I told them to."

"And they listened to you?"

"You're important in your world, I'm important in mine."

WE CARRIED ON LIKE THAT, HIM ASKING QUESTIONS AND ME ANSWERING them, until we noticed the room beginning to lighten. I'd finished my bread long before, and had started toying with my Order ring while we talked. I could tell he was still a little uncomfortable with me owning it, being just a lowly thief. When the room started lightening, I sighed.

"I should go."

Tannix nodded. "Yes, you should," he agreed, getting to his feet. "Come back here afterwards, if you can."

"I will." I put the ring back on my little chain and draped it over my neck. I went to the desk to glance over the drawings one last time, and picked up the letter. "Shouldn't take too long." I slipped the letter under my tunic and walked over to his window. I briefly remembered the last time I'd climbed out of this window, while in a panic and trying to escape. This time, I was more careful about it. I climbed back up to the familiar roof, where I could stop to figure out what to do next.

The director's office was on the fifth floor, and his window was facing the opposite side of the building as Tannix's. I walked across the roof and peered over the edge. One floor down, two windows across. I thought I had the right one. I rolled my shoulders before starting down the wall cautiously. I reached the window easily and risked a quick glance in. The room seemed to be empty. Carefully, I stepped onto the thin windowsill. I tentatively pushed on the window, but just as I expected, it didn't swing open. I could see that it was held shut by a little latch on the inside.

I shifted so that I was only holding onto the wall with my right hand and carefully pulled out my dagger. I dug the tip into the wooden window frame, as close to the glass and the latch as I could. After some wiggling, I managed to get the tip to poke out the inside of the frame. I nudged at the latch until it came loose. I grinned, let go of the dagger, and pushed the window open. I waited until I was standing in the room to reach around and tug my dagger out of the wood, so that there would be no chance of me losing my balance and falling.

I then turned to the room. It had a large wooden desk in the middle of it, piled with papers. There were various other things sitting on the desk, as well as a quill, resting in a little pot of ink. The far wall of the room was covered entirely by bookshelves. Large paintings hung on the other walls. Pushed in one corner was a cushioned chair similar to Tannix's. The thief in me wanted to explore every drawer of the desk, but I fought the urge.

I walked across the room cautiously and placed the letter in the centre of the desk, where it could not possibly be missed. I was just turning around when something caught my eye. One of the objects on the desk was a tiny sword. Confused, I stopped to pick it up. It was barely as long as my hand, and very dull. I ran my finger down the blade, and felt wax at the end. It suddenly dawned on me, as I looked at the letter and remembered Tannix breaking the seal with the tip of his knife. The little sword was made to open letters.

The door swung open suddenly, before I had even registered it moving. The little sword dropped from my hand, and for a moment I was frozen, staring into the confused eyes of the man at the door. Then instinct kicked in, and I ran for the window. The man charged across the room after me, but I had grabbed the bricks above the window and pulled myself up before he could reach me. I was almost to the roof when I glanced down and realized that he was following me.

Panicking, I hauled myself onto the roof and ran across it as fast as I could. I swung myself over the other side, scraping my right palm across a rough brick in the process. It hurt, but I couldn't waste time favouring it. I descended more rashly than I usually would have, but I reached Tannix's window, jumped into his room, and closed the glass before the man could make it to the wall to see where I had disappeared. I leaned against the wall and sank to the floor. My heart was racing, and it took me a moment to get my breath back.

I had just calmed down when I heard footsteps outside of Tannix's door. Startled, I dove for his bed and crawled under it, ignoring the dull throbbing in my palm. I tensed as the door opened and someone walked in. The door was closed, and to my relief, Tannix said my name.

I rolled out from under the bed and got to my feet. "Thank Zianesa it's you." "You were seen?" Tannix asked. "How? What happened?"

"I know," I groaned. I sank down into the comfortable armchair by his window. "He walked in just as I was leaving. He tried to follow me, but I was too quick."

"Good. But now the alarm's been rung and the guards are checking all the rooms for signs of you."

My stomach dropped. As much as I liked to think of him as a friend, it had still been four years since we had last seen each other. I glanced up at him. "You're not going to turn me in?"

"No, of course not," Tannix said. He began to pace in front of his door, but stopped. "I hear them in the hallway, get back under the bed."

I dropped to the ground and rolled under the bed just in time, as there was a knock on Tannix's door. It creaked as he swung it open. I could see, between the edge of the blanket and the stone floor, two sets of shiny black boots. One set stepped into the room, and Tannix moved out of the way.

"May I ask what is going on?" Tannix asked, politely but with all the authority his position offered him.

"There is an intruder," one of the men replied. "We're checking all the rooms, sir."

"If there was an intruder in my room, I think I would know," Tannix said dryly.

"We're just doing our job, sir," the guard said. The second set of boots had stepped into the room by then, and was walking over to Tannix's closet.

"Gentlemen, that was my subtle way of telling you that I am a busy person and I would like not to be disturbed. If there were an intruder in my room, I would know. You would be better to check the next room."

"It'll just be a minute, sir."

"Do you know who I am?" Tannix asked. I could hear that the second man was opening the doors of his wardrobe.

"Orders are orders, sir."

"I am Lord Tandrix of West Draulin," he said. "And I would like to get back to work."

The noises I could hear from the man rummaging through the wardrobe suddenly stopped. Tannix's name had worked like magic. The two men swiftly left the room.

"My apologies, my lord. We did not mean to dis—"

"Of course you didn't," Tannix interrupted. "Carry on your search, then. Good luck." He closed the door without letting the man stammer out another apology. "Finn, you're lucky you made friends with someone so important."

"I know," I replied, once again rolling out from under the bed. "Thank you."

"What did you do to your hand?"

I glanced down at my bloodied palm. There was dirt in the cuts, but I assumed it would be all right. It wasn't the first time I'd hurt my hand while climbing. "I scraped it. It'll be fine."

"Let me see."

I reluctantly got to my feet and offered Tannix my hand. He looked over it for just a moment before gesturing to the armchair.

"Sit down. I have to clean it out."

"No." I pulled my hand away from him.

"Finagale." He sighed my name. "Don't fight me."

I met his gaze for a moment, then groaned and plopped myself down on the chair. I watched warily as he went to his wardrobe and pulled out a fancy golden pin meant to hold his cloak in place. He moved the chair from his desk over so that it was sitting in front of the armchair, and once he was settled down, he held out his hand. I timidly placed mine in it. "Please don't hurt me."

"I'm not going to try to hurt you. Don't sound so afraid."

"I tend to avoid getting hurt," I said. "Or at least I…" I stopped when Tannix poked the pin into my cuts.

"And yet you lead such a dangerous life," Tannix said.

"I avoid conflict. I run away from danger. I'm a coward, really. I'm only as brave as I have to be to survive." He poked me again and this time I flinched and pulled my hand from his grasp.

"Give it back," Tannix said.

"No. I need a distraction," I muttered. "Can I see your ring?" He looked confused. "I like rings."

He slipped the ring from his finger. "My father would kill me if he saw me handing my crest ring to a thief." He dropped it into my left hand, and then grabbed my right before I could try to move it out of reach.

"I can't exactly get away." The ring was doing its work, and I almost didn't notice when he poked into my hand again. I slipped it onto my middle finger and absentmindedly started twirling it with my thumb. "Tannix?"

"Hmm?"

"Are you still training with Malte? Wrestling in the courtyard and climbing walls?"

He shook his head. "No. First year is just basic knowledge, and they assess us to see where we would be most useful for the kingdom. I have more specialized instructors; Malte only deals with first years. I've been training with swords, daggers, and hand-to-hand combat. I've been trained to fight on foot or on horseback. I've had lessons in battle strategies and how to handle troops. I've been studying the strategies of Deorun and Navire. With my lineage and talent, I'm pretty much guaranteed to become a ranking military commander. You would have found it all quite boring, I imagine."

"If I had been a lord and I was still training here, what would I be doing?"

Tannix was silent for a moment. "Second year they would have probably trained you to be a spy. If you were any good with weapons, they'd try to have you be an assassin, but as I recall, you aren't. You would most likely just be a normal spy. By now, you'd be able to speak, read, and write Teltish—which actually you should have already learned as common education—as well as Deoren and Navirian. You would be learning about codes, making them up and decoding them. You would be practicing your climbing ability, different ways to sneak around. Knot tying, lock picking… Can you pick locks?"

I shrugged. "Sometimes, depends on the lock."

"You'd be training in close combat fighting skills, just in case you were captured or attacked. Not as much as if you were an assassin, though. You would also learn about Navire and Deorun, their cultures and customs, things like that, so that you'd be able to blend in."

"Sounds less boring."

"You would think that," Tannix agreed. He put the pin aside and grabbed a piece of white cloth I hadn't noticed earlier. He began to gently wipe the blood away from the cuts. As I watched, he put that cloth aside and grabbed another one, which he used to wrap around my hand. "There, that wasn't so bad. Can I have my ring back?"

I placed it into his hand. "Do you think it's safe for me to leave now?"

"Not with that hand," he replied. "Even if you do manage to climb with it, you won't be able to outrun anybody. Stay here for a while. You look exhausted."

I nodded, suddenly realizing just how tired I was.

"Go to sleep, then. I'm on my own time, so I'll stay here to watch over you," Tannix said. "Tonight, if the guards have given up searching, you can go."

"All right." I nestled further into the chair, trying to get comfortable.

"You can use the bed, you know."

"I can?" I looked at him, shocked. I couldn't remember the last time I'd slept in a bed. "Are you sure?"

"Yes," he nodded towards it. "Go ahead."

Gratefully, I climbed out of the chair and collapsed onto his bed. I pulled the blankets up over my body, rested my head on the pillow, and marvelled at the comfort and warmth. I was asleep almost instantly.

I SLEPT ALMOST THE WHOLE DAY. WHEN I OPENED MY EYES, IT WAS ONCE again dark in the room. Tannix was sitting at the desk, leaning back in his chair with his feet propped up on the table. I moved slightly and muttered, "Are you allowed to sit like that?"

He didn't seem startled to hear my voice, and didn't bother turning around to face me. "Why wouldn't I be?"

"You're a Telt," I said. "You're supposed to be proper and well mannered."

"I think you've only ever seen Teltans at formal occasions," he replied. "We're just as badly mannered as the rest of you when we're alone, which you'll notice if you plan to spend any more time in my bed."

I groaned and buried my head under his blankets. "Tannix," I began, sure my voice was muffled, but not caring to move to blanket out of the way. "I sleep on a pile of clothing, pushed into the corner of a ruined stone room, with a fire in the middle being the only thing keeping me warm. If I could figure out how to steal this bed from you, I would do it. I just might have trouble getting it out the window."

"And getting it down the wall would be no trouble at all," Tannix said sarcastically.

"After getting it out the window, the wall would be easy."

"Of course." I heard the chair legs scrape against the floor and when I poked my head out from under the blankets, Tannix had gotten to his feet. "I'm going to go get you some food, and then you should go."

I reluctantly tossed back his blankets and sat up. "Yes, you're right."

"Don't be so disappointed, Finn," Tannix told me. "Maybe you've noticed that I haven't slept yet? You're lucky I didn't make you leave earlier."

"I'm lucky about a lot of things, I think," I said.

Tannix nodded. "I suppose you are. Stay here," he said as he left the room, as if I would leave when he was bringing me food. When he returned, I had moved, but only so that I could sit in his comfortable chair. He was holding a bowl and a spoon, which he handed to me. It was some kind of stew, and I gladly started eating.

Tannix sat on his bed and watched me. "You don't ever get enough to eat, do you?"

"Not since I stayed here," I said. The stew was already half done by then.

He was silent until I had finished the whole bowl. I scraped the edges to get as much of the sauce as I could before holding the bowl out to him. "Thank you."

He took it. "If..." he paused. "If I gave you some money..."

My eyes widened in shock. "You'd give me money?"

Tannix shrugged. "If you wanted some."

"I do," I said quickly. As an afterthought, I added, "But I don't need it." Our friendship had never been about money and I didn't want him to think it was.

"I don't want you going hungry." He placed the bowl on his bed and went to the desk. He spent a moment rummaging through the top drawer before pulling out a small blue pouch, which he tossed towards me without warning. It was heavy despite its small size. "You can have it, if you want it."

I wanted to protest; for once in my life, I was hesitant about taking someone else's money. But then I thought of Baisan and the rest of my little family, and I nodded. "Yes... yes, I do. Thank you, Tannix," I said. It would have been selfish to turn away the money because of my own sense of pride.

Tannix looked a little uncomfortable and shrugged. "I don't need it. Don't overthink it, I'd like to help you... So, come back in a couple of days, if you can."

I nodded as I slipped the money pouch into my pocket. "I will."

"Goodnight, then. Be careful. Don't fall."

"I will," I promised again. "And I never fall." I paused at the window to wiggle the fingers on my right hand. It hurt, but it wasn't excruciating and I knew I could make the multiple climbs that would get me home. "Goodnight." I glanced back quickly before carefully climbing onto the windowsill and starting my descent.

CHAPTER
Twelve

"**I** told you to get back during the day."

I waved my hand dismissively. "You didn't, really. You said tomorrow. It is still tomorrow." Baisan had found me almost as soon as I gotten to the lower city. Lothian Dusk had just fallen, but that wasn't the true end of the day, not for those used to Zianna.

Baisan muttered something insulting about me under his breath, but I didn't catch it. "So," he added, louder. "Was the letter important?"

I hesitated, unsure of what exactly to tell him. "We're looking into it," I finally said.

"We?"

"Yes, me and the friend I went to."

"The one who can read."

"Yes."

"When did you become friends with somebody who can read?"

I sighed. "I'll explain when we get home. I'm sorry for worrying you, Baisan, I really am. But you know by now that sometimes I need to do things on my own."

"And there's no way I could have stopped you," Baisan said. "I know."

"Besides," I draped my arm over his shoulders, "I wasn't in any danger, not really. I was going to see a friend."

"Of course." Baisan shrugged off my arm.

I laughed. "So, are the others home?"

"Leker and Castin just went out. Orrun and the girls were working all day and got back before I came out to find you."

"Do you think we could find Leker and Castin before going home?" I asked hopefully. "I have something to show everyone."

Baisan was obviously annoyed, but after a moment of thought, he nodded. "Come on, they were going to wander around near the gate to the main road." He turned and led me off in another direction. When we reached the gate, it was clear that the two boys had decided on begging. I tended to stick to pick pocketing, but the rest of them would occasionally switch if they believed it would work better.

Baisan and I, from our vantage point on a nearby roof, could see Leker working the crowds of people who were leaving the lower city. Many of them were probably poorer merchants who had decided to sell their goods in the lower city instead of trying to find room in the real market. Others were visitors, mostly the working sailors who had come in for some food, drinks, and probably a stop at one of the brothels. Leker seemed to be doing well. He was still young enough that he could work on people's pity to get things from them. As we watched, we saw a few people give him coins.

Castin, on the other hand, couldn't manage the cute, poor little street child any better than Baisan or I could. He was leaning against a wall, just out of sight of the guards who were standing at the gate. He was watching Leker carefully, ready to run in and help if the need arose. He had his little knife out to warn any other thieves to leave him alone. He didn't need to worry; Castin had quite the reputation among the thieves as a dirty fighter. Most people knew better than to bother him. He had even managed to teach me a few things over the years, though he quickly got frustrated with my lack of talent.

Baisan leaned over the edge of the roof and whistled loudly. It was a particular whistle, a quick high-pitched note followed by a longer one that started high and ended low. Different groups had different signals, and that was ours. Castin glanced up when he heard it, and after a minute, he had located us. Baisan motioned for him to join us and Castin responded with a nod. He went off into the crowd to get Leker. Within a few minutes, they had joined us on the roof.

"What is it?" Castin asked.

"Finn wanted to talk to all of us together," Baisan replied.

Castin glanced at me. "About?"

"I'll tell you when we're all together," I told him. "Let's go." I didn't wait to see if the others would follow me, instead I just took off back towards our home.

When we got back, the girls and Orrun were sitting around the fire. Stria was tending to it, poking it gently with a longer stick, while the other two were dividing up whatever they had gotten earlier in the day. They looked up when we entered.

"Thought you two were staying out until real dusk," Orrun commented.

"The greatest thief wants to tell us something," Castin replied. "You three did well." He reached down to pick up a few of the coins Orrun had been piling up. "Leker has some too."

"Well, Finn?" Baisan sat down beside the fire. "Talk."

Instead of talking, I pulled Tannix's little pouch of money from my pocket and tossed it to the floor in front of Baisan. The noise it made when it hit the ground, a dull thud due to the weight, combined with the tinkling of coins hitting each other, grabbed everyone's attention. Baisan picked up the pouch, opened it, and poured some of the coins out onto his hand. They glinted in the flickering light from the fire, drawing everyone's eyes. Mostly they were copper, but I saw two brass ones, their shine less red in the light. Baisan handed the pouch to Castin and glanced up at me. He didn't say anything, so I started speaking.

"That was given to me by the friend I went to visit last night."

"In payment for the letter?" Baisan asked.

"No," I shook my head. "We're unsure about the letter. This was just a gift."

"How did you manage to become friends with someone who could part with this much money?" Leker asked. Orrun had just handed him the pouch to look at, and he had pulled out a few of the coins to inspect.

"Must be royalty," Castin muttered under his breath.

"He isn't royalty," I protested, before really thinking it through. They all tore their gazes from the pouch to look up at me again. I sighed and moved over to settle myself beside the fire with them. "Of course you remember that I vanished for some time before joining you, Baisan?"

He nodded.

"That's when I met him," I said. I briefly described my time at the Order. I reminded Baisan of how I had helped him get away from the merchant in the marketplace, and how soon after that, he had run by me with the guards in tow. I explained that after distracting the guards and climbing over the wall, I had found myself dragged into the strange group. I showed them the gold ring that had allowed me to blend in. I told them about Tannix, and how we had quickly become good friends. I ended the story the day I was forced to run away, and I had shown up with the cloak for Ninavi.

"So you really can pass for a Telt?" Castin asked.

Baisan nudged him. "That isn't the point, Cast. That day we found you wandering around with those two Telts?"

"The younger one was Tannix."

Baisan laughed. "You made friends with him? He would have been cornered and robbed instantly if you and that huge man hadn't been with him. So he's not royalty? Then who is he?"

"He's from West Draulin."

"West Draulin? That's royalty," Orrun said.

"So you want us to believe that you, a thief, became friends with a lord from West Draulin?" Baisan asked. "And he just decided to give you money."

"He doesn't need it," I said. "I know it might be hard to understand, but people can't help who they make friends with. He didn't know I was a thief at first."

"I believe you," Ninavi said. She was wearing her red cloak, and during my story had started fiddling with one of the sleeves. "Where else could you have gotten this?"

"I do too," Stria added. Leker and Orrun agreed. Only Baisan and Castin still looked a little skeptical.

"Do you think he'll give you more money?" Baisan asked. The pouch had made it around the whole circle, and it was sitting in his hand again.

"I can't ask him for money," I said. "Baisan, look at how much he already gave me. How much is in there, forty, fifty siyas? That was nothing to him, but it can easily last us weeks. We can buy good food tonight for dinner, and tomorrow night, and many nights to come." I hesitated and glanced around the fire, briefly making eye contact with all of them. "We learn to hate Telts. They're rich, they do no work, and they don't care about or even notice our problems. Tannix, well, he's not royalty, but I suppose he's close enough. We still became friends. In a couple of days, I'm going to go back to speak to him about the letter again. Baisan, why don't you come? Maybe if you meet him for yourself you won't mind this so much."

Baisan stared thoughtfully at the coin pouch. "We'll be safe?"

"You know me, Baisan. Have you ever seen me take a risk I didn't think I could get out of?"

"No," he admitted.

"It's easy to get in and out when you know how," I assured him. "And he's expecting us."

"Then I'll meet him," Baisan agreed. He slipped the pouch into his pocket and stood up. "Leker, Orrun, let's go see what food we can buy."

I WOKE UP THE NEXT MORNING TO ORRUN SHAKING MY SHOULDER. "FINN, get up. Baisan wants us to go out. We're supposed to find more blankets."

More blankets sounded amazing. In my half asleep state, I imagined Tannix's wonderful sheets before being sharply brought back to reality when Orrun shook me again. I groaned and sat up. I'd been huddled into my little pile of clothing in the corner of the room. It was empty, aside for Orrun, the remains of our fire, and our own little sections. When it came to food and money, we were always certain to split it evenly, but other things we tended to claim for ourselves as prizes, such as Castin's little knife or my dagger.

"Why don't we just buy some?" I asked grumpily, even though I knew the answer. Baisan didn't want to waste the money on things we could easily steal. Orrun didn't bother replying to me, he just watched as I reluctantly got to my feet. I slipped my feet into my boots and picked up my cloak. "Where are we going?"

"I thought we could check the stalls," Orrun said. "There might be someone selling cloth. That would be the easiest. If not we could go to the residential sections and hope for an open window."

"Or an unlocked door." I nodded in agreement. My belt and dagger were tucked up against my pile of old clothing, so I picked that up next. I wrapped it around my waist and did up the buckle while starting to walk towards the door. Orrun followed me.

We quickly got to the busiest section of the lower city, the slightly wider road with all the little booths. As we walked down it, we glanced over every cart. Just because we had only been told to find new blankets, didn't mean we needed to ignore easy pickings. At one point, we wandered past Ninavi, Baisan, and Leker, but didn't acknowledge them beyond a quick nod. Ninavi was working all of her charms on a small group of foreigners, and we knew better than to get in the way of her act. Baisan and Leker were acting both as guards and trying to pickpocket people who walked past.

To our disappointment, none of the stalls was selling cloth. "Why did he give us the hard job?" I said to myself as we left the main road to go search the houses.

"Because he's upset with you," Orrun said. "Not about the money, of course, he's delighted about that. But he's worried about you getting cocky and challenging him for control."

"Yes, he's always worried about that." I couldn't help but smile. Baisan and I tended to switch between being friends and being rivals, though I had never tried to overthrow him as leader. Sometimes my more elaborate ideas concerned him. "So maybe I deserve it. I understand him wanting to pull me in a bit. What did you do wrong?"

"I volunteered." Orrun grinned. "It was go out with you, or be the one keeping an eye on Ninavi."

"And I was the better choice?"

"To watching Ninavi beg and cry so that people will give her a little bit of food? Yes. When my mother… I never begged for her to give Leker more food. I won't beg now. I like to think we're a little above that. I can hope, at least."

"Of course you can," I agreed. "I like to think we're above that too."

Our deep discussion was interrupted by a scream from nearby. Normally we would both ignore it, but this time it was Stria. We broke into a run. Sometimes it was hard to figure out exactly where a sound had come from amongst all the winding streets and little buildings, but we were lucky. As soon as we reached the next intersecting street, we saw her.

Arow had Castin pinned against the wall. Castin's knife was lying on the ground near their feet, and it was obvious he'd been taken by surprise. Stria was tugging at one of Arow's arms, but to no avail.

"Arow!" I yelled as Orrun and I reached them. "Let him go." I pulled out my dagger and tried to look as menacing as possible. Orrun grabbed Stria and pulled her out of the way. She fought against him, frantically trying to get back to Castin, but he held onto her tightly.

Now that I was closer, I could tell why she was so distressed. It wasn't only because Arow had Castin trapped, as I had initially thought. There was a jagged rip in Castin's tunic just above his hip, the edges of which were stained red. I couldn't see the actual wound, not from my position, so I cautiously moved a bit closer.

"Stay back," Arow growled at me. He shook Castin slightly, drawing my attention to how limp he'd gone. "Or I'll do worse. You still owe me, Finn. Your little band of thieves all owe me. I think that maybe ridding your group of this one might make you a little less troublesome."

Stria jerked against Orrun again, and he barely managed to keep his hold on her. I held my right hand up to try to ward her off.

"Let him go, Arow," I said again, trying to sound calm.

"You can't fight," Arow said with a cruel grin. "You wouldn't attack me."

I would for Castin. At least I would try. I shifted the way I was holding the dagger slightly, trying to remember what Tannix and Castin had attempted to teach me. Castin had, by then, closed his eyes. He was still breathing, but faintly. I knew I had to get him away from Arow. I took a deep breath, gripped the dagger handle a little more tightly, and rushed forward.

I took Arow by surprise. He dropped Castin and had whipped out his own knife by the time I reached him. I barely managed to duck away from the first swipe he made towards my head. The second slash, however, got me across the forearm. For such a big man, Arow was quick when he had to be. Speed had always been my advantage against him, and without it I knew I would lose. Maybe if I could distract him long enough so that Orrun and Stria could get Castin away, I could run.

Arow lunged at me again. Instinct kicked in and I dove to the side, rolling to my feet behind him before he realized what I'd done. I took the chance to jump onto his back. It wasn't the most effective attack. I wrapped my arms around his head. Orrun and Stria were crouched over Castin, but they weren't leaving. They weren't taking advantage of the time I was giving them. Arow started trying to pry me off.

"Orrun! Get him out of…" I was cut off as my grip slipped and Arow threw me to the ground in front of him. I scrambled to my feet just in time to avoid a kick to the head, and hopped backwards out of his reach.

Suddenly, there was someone else at my side. Arow instantly stopped fighting. He never liked to take on more than one of us at once, preferring to pick on us when we were alone. The appearance of the stranger must have worried him. He fixed me with a glare for a moment, and then he turned and walked away calmly, assuming that I wouldn't go after him. He was right. I ignored the person at my side and rushed back to the others. They'd moved Castin so that he was sitting up with his back to the wall. Stria was hysterical and Orrun looked panicked.

"I… I don't know what to do," he stammered, staring up at me. His hands were red, and I knew he'd been trying to cover Castin's wound.

I felt strangely calm. "Go find Baisan," I told him. He was off in a heartbeat, and I took his place kneeling beside Castin.

The girl, I had vaguely noticed that she was a girl, crouched beside me. "You have to cover his cut." Her voice was light and gentle. "We'll use his tunic." She picked up Castin's little knife and reached over to grab the corner of his shirt. She paused, and after a moment I realized she was waiting for my permission.

I shook myself back into the moment and nodded. "Yes, use his tunic." With my own dagger, I helped her cut it away. She took the scraps from me and started to wrap them expertly around his waist so that they would stay in place over the cut.

Stria had stopped crying by then, but she was still tightly holding on to Castin's hand. "He'll be fine, Finn. Right?"

"He's strong," I murmured, which in no way answered her question, but seemed to make her happy. I watched as the girl finished tying a knot in Castin's makeshift bandage.

"Your arm?" She took my left arm gently and I didn't protest. She rolled my sleeve up carefully to get a better look at the slice. It wasn't as bad as I thought. It was quite shallow and had almost stopped bleeding. "Do you want me to bind it?" she asked.

I shook my head. "No, I'll be fine." I pushed my sleeve back down and when I looked up I accidentally met her gaze. Her eyes were brown, just like any other Native's, but with a ring of orange around the centre. Intrigued, I had to ask. "Who are you?"

"Kassia." She broke the eye contact to look down at Castin.

"Are you from the streets?"

She hesitated, and then nodded. "Yes, I guess I am now. I used to live with my mother, but she just died and I…" She hesitated again. "I was kicked out. Your friend needs help."

Just as she finished talking, Orrun reappeared with Baisan and the others. Baisan took in the scene quickly. "Finn, help me pick him up. We'll take him home. Orrun, Leker." He paused to pull the blue money pouch from his pocket and hand it to Leker. "See what you can find for bandages. Clean ones. Girls, run home, get a fire going and prepare his bed."

We all obeyed. The boys ran off in one direction, the girls in another. Baisan and I carefully lifted Castin. Baisan hadn't acknowledged Kassia, or maybe hadn't noticed her in the panic, so I motioned for her to follow us.

CHAPTER
Thirteen

aisan and I slowly lowered Castin onto his pile of blankets. Despite how gentle we were being, my heart was racing. I was sure Baisan felt the same. Worse, even. Castin was his best friend, and now he… I let the thought trail off as I crouched down next to the injured boy. Baisan had stalked off as soon as putting him down, into a corner of the room. I distracted myself by looking over the binding on Castin's waist. It was well done, still tightly in place. I barely took notice of Kassia kneeling beside me, but then I tore my gaze from Castin to look at her.

"The girl who was with us?" she questioned quietly.

"Stria," I replied.

Kassia looked over at the two girls. "Stria," she called out, breaking the near perfect silence. Stria flinched and looked over at us. Her eyes were red from crying, but she had managed to stop the tears. Kassia motioned for her to join us, and she did.

"What?" Stria asked shakily, clearly holding back more tears.

I was aware of Baisan staring at us from across the room, and Ninavi wrapping her cloak around herself as if it would protect her from what was happening. I watched as Kassia reached across Castin to take Stria's hand.

"He's special to you," Kassia said gently. "So you will be able to reach him best. We want him to wake up, so you should talk to him. Remind him that we're here for him and draw him away from Siour's chariot." Siour, the god of darkness and death. I couldn't help but flinch slightly at the sound of his name.

Stria nodded solemnly. She pulled her hand away from Kassia to pick up Castin's. She paused nervously before beginning to talk. I felt awkward sitting there, listening to the personal things she was telling him. Luckily, I was given an excuse to leave when I heard Baisan hiss my name. I got to my feet as quietly as I could—somehow making too much noise seemed disrespectful—and joined Baisan in his corner.

"Do you think he'll make it?" he asked in a near whisper.

I shrugged. "I think if he wakes up, he'll survive."

Baisan nodded. "When the others get back with the bandages, I'd like you to go out and try to find some sort of medicine that will be useful. I trust your judgment more than theirs."

"I'll do my best."

"I know," Baisan said quietly. "Who is she?"

"Her name's Kassia, she helped me fight off Arow. You know how he doesn't like dealing with two of us at once. She wrapped Castin's wound too."

"She did a good job, she might know something about medicine," Baisan said. We both knew it was a faint hope, but at least it was something. "Take her with you. But don't believe everything she says until we know who she is."

That was common sense, but I didn't say anything. Baisan was worried and of course he was going to over think things. Instead, I nodded. "Of course."

Noise at the entrance to our home startled all of us, and we all glanced at the door. Leker burst in, his arms wrapped around a bundle of clean bandages. Orrun followed him a moment later. Both were panting, as if they had run the whole way.

"We got the best ones we could find," Leker explained with a quick glance towards Baisan and me. Then he went over to the others and dropped the bandages near them. "Are they good?"

Kassia nodded. "Yes, they're perfect. Can you get me some water so I can clean his wound?"

Leker nodded and ran out of the room, just as Orrun approached us and handed over the pouch of money. Baisan put it into my hand. It felt distinctly lighter than it had before, but it was still a large sum of money for us. I slipped it under my cloak.

"I'll wait until she's given Castin a new bandage?" I formed it as a question, even though I knew the answer. Baisan nodded.

Using the water Leker had returned with, Kassia cleaned out Castin's cut. I noticed that Ninavi had moved forward to help the other two girls, whereas Leker, after putting down the small bowl of water, had backed up to stand with us near the wall. Whether it was instinctual or us just knowing we'd get in the way, I couldn't tell. When Kassia finished cleaning, she wrapped one of the clean bandages around the cut. As she was tying it off, Stria gasped.

"Castin?" she asked, drawing all of our attentions.

"Did he do something?" Baisan broke away from the rest of us to join the girls near Castin. After a brief hesitation, I followed, but the younger boys stayed behind.

"I thought he moaned," Stria said quietly.

"He might have," Kassia said, her voice gentle.

Baisan crouched beside Stria and put his hand on her shoulder. "Stria, that's good, if you heard him moan. That means he felt the bandage getting tied, and it's a good sign if he felt it." He glanced up and me and nodded towards the door. He lowered his voice and continued to talk to Stria. She didn't look away from Castin, but his words seemed to be calming her down.

I nudged Kassia and when she looked at me, I motioned for her to follow. I walked out of the room and waited outside for her to catch up. It was still light out, but the sun was just beginning to fall behind the cliffs. A moment later, she appeared at my side. The slight wind picked at her dark hair and I couldn't help but be distracted.

She broke the silence. "How is your arm?"

"Fine," I replied, after having to remember what she was talking about. "It was nothing, just a scratch."

"So then, why did you bring me out here, Finn?"

I was startled by her use of my name because I couldn't remember telling her what it was. Then I recalled both Stria and Baisan addressing me by name. "Finagale," I said as if I was correcting her, not really sure why. I almost never told people my full name.

"Oh." Kassia drew out the word a little and nodded. "Fancy name for a street boy, isn't it? But that's not what the others call you, so I don't think I will either. Why did you bring me out here?"

"Baisan wants me to find some medicine for Castin. We thought you might have some idea as to what we should get."

Kassia looked thoughtful for a moment. "Yes, I know something that might help. It's a paste that will keep the cut from going bad. I got a better look at it once I'd cleaned it, and for all that blood I don't think it's really that deep. It should heal on its own, so all we need to worry about is sickness. That said…" she paused and looked at me. "I might be wrong, so let's not tell any of the others until he wakes up. Anyway, I don't think we can find the paste down here. It's more of a Teltan thing."

"That's not a problem."

Kassia glanced at me quizzically. "How is that not a problem?"

"We can just sneak into the upper city," I said. "Can you climb?"

She nodded.

"Wait, stop," I reached out and grabbed Kassia's arm just before she walked out onto the marketplace court. I pulled her back into the shadows of the building, which had only grown as we'd made out way into the upper city.

"What?" Kassia shook off my arm. "There was no one looking."

"We can't just walk around looking like this." I gestured down at myself. "We might as well tell them all that we're Natives." Under my cloak, I was still wearing the darker clothing that I had used to look like a Telt earlier. I untied my cloak and tossed it into the corner of the alley, motioning for her to do the same. Kassia reluctantly followed my lead. She was dressed in a similar fashion, but her tunic was light green and a little looser than mine was.

She crossed her arms, looking annoyed. "Don't look at me like that."

"Like what? I was just wondering whether or not you look like a Telt." I pulled my hair tie out from one of my pockets and tied my hair back, hating the way it felt. "Let me talk, I've done this before." For all I knew, she might also have experience lying, but it wasn't exactly the right moment to test her.

"Fine."

I peered around the edge of the alley. When I couldn't see anyone looking in our direction, I walked out and started down the street, doing my best to look like a Telt. Kassia walked up beside me, but hung back just slightly, letting me lead the way. I walked to a building that I knew from eavesdropping was called an apothecary. Before pushing open the heavy door and walking in, I reached back to take Kassia's hand. She flinched and tried to pull away from me.

"You're my sister," I told her quietly, and I felt her relax. Then, taking a deep breath to calm my nerves, I pushed open the door and walked in, tugging Kassia in with me.

I saw the owner leaning over a table in the back, and he glanced up at the sound of movement. The room was lined with shelves covered in various bottles and boxes, but I ignored all of them and approached the man. The room smelt strongly of odd dried herbs, making my head ache a little. "Excuse me, sir?" I asked timidly, stepping up to the table.

"Yes?"

"One of our father's guards got hurt while training." Luckily, the nervousness I was feeling fit the character I was trying to portray perfectly, so little acting was involved. "Our father sent us to buy something that would keep the cut from going bad while it healed."

The man looked us over, no doubt taking in every aspect of how we looked. He turned around and walked back to one of his shelves, motioning for us to follow him. I pulled Kassia over as the man reached up and picked a small jar from his shelf, which he then put on the counter in front of me. "This is the most expensive salve I have that protect wounds from going rotten. It is guaranteed to work."

"Do you have anything less expensive?" I asked.

"Yes," he picked up another jar, which was nearly identical to the first except for the label on the lid. "This will help protect the wound, but if it's bad, the salve might not be able to do much."

I reached out for the second jar, knocking a wooden box with my elbow as I did. It dropped to the floor and the side of it cracked, spilling out the leaves of a dried plant. "I'm sorry," I yelped, startled by the sound.

The man narrowed his eyes, and then crouched to start picking up the leaves. Kassia slipped her hand from mind and knelt beside him, scooping up some leaves and dropping them into the box. While they were distracted, I pulled the lid from the jar I was holding and tentatively smelled whatever it contained.

A moment later, Kassia and the man stood back up. "Sorry," I repeated. "I'll take this one." I held up the jar in my hand. "I'm sure his cut won't need much protection."

"Twenty-five siyas," the man said.

I took out the little coin pouch and carefully counted out the right amount of money before handing it over to the man. "Thank you very much. Come on, Kassia." I took her hand again and led her from the apothecary.

Neither of us spoke until we had ducked back into the alley with the cloaks. I was putting mine on when I noticed her looking at me. "What?"

"What did you do?" she asked. "You didn't knock that over by accident."

I couldn't help but smile as I carefully tucked the little jar away in my cloak. "I switched the lids."

"So we got the more expensive salve," Kassia said, pulling on her own cloak.

I nodded.

"You know that some person will now buy the weaker one and think they're safe?"

I shook my head. "They smell different. The owner will notice when he sells it, but we'll be long gone by then."

Kassia stared at me a moment longer, then nodded slowly. "You're good."

CHAPTER
Fourteen

Baisan was waiting at us at the entrance. Arms crossed, he leaned in the doorway as if he was guarding Castin against Siour. I held out the jar. "The best available. It'll stop the cut from going bad."

Baisan nodded without bothering to take it from me to inspect it. "I've got another favour to ask of you, Finn. Take Stria to the temple."

Kassia took the jar from my hand and gently pushed her way past Baisan. We both watched her go.

"She's hysterical and worrying the others. Take her, have her talk to Anniva for a bit. I'd do it myself, but…" He hesitated and glanced over his shoulder. "We've been together for, I don't know, seven years? I don't think I can… If I leave, and he…"

"I understand. He's my brother too." I clapped Baisan on the shoulder as I walked past him. Inside, the room was much as I'd left it. The girls were crowded around Castin. Kassia was unwinding his bandage to add the salve. Orrun and Leker were sitting quietly in the corner. I nodded at them and walked over to the others. "Stria, come with me."

She glanced up at me in a panic, her eyes wide. She was still tightly holding Castin's hand. "What do you want?"

"Come to the temple with me." I spoke as calmly as I could. "We should ask Anniva for help."

"You go." She turned back to stare at Castin's face. He was pale, and I tried not to look at him.

"No, Stria. You need to do it." I crouched and touched her arm. "Anniva will feel how strongly you care about him, and that'll convince her to help. There's nothing you can do here for now, in any case. Kassia's putting the salve on him and Baisan's watching the door. Trust me, Siour's not getting through anytime soon, so come with me."

I let her think about it. A few minutes passed before her grip on Castin's hand relaxed and she shakily stood up. I got up with her and put an arm over her shoulders.

IT WASN'T REALLY A TEMPLE. BEFORE THE TELTS HAD LANDED, ZIANNA had a large temple in the upper city, and many smaller shrines spread around the rest of the city. The Telts hadn't approved of our beliefs, and tried to destroy the temples throughout the entire kingdom. Three of the statues had been rescued from Zianna's great temple and hidden away.

Their current home, the building we called a temple even though it wasn't one, used to be a medium sized administrative building for a trading company. I had to guide Stria through the wooden doors as if she was sleep walking. The first room was small and empty aside for a small table holding some candles. They were all lit, as usual, since the priest often checked on them. I picked one up and gently took Stria's hand.

The second room was larger. It was lit by the raised trough that ran down the centre of the room. It held wood and oil, which burned gently, casting a warm glow on the statues at the far end of the room. The three statues were a little bigger than life size, and were the only ones remaining from the ancient temple. In the middle stood Zianesa, the goddess of the earth and patron to the kingdom. She was wearing a dress that had once been green and a crown carved to look like it was made of wood. Her hands hung down at her sides with her fingers spread to meet the vines that were reaching up from around her feet.

Her sister Kitsa, the goddess of the air, was to the left. Unfortunately, her statue was not in good condition. Her hands had once been clasped in front of her chest, but long ago had broken off and left two stumps that cut off near the elbow. There was no paint remaining on her dress, but it would have been white. She was staring up at the ceiling, towards the sky she ruled.

Their brother, Roe, stood on the right. Like Kista, he was worn down, so much so that it was impossible to tell where the cloth wrapped around his waist was meant to start. His right hand held the remains of what was once a spear, and his left hand was stretched out and held open. He was supposed to be holding a small ship, but it had been stolen and I'd never seen it. He was the god of the ocean.

Stria ignored them. Along the walls of the room were small niches, each holding a figure of a god or goddess. The smaller statues had been carved after the Telts' arrival, to replace the larger ones that had been lost. Stria quickly picked out the niche she wanted. The figure was a woman holding a box and sitting in a crescent moon. It was Anniva, the goddess of the moon and healing.

Stria knelt in front of the little statue and began to pray quietly under her breath. I walked away, giving her a little bit of privacy, and found the statue of Siour. He was carved entirely from a black rock, and was depicted as he usually was, standing in his chariot. It was pulled by two skeletal creatures that looked a bit like horses. Although the trip into the underworld wasn't supposed to be scary, Siour certainly was. Every Native child had nightmares about him pulling them onto his chariot. I sighed.

"Don't take him, Siour, please. We need him." I hesitated, and then started to mumble one of the traditional prayers to him in Old Ziannan. I didn't understand the words, no one did anymore, but we memorized the sounds as best we could. I often wondered if they'd been altered over the years, the meaning completely lost.

There was movement at the door and I moved back beside Stria protectively. Two women walked in, but paused when they saw us. Stria paid them no attention and I nodded a quick greeting. Getting interrupted was one of the downsides of a small temple, but everyone did their best to ignore each other. The women nodded in return and made their way across the room, stopping in front of the little statue of Lovi. I watched them a moment longer than I should have, and noticed them place a small stone in front of the statue.

I looked away before they would notice me watching. Our wedding ceremonies were fairly private, and I didn't want to interrupt their moment. Lovi had brought those women together, just as she'd brought Stria and Castin together. With a sigh, I glanced at the statue of Anniva. She had to help Castin. We annoyed each other constantly, but that's because we were brothers. He meant even more to Stria.

Stria finished her prayer, stood up and grabbed my hand. Her eyes were red and puffy, but she was no longer crying. Praying to the statues didn't make a huge difference in whether or not the gods would listen, but it certainly made us feel better.

The women both glanced over as we moved. One of them cleared her throat. "May Anniva heal your loved one," she said kindly, having clearly overheard.

"Thank you," Stria murmured.

"And may Lovi bless your union," I added, before squeezing Stria's hand gently and leading her from the temple.

ON THE WAY HOME, I STOLE A FEW SLICES OF BREAD AND ALMOST HAD TO force Stria to eat them. We saved one to try to give to Castin. Baisan was still hovering outside. Stria walked past him without a word, but I stopped.

"So?"

He shrugged dejectedly. "I don't know. Stria seemed calmer."

"A little."

"Can I talk to you two?" Kassia stepped outside and shivered. As usual, it had gotten colder once the sun had completely set. "You're in charge, aren't you?" She correctly looked to Baisan, who nodded slightly. "Right, well, I think he'll survive. The cut isn't as bad as it looked, and the salve Finn took should protect it from rotting. If you want, I can show the other girls how to properly bandage it up, and then I can get going."

Baisan glanced at me. I was unused to being consulted; usually he and Castin made all the decisions. I didn't know how to react. Baisan sighed. "Kassia, do you have somewhere to go?"

She looked a little shocked by the question. "I guess not. I lived with my mother, but she died and our landlord won't let me stay in the building." She shrugged. "So, I'm alone."

"You can stay with us," Baisan offered quietly. He didn't like letting others join us, hence why in the past four years only Leker and Orrun had been allowed. We'd become a family, the only family most of us had, and it was hard to let people in, but he was desperate. I could see it even though he pretended he wasn't. "At least until Castin's better. Then if you want to move on, you can."

Kassia smiled. "I'd love to stay, thank you."

Baisan looked at me. "Finn will answer any questions you have." Without another word, he turned and walked back into the building.

I stared after him with narrowed eyes. This was Castin's sort of job. I wasn't sure if I liked being second in command.

CHAPTER
Fifteen

*K*assia and I spent most of our time together for the next few days. I realized that this served two purposes. I could answer any questions she had about our lives, but I could also keep an eye on her for Baisan. Every morning, she cleaned and re-dressed Castin's wound. On the second day, he woke up briefly and Baisan managed to force him to eat a bit of bread before he went back to sleep. We all saw it as a good sign.

For the rest of the day, Kassia and I either stayed home or went out, depending on where Baisan wanted us. No matter where we were, she asked me questions constantly. Mostly, they revolved around the hierarchy of our family, or the way we did certain things. One afternoon, four days after her arrival, she locked on to the topic of our pasts.

We were on the main street, I was looking for a stall I could quickly grab some food from, but she kept distracting me.

"So Orrun and Leker are actually brothers, right?"

I nodded and turned my attention to a nearby stall, but she nudged me sharply, meaning she wanted an elaboration. I flinched and rubbed my side. "All right, calm down. Their father was having an affair. He was married to Orrun's mother. They were born only a few months apart."

"What happened to their parents?"

"Um…" They'd told me the story before, but I couldn't remember the details. "Somehow they both ended up living with Orrun's mother and his siblings. He has a bunch, five or six, I think. Anyway, I think their father died and Orrun's mother hated Leker so she made him leave and Orrun went with him. Something like that. Their siblings never came to look for them, so…" I trailed off and shrugged.

"That's horrible."

"It's common. When you're poor, taking care of children is difficult." I slipped up between a few people and grabbed a few oranges from the basket I'd been eyeing. After moving away from the cart so we wouldn't be noticed, I grinned and handed one to Kassia.

She smiled. She was really pretty when she smiled. "Thank you. So tell me about Baisan."

I started peeling my orange and tossing the peels to the ground. A rat would probably appreciate them later. "Baisan lived with an uncle because his mother died and his father was a sailor. Then his father died at sea and his uncle refused to care for him, so he ran away. He's the only one of us who has any sort of education, but it's nothing useful as far as I can tell. He was young when this happened, I think around eight. Then," I paused to eat a piece of my orange. "Then he met Castin and they've been together ever since. That's why Cast's second in command instead of me, when I'm clearly smarter and better for the job."

"You don't think Castin's smart?"

I shrugged. "Sure, he is. But he and I have this rivalry, you know."

"I hadn't noticed. With him being unconscious and all," Kassia said.

"Right, well… Anyone else?"

"How about Castin?"

"He's like me, I guess. Son of a prostitute and some man. We think his father was Native, or a foreigner, based solely on his skin. He's darker than me and Ninavi, so we're probably half Telt, but it's impossible to find out."

Kassia looked thoughtful. "So he might be part Deoran or Navirian?"

"I suppose so."

"And is he the same age as Baisan?"

"We guess so. See, Baisan, Stria, Leker, and Orrun all know how old they are, since they had real families. Ninavi, Castin, and I don't. I'm pretty sure I'm the oldest, though." I paused, remembering how old Tannix had guessed me to be. "Sixteen or so, I think. How old are you?"

"Sixteen." Kassia wiped the orange juice off her hands as best as she could on her tunic. "So what about Stria, then?"

"Her family all died from some sickness, so she ended up alone and found Baisan and Castin." I glanced down at my own sticky hands. "Let's go find a pipe. Can I ask you some questions?"

She nodded as she followed me down the street. "Go ahead."

"Thanks. So, you said you were alone because your mother just died?" I realized how painful of a memory it must be as soon as I'd said it. "Sorry, I mean…"

"No, it's all right. Yes. She was a seamstress. She cut her hand while trying to cut some cloth, and it went bad. She died not long afterwards. There was nothing I could do. We didn't have enough money for me to buy her any medicine, and I don't have your particular skills."

"What about your father?"

"I haven't seen him in years. He might be dead, I don't know."

We'd reached one of the many water pipes that were spread around the city. They were fed by underground rivers from the Cliffs of Loth, so the water was clean and cold. I held my hands under the flow for a few seconds to wash off the juice, then moved aside so Kassia could do the same.

She dried her hands on her pants. "Anyway, we're in this together now, aren't we? Is there anything else we're supposed to be doing?"

I gestured back down the street, towards the stalls. "I was supposed to be getting food."

She grinned sheepishly. "Right, sorry. Maybe I can help you out, if you show me what to do." Without warning, she slipped an arm through mine and started to lead me back up the street.

When we neared the stalls I pulled my arm away from her. "You talk to the owners, be distracting, and I'll see what I can do."

Kassia nodded. She walked up the street, looking around curiously before stepping up to one of the stalls selling vegetables. "Hello!"

While she struck up a conversation, I slipped behind the stall. The system worked well, and we made it to four different stalls without any problem. At the fifth stall, I made a mistake. Encouraged by our success, I didn't notice until it was too late that there were two people working at the stall. I was reaching into a basket of potatoes when a hand clamped around my wrist. I pulled back, but the woman's grip was too strong.

"Thief!"

"Sorry," I managed to say. She was holding a knife, which she had been using on her vegetables. She probably wouldn't use it on me, but it was still frightening. "I was just trying to, uh… my brother's hurt and-"

"Let go of me!" Kassia was struggling in the man's arms. "I've done nothing wrong, you-" she growled something that didn't sound Teltish.

Kassia provided the perfect distraction and I wrenched my arm away from the woman. She lunged for me but I ducked out of her way and hopped over the stall. By then the commotion and shouting had gathered an audience. Thank Zianesa not many guards patrolled the lower city.

Other merchants along the road were starting to recognize Kassia. Through the babble of the spectators, I heard a few cries of accusation as the stall owners realized what had happened.

The woman was coming around the stall, brandishing her large knife and shouting at me. Seeing no other option, I threw myself at the man holding Kassia. All three of us crashed to the ground. He let go of Kassia in an attempt to catch himself. I hopped to my feet and dragged Kassia up beside me. I gave her a sharp push towards the crowd. "Go."

She didn't argue and bolted. When I turned the man had gotten to his feet and taken the knife from his wife. The crowd around us was getting more excited, but I relaxed. It was easier to think when I only had to worry about myself.

When the man stepped towards me, I did my usual trick by diving out of the way and rolling to my feet behind him. I hopped onto his stall, which made it easy to jump to a higher spot on the wall. I climbed quickly and pulled himself onto the roof before anyone had managed to throw anything at me. I took a moment to catch my breath. From there, it was easy enough to jump to the next building, and the one after that.

Since I hadn't managed to steal anything from them, and man and his wife didn't follow me for long. Once the coast was clear I climbed back down to the cobbled streets and went to find Kassia.

SHE WAS WAITING NEAR THE WATER PIPE, HER ARMS CROSS TIGHTLY AS she stared down the street towards the stalls.

I hadn't come from that direction and stepped up behind her before I spoke. "Looking for someone?"

She spun around, shock giving way to relief. "Thank Zianesa." She pulled me into a quick hug. "I thought I'd gotten you killed."

I shrugged. "I was my fault, I got cocky. Are you hurt?"

"No. You?"

I shook my head as we began walking back home. "I'm fine. What did you say to that man? It wasn't Teltish."

"Oh, I just called him a dumb fat pig in Deoran. Something my mother picked up from a sailor when I was a baby," she said, waving her hand dismissively.

"Seems pretty accurate," I said.

Kassia laughed. "It was pretty fun before that, anyway. Did you manage to keep everything else?"

I nodded and patted the pockets of my cloak. "We did a good job."

WE COULD TELL SOMETHING WAS GOING ON AS WE WALKED THROUGH the front door of our home. When we reached the room, we were surprised to see Castin on his feet. Stria was supporting him with his right arm over her shoulders.

The only other person in the room was Baisan, and he was clearly annoyed. "Sit down, Castin."

"Come on, I need to move around."

"You just woke up!" The two of them hardly ever argued. That was proof enough that Baisan was serious. I stepped up next to him.

"Baisan…"

He replied without looking at me. "Tell Castin to sit down."

"Uh… Cast?"

"For the love of Zianesa, be quiet, Finn," Castin muttered. He slipped and I dropped the food I was holding, springing forward to catch his left arm. He glared at me. "Thank you."

"You're welcome. How about you sit down before Baisan kills us both?" I didn't wait for a reply, and instead pulled him away from Stria and carefully lowered him to the floor.

Kassia joined us and handed him a piece of bread. "Eat this while I check on your cut."

Castin eyed her. "Who are you?"

"Castin, do what you're told!" Baisan growled. "Don't be like Finn."

I started to argue, but Kassia smacked my shoulder lightly to stop me.

"Boys, you're not helping anything," she said sternly. "Baisan, Finn, give me some space. Stria, please make him eat that bread."

Reluctantly, Baisan and I backed up and let Kassia take control of the situation. Baisan finally noticed the food I'd dropped. "How did you manage that?"

"Kassia and I make a good team," I replied, decided to leave out the fact that we'd nearly been caught.

We were both still watching Castin, so we saw when he flinched and swore. "Tufa! Don't touch it." The curse was one of the few words from Old Ziannan that was still regularly used. Castin glared at Kassia. "Who are you?"

"My name's Kassia. I've been here since you got hurt, and I've been taking care of you. So stop fighting with me and let me put this salve on your cut."

"Baisan," Castin complained.

"I will call Siour myself if you don't stop being impossible to deal with," Baisan said.

The threat did its job and Castin fell silent, though he still flinched when Kassia touched his cut. Despite his annoyance, Baisan was clearly relieved. For the first time since he was hurt, we could be sure he was going to make a full recovery.

CHAPTER
Sixteen

My main job changed over the next few days. Instead of keeping an eye on Kassia, I was told to watch Castin. Even though we liked to argue with each other, I was the only person other than Baisan he'd listen to. Even Stria couldn't get him to stay still; he seemed to get his way whenever we left her in charge.

I was sitting beside him, bored, listening to him complain about not being allowed to leave. He'd been up and walking around the day before, even though moving hurt him and aggravated the wound.

"Finn, that's not..." he trailed off with an annoyed sigh. I had pulled out my knife and was poking at the brick floor with it, running the tip of the blade along the mortar lines. "You're going to ruin that knife."

"I've done it before," I pointed out. "It's a good knife."

"Right," he crossed his arms and winced a little, though he tried to hide it. "It is. Doesn't mean you should go dragging it through... Stop it."

I grinned mischievously, having just pressed the tip of the blade a little further into the crumbling mortar just to bother him. "Stop what?"

"By the love of Zianesa, Finn..."

"I doubt she'd care," I said. "Tros is the god of war, after all, not her. He'd probably be furious at me."

"He probably decided to ignore you years ago when you proved you're incapable of holding a knife properly."

"Probably, but I still managed to chase Arow off, didn't I? And you managed to... Do what again? Oh yes, get stabbed."

Castin nodded. "Right." He put on a high-pitched voice. "Oh, Finn's so brave, he's a hero! I bet you enjoy that."

"What was that?"

Castin smirked. "Maybe you've noticed that when the girls are around, they like to clump around me as if I'll die when they turn their backs. Sometimes I like the attention, I'll admit it, but sometimes the conversation turns to you and how much of a hero you are."

"I'm not a..." I trailed off uncomfortably. "Who were you mimicking?"

"Oh, they all say that. Mostly Ninavi, though." He grinned at my obvious discomfort. "Are you going to stop torturing me by ruining that knife, or should I tell you about the rest of what they say?"

"I'm done," I said, slipping the knife back into its little sheath.

"Play nicely, boys." Kassia's voice shocked both of us, and we looked towards the door to see her walk in with Baisan.

"They don't have to," Baisan said. "Cast could probably take Finn out, even given his condition. How are you feeling?" he asked, cutting off my protest before it started.

"Better," Castin replied. "When can I start helping out again?"

"When you can move without wincing," Baisan replied simply. "Finn, a word."

"All right, speak," I said, without bothering to move. Castin punched my shoulder, not hard enough to hurt, but harder than I'd expected.

"Thank you, Cast." Baisan was smiling.

"The least I can do is help keep his majesty under control." Castin smirked at me.

I didn't reply, just got to my feet and followed Baisan from the room. I could hear Kassia start asking Castin her usual questions about how his wound felt and if anything had changed. Their voices faded when Baisan and I stepped outside. "Yes?" I asked.

"When were you planning to see your friend?"

His question surprised me. In the panic surrounding Castin's injury, I had completely forgotten my promise to Tannix. "Soon. I don't know." I glanced at the sky to see that the sun was just starting to disappear behind the Cliffs of Loth. "Now?"

"I know I agreed to come with you, but we can't both leave when Castin's in this condition," Baisan said.

I nodded. "But you don't mind if I go now?"

"No," Baisan replied after a brief pause. "Have you eaten?"

"No."

"Are you hungry?"

"Of course, but I'll be fine."

"Then you might as well go," Baisan decided. "Be back by midnight." It sounded more like a question than an order.

"Of course."

I KNOCKED ON THE WINDOW GENTLY, HOPING THAT IF HE WERE INSIDE, he would hear it. It was a little windier out than I liked, and the windowsill was thin. I didn't want to make any sudden movements. After a moment of nothing happening, I reached out to knock on it again just as it opened. Taken slightly by surprise, I flinched and just for a moment felt my balance wavering. I grabbed the inside of the window frame to steady myself.

"A couple of days means a week now, does it?" Tannix stepped out of the way so I could climb into the room. "I thought something had happened to you."

"Between you and Baisan…" I muttered to myself, but I let the thought trail off. "I was busy. One of my group got hurt."

"Oh." Tannix closed the window and did up the latch. "Do you need anything for him?"

"No." I settled into the comfortable armchair. "I did want to come, you know."

"Did you?"

I nodded. "Actually, this whole letter thing…" I paused, wondering if I really should tell him. "I did hope it would be worth something. The thief in me always hopes things are worth something." I shifted slightly in the chair. "But I also, partially, used it as an excuse."

"Did you?" Tannix repeated. He was leaning against the window, somehow managing to look both relaxed and alert at the same time.

"Yes. I know four years is a long time, but I did want to visit you. I was just afraid of what you might do. With the letter, I thought, at least there was a reason for me to show up. I didn't really become friends with people back then. You were one of the first."

"You were one of my first too."

"I don't believe you," I said. "I'm sure the son of Lord West Draulin has lesser lords constantly falling over themselves to be his friend."

"That's true," Tannix agreed. "But just because they try doesn't mean they succeed. You weren't looking to benefit from my wealth or my status, and that's why I liked you. Still do."

"Well, now that we have that settled." I spun around so that I was kneeling on the seat and crossed my arms on the back of the chair. "Has anything happened with the letter? Does the king want to give me a reward?"

"Unfortunately not," Tannix replied. "On both accounts. Although I had some free time yesterday when I was supposed to be studying military tactics, and I made a list of things I thought were important about the letter."

"What are they?"

He walked over to his desk and picked up a piece of parchment. "I wrote down the last line, 'a king leads a country. Without a king, the war begins, and a country falls.' The wax was stamped with the Navire seal. We know that the recipient is supposed to meet someone called M. We know that they're a foreigner."

"No, we don't."

Tannix looked up from the parchment. "Yes, we do. They need a map and they are unfamiliar with the Lothian Dusk."

"They write in Teltish," I pointed out.

He hesitated and glanced down at his notes as if they would give him an answer. "Navire and Deorun both speak Teltish," he said slowly, still confused.

"Politically," I agreed, "but the Telts only took over what was old Zianna. We used to have our own language, just as Deorun and Navire did and still do. Old Ziannan is lost; it was beaten and forced out of us until we entirely forgot how to speak it. But they didn't, because the Telts never took them over. They don't use Teltish as an everyday, common language. Why would they write letters to each other in it?"

"How do you know that?"

"It is really that shocking that I know something?" I asked. "You have your fancy education, but I listen to people on the streets. I learn things."

"I didn't mean…" Tannix looked back down at his parchment. "I'll add that they write in Teltish. That doesn't necessarily mean anything, though." He dropped the parchment on the desk and sat down. I saw him grab a little inkpot, and then he picked up a fancy quill. I couldn't help but climb from the chair, walk over to his desk, and pull the quill from his hand. He almost started to protest, but then seemed to decide it would be useless. I'd backed away from the desk a bit so that he couldn't take it from me.

The feather itself was blue and attached to a silver piece that served as both the place to hold the quill and the tip. Where the feather and the silver piece met, there was an intricate miniature feather carved into the silver. "Why is it," I asked after inspecting the quill thoroughly, "that even your quill is more expensive than anything I've ever owned in my life?" I looked up to see that Tannix had turned around in his chair and was watching me.

He shrugged. "I've never noticed."

"You've never noticed how expensive your quill is?"

"I'm used to it," he said. "I've never really thought about it. Are you trying to make me feel guilty?"

"No." I shook my head. "No, it's just, sometimes I see things like this and I wonder why people are born who they are. Why do you get this," I shook the quill a little, "when I get nothing? Why couldn't I have been born the rich one? Don't you ever look at a poor person and wonder why you're so lucky?"

Tannix seemed a little reluctant to answer, but finally said, "No."

"Of course you don't. Why would you want to imagine having nothing? I guess only the poor would imagine living a different life. It makes sense."

"Do you want to be rich?" Tannix asked.

I shrugged, dejected. "I don't know. Sometimes. Not for the power that would come with it, but just so I could own something, so I could buy my own food—and enough food."

"I'm sorry, Finn."

"It isn't your fault." I sighed and handed the quill back to him.

"But it's true that I've never thought about it before," Tannix said. "For what it's worth, I'll do what I can to help you. Are you hungry?"

"Of course I'm hungry."

"I'll be right back." He got to his feet and left quickly, leaving me still standing by the desk. While I waited, I distracted myself by looking over his piece of parchment. Upon it were the little shapes and symbols that I knew meant something, but looked like complete nonsense to me. I traced my finger along one of the lines, wondering what it said. Tannix returned sooner than I expected. He handed me what looked like a tiny loaf of bread and sat down at his desk again.

"What is this?" I asked.

"Some sort of pastry," Tannix replied. I started eating it and watched over his shoulder as he opened his little bottle of ink and dipped the tip of the quill into it. He then moved it over and made another row of letters underneath the others.

"Is it hard to read?" I asked.

"Not once you know how," Tannix replied. "Writing can be a little harder just because the ink is messy. Do you want to see your name?"

The offer caught me off guard, and I even stopped eating for a moment. "You can write my name?"

"I don't know how you'd spell it, but I can try phonetically."

"I don't know what that means," I admitted. Often I could figure out strange words by their context, but for once, I was at a complete loss.

"It just means that I can write it out the way it sounds."

I nodded. Even though I had never cared about what my name looked like, I was suddenly curious. "Do it."

Tannix ripped off a piece of the parchment. He dipped the quill into the ink again and then wrote out two groups of letters. The first was four letters, the second was eight. He pointed at the smaller one. "This says Finn.

The longer one is how I think you would spell Finagale. Do you want to try writing it?"

I eyed both of the names. "I'll try writing Finn," I decided.

Tannix smiled. "All right." He dipped the quill into the ink again for me. "Here, most people would hold it in their right hand, but you can use your left. Just try to copy the shapes."

Tentatively, I took the quill from him. I tried to copy the way he had arranged his fingers. When I believed I'd gotten it right, I lowered the quill and slowly drew the first letter. My hand was a little shaky, so it turned out wobbly. When I was finished, I put down the quill and admired my writing. It wasn't neat as Tannix's had been, but it was recognizably the same thing.

"There, you wrote your name."

"Show me yours," I said.

Tannix picked up the quill again. Underneath my name, he wrote out a six-letter word. Then beside it, he wrote four letters, and then seven. He pointed to them in turn as he said, "This says Tannix, and these two say Lord Tandrix."

"I'll write Tannix," I decided. "Some of the letters are the same." I took the quill and went through the same process of slowly drawing each letter. When I was done with his name, I tried mine again. "I can write," I declared proudly. "My name, at least."

"You can write," he agreed. "Now you just need to learn how to read."

I shook my head. "No. I'll just remember my name and your name."

"And that will get you through life?"

"Yes. Why would I need to know anything else?"

"I guess you don't. I might teach you anyway," he said.

"Good luck." I glanced towards the window. It was getting dark enough that I knew real dusk was starting to set. "Are you allowed to leave? We could go for a walk in the upper city."

Tannix followed my gaze. "I don't have time, but we can still talk. Come on."

CHAPTER
Seventeen

"Why do you need your sword?" I asked. "Where are we going?"
Tannix was just finishing buckling his belt. Without looking at me, he went to his closet and pulled out a deep blue cloak. "I told you we didn't have time for a walk," he said unhelpfully, as if that answered my questions. He draped the cloak over his shoulders.

"Yes," I said. It was clear he wasn't going to elaborate. "When you're in a hurry, do you always decide to waste time by bringing your sword?"

"We're in a hurry because I'm on guard duty tonight, and soon I'll need to relieve one of the guards near the main gate. For that, I need my sword."

"You have guards? I've never seen any."

Tannix sighed as he crouched to tie his boots. "We post guards by the main gate. When we get older, we gradually start to take shifts. We don't guard the walls because it is assumed that they're impossible to get over. Obviously a design flaw, and I would report it, except that I enjoy your visits." He hesitated as he stood up. "So yes, we have guards."

"Should I avoid the gate?"

"Usually, but now I want you to meet me there. We can talk until I have to go on duty, and then you'll have an easy route out."

"And if the other guard sees me?"

"He won't," Tannix said. "I can plan better than that. Do you want to see a map?"

I shook my head. "No, I'll find it on my own. How long will it take you to get there?"

"Ten minutes at the most."

I turned towards the window and stepped up onto the sill, not saying anything for a moment. "That long? I'll be there in five." I pulled myself outside before he could come up with anything to say in response. Considering I didn't really know where I was going, I actually doubted I would get there before him. I heard him close his window once I was out of the way, and assumed he would leave the room right then.

When I reached the roof, I looked around for the gate. Most of the wall was tall and solid. If not impossible to get over, it was at least hard to climb. Then again, anyone trained to climb at the Order could potentially make it over, and I wondered why no one had thought of it before. I finally found the gate and shook the thoughts from my head. The whole area seemed deserted, so I wasn't worried about being seen as long as I was careful.

I climbed down from the roof, planning my route in my head. I would take the thin cobbled walkway that ran between the wall and the ring of buildings. Deserted as it looked, it wasn't worth the risk of sauntering right through the courtyard. When I reached the path, I couldn't help but remember the last time I'd been there, when I'd told Tannix the truth about who I was. I did my best to ignore the memory as I continued along it. A few times, I heard voices and pressed myself into a shadow, but no one stepped out onto the walkway. I thanked Zianesa silently each time it happened.

The gate itself was arched and seemed unnecessarily tall, because it had more than enough room for a man on horseback to ride through. The opening was blocked by a sturdy metal portcullis that could be drawn up to allow people though. I knew that within the portcullis was a smaller hinged section about the size of a normal door, which was used more often. There was one guard near it, standing against the stone wall and lazily holding a spear in his hand. This part of the wall was thicker, unlike the rest of it there was quite a lot of room for people to walk and move around. There was even a little building on top of which I assumed was a guardhouse. I could make out two guards standing near it, one on each end of the platform.

I wondered which guard Tannix would be replacing and where I was supposed to meet him. The problem was solved for me as I heard his voice coming from near the little guardhouse. I backed away from the gate to where I couldn't be seen by any of the guards, and made my way up the wall. Once on top, I carefully walked along it until I could pin myself against the wall of the little guardhouse.

I could hear Tannix talking to one of the guards on the other side. The discussion seemed to be a mix between a professional report and a casual conversation. It wasn't until I heard the other voice say goodnight, and then footsteps walking away, that I peeked around the corner. Tannix was standing by himself, half leaning against the guard house wall. His left hand was resting on the handle of his sword, giving him the appearance of attentiveness even when his posture didn't. A torch flickered nearby, casting strange shadows.

Feeling relatively confident that I was safe, I stepped around the corner. "Tannix?" I whispered to get his attention.

He glanced up at me, then looked around, and motioned for me to come closer. When I had reached his side, he said quietly, "That was not five minutes. And now I actually am guarding, so we shouldn't be talking."

"My apologies. Next time I need to sneak across a courtyard, I'll throw caution to the wind and just run over. Would that make you happy?"

"Would you get caught?"

"Me?" I shrugged nonchalantly. "Never."

"Of course, my mistake." He nudged me with his elbow, an action he managed to make seem both affectionate and condescending. "I suppose I'll forgive you for being late, this once."

I rolled my eyes, but I doubted he noticed in the growing darkness. "Do people bring horses up here?" I asked. I had noticed a ring set into the wall near us, attached to which was a neat coil of rope. I'd seen rings similar to it before, and they were usually outside of buildings and meant to tether horses.

Tannix nodded. "Sometimes the more important men like to ride up here to flaunt their power. It's unnecessary, and not very easy. Of course, the horses can't take the stairs and they don't particularly like the ramp. It's only happened two or three times since I got here."

"Horses can't use stairs?"

Tannix paused. "I suppose they could, if it was only a couple. But we're nearly two storeys up. I think getting them back down would be the real problem, anyway."

"You're important, so why don't you ride up here?"

"My horse is back in West Draulin."

"I'd think the son of West Draulin could just buy a new horse."

"I could," Tannix said. "But I don't want to." A noise nearby, like someone kicking a small stone, grabbed our attention. Tannix pushed me away and without complaint, I disappeared around the corner of the little guardhouse. I pressed myself against the wall once I was out of sight. The silence almost seemed to draw out forever, until I heard Tannix speak. "My lord," he said, greeting whomever it was who had walked up. "I only just took over the watch; I have nothing to report yet."

I heard a noise I couldn't place for a moment, and then the loud clang of two metal objects hitting each other. I flinched at the suddenness of the noise. Then Tannix was yelling for guards and I had to look around the corner of the guardhouse. He had his sword out, and it flashed in the moonlight as it met the blade of his opponent. I would have thought it was a training exercise; I even tried to persuade myself that it was, but Tannix's yelling convinced me otherwise. I was frozen in both shock and fear, unsure of how I was supposed to help him. Despite that, I was comforted slightly by the fact that he was the better swordsman, which even I could tell. He'd only gotten better during the last four years. It looked like he was winning until the second stranger appeared.

The idea appeared in my head and I started moving before really knowing what I was doing. I slowly walked closer to the fight, using the shadows from the wall to hide. When I reached the horse ring I had noticed earlier, I crouched and wrapped the end of the rope around my right wrist a few times before clenching the end in my fist. I waited for the perfect moment. It came when Tannix plunged his sword into the stomach of one of the strangers. At the sight, I almost lost my nerve, but while he was struggling with the body, the second man was stepping up behind him.

I took my chance, rushed forward, and threw myself at the second attacker. Had he been expecting it, he could have braced himself against me, but as it were, my momentum carried us both over the edge of the wall. The rope jerked against my wrist and I turned just in time to use my legs to protect myself from slamming into the wall. The stranger, with no rope to hang from, fell screaming to the ground far below us.

My wrist throbbed furiously, and I could feel my hand tingling as it went numb. The rope was tight enough that it was digging into my skin. It was supporting almost my entire weight and I couldn't take it off while hanging there, so I did my best to lessen the load. I found footholds in the wall and a good handhold, but without the use of my right hand, I couldn't climb any higher. I closed my eyes and tried to block out the pain. A heartbeat later, I opened them when I heard noise above me.

"Finagale." Tannix's voice was laced with concern as he crouched at the edge of the wall. He reached out a hand to me and I grabbed at it desperately. We caught each other's wrists, and he pulled me up. Once I was up, I crawled away from the edge, almost forgetting about my wrist until I put weight on it.

"Stop." Tannix gently lifted my wrist and unwound the rope. Even the slight movement shot pain up my arm. I flinched and pulled away from him, cradling my arm against my chest. I caught sight of his sword, lying abandoned near us, its blade red.

"You killed him," I managed.

"He was trying to kill me." Tannix sounded calm, but I got the impression he was more shaken than he was letting on. "You killed the other one. Why did you do that? You could have died."

"You *would* have died." I couldn't keep the tremor from my voice. I felt sick suddenly, realizing what I had just done. My mind started racing. I imagined Siour gathering the man in his chariot and taking him to the underworld. I started to shake.

Tannix put an arm over my shoulders, drawing my attention. "Finn, you need to get out of here. I think these men killed the other two who were guarding the gate, but there is no way nobody heard me yelling." He stopped talking and looked up suddenly. "I just heard them. Get up." he got to his feet and almost had to lift me to get me up.

"I… I can't," I protested.

"You have to."

"I can't climb with one hand," I said. I looked up at him, panicked. "I can't get away."

"My lord!" The call startled us both, but I recoiled and almost fell over when Tannix's grip loosened.

I knew then, for sure, that there was no way I could get away. My mind was suddenly clear. "Tannix. Can you get me out of jail?"

He hesitated, and then nodded. "Yes, I can get you the key."

"Then arrest me."

"Finn," he began to protest.

I cut him off by shaking my head. "I can't get away. If I try, they'll catch me and they'll probably kill me in the process."

"Lord Tandrix?" The guards had evidently found the other guards' bodies and knew who it was they were looking for.

Tannix stared at me, looking torn between his two options. He nodded as he made up his mind. "Guards! I'm here!" he called. He then grabbed my little dagger and tucked it under his own belt. Understanding the action, I slipped the chain with the Order ring from over my head and dropped it into his hand.

As soon as we'd finished, three guards appeared from the other side of the gate. They each had their swords out, looking around wildly. I could tell when they noticed the bleeding body on the ground, as well as when they noticed me. Tannix was not supporting me anymore, but he was still holding my left wrist tightly.

One of the guards stepped forward. "My lord, are you hurt?"

Tannix shook his head, then launched into an emotionless report. "Two attackers, both dead. The other fell over the side of the wall. Neither spoke. Dressed similarly, black clothing, I assume to blend in. I heard no cries of alarm from the other guards. Were they killed?"

The same guard nodded. "What of him, my lord?" He used his sword to gesture towards me, and I flinched.

"A petty thief," Tannix replied. "I highly doubt he had anything to do with the attack. I believe he was trying to climb over the wall and was drawn into the action. He has no weapons and did not try to attack me."

"Very well." The guard didn't sound entirely convinced, but luckily he didn't seem willing to question a lord. He turned to his companions. "Escort Lord Tandrix back to the building. Call an alarm if you see or hear anything suspicious. I'll take the boy off your hands, my lord," he added.

Tannix nodded slowly. "Yes, thank you."

The guard walked over to us and roughly grabbed my right forearm. His hand missed my wrist, but the movement alone was enough to shoot pain through my arm. I managed to not make any sound, but Tannix must have noticed a reaction.

"He's injured, try not to make it any worse. I would like to speak to him later about what just happened."

The guard finally seemed to notice the way I was holding my right hand. "Of course, my lord." He took my other arm, not gently, but at least it didn't already hurt.

Tannix seemed like he wanted to say something else, but then reconsidered. He picked up his sword from where he had dropped it earlier. "Lead the way," he said. My panic started to build up again as I watched him disappear into the darkness.

CHAPTER
Eighteen

We left the Order and went to the city's main jail. It was a place I had always hoped to avoid, but part of me was resigned to the fact that I'd likely die there. I just never expected to be caught so soon. I was dragged through the front gate and down multiple hallways before the guards stopped and one of them unlocked a cell door.

It was cold and dark, but so was almost every building I'd ever lived in. I was tossed in unceremoniously, and only just managed to not land on my hurt wrist. In an instant I was on my feet, facing the door and the guards, though I knew I would be powerless if they decided to hurt me. I held my injured arm near my body where I could protect it. Vaguely, I was aware of a few other people in the cell with me, but I could only deal with one threat at a time.

The two guards didn't close the door right away. Instead, the one who seemed to be the leader stood in the doorway, while the other leaned back against the metal bars that made up one side of the cell. By the way they were eyeing me, I knew they were hoping I'd give them a reason to beat me. It was well known that bored guards would turn to petty criminals for amusement.

"That lord told you to leave me alone," I pointed out, managing to disguise the nervousness I was feeling.

The two guards exchanged a glance and then began chuckling. "Do you even know who that lord was?" the leader asked me.

I shook my head. "No." After a moment's thought, I timidly added, "Sir," hoping that it would please him.

"That was Lord Tandrix, of West Draulin. I highly doubt he'll want to waste time with the likes of you. He'll probably ask us to question you ourselves."

Probably not, but I kept up the scared prisoner look. It really wasn't difficult. "Oh, is he important?" I decided that the less intelligent I seemed, the less likely they would think I was in on the attack.

"Is West Draulin important?" The leader laughed, and it took him a moment to continue. "The closest you'll ever get to royalty, boy."

"Maybe the closest we'll ever get," the second guard added.

"We could very well guard for the king."

"Well, yes. But he probably wouldn't talk to us personally as Lord Tandrix did."

"I suppose so," the leader said.

"So..." I said carefully. "So if he's so important, and he told you not to hurt me, you probably shouldn't risk it. It seems to me that someone so close to being royalty could easily have you two arrested yourselves if you displeased him. Couldn't he?"

The two guards looked at each other, but this time I detected a sense of uneasiness. Without another word to me, they turned away. The door clanged shut and the lock snapped closed, and they walked away talking quietly to each other.

I waited until their footsteps had faded away and rushed forward. I didn't know how long they would be gone, so I had to be quick. I reached my good arm through the bars and ran my fingers over the lock, trying to understand what it looked like. Until I could move the fingers of my right hand, I knew I wouldn't be able to pick, but at least I would be prepared.

"Can you open it?"

I'd almost forgotten about the other people in the cell. Startled, I spun around. There were three other men locked up with me. They were all

Native. Two appeared to be around Tannix's age, one of them possibly part Telt, and the third...

"Arow."

"Finn."

I glanced at the bars behind me. "I can try to open it."

Arow scoffed. "You can try? We've all *tried*." He looked like he'd been in the cell for a few days, and I tried to remember if I'd seen him around the lower city recently. Of all the people to be locked up with, it was just my luck to end up with the one man who hated me personally.

"I'm a thief," I replied. "Not a lock picker."

"Picking locks comes with the territory, I thought."

"Sometimes."

Arow got to his feet. "You did well, scaring away those guards."

I shrugged, feigning indifference while I watched Arow and his companions warily. "The lord who arrested me said I wasn't to be hurt, and the guards told me that he's important. I assume no one would want to risk angering him."

"He's threatening you, Arow," one of the men said.

"Look at him. What could he possibly do to us? But he's quite the thief. We should see if he's got anything good on him before the guards come back and check him."

"It was a threat." I sounded braver than I felt. "The lord wants me for some reason. If the guards were afraid of angering him, you should be too."

"You seem to have a lot of faith in this lord," Arow said. "You know he probably just wants to beat you himself?"

"Maybe he does, but that probably won't happen for days," I said. "I'd like to hold out as long as I can." Arow had moved a little closer to me while we were speaking, so I sidestepped away from him. "Arow, our energy would be better spent trying to find a way out of here. I am not looking forward to being hanged, and I don't think you are either." I spoke slowly, like I would to a frightened child. I backed up a little more, fully aware that he was driving me into a corner. "I think, together, we could come up with something. You know I'm the greatest thief in Zianna. I'm very good at sneaking around places I shouldn't be."

Arow narrowed his eyes. "Let's see what you come up with. Don't think getting me out of here will pay off your debt, though." He walked back over to the others, and settled back down on the floor. "If you don't have a good idea by tomorrow…" He let the threat trail off, which only gave my imagination free reign to make up the ending.

I DIDN'T SLEEP AT FIRST. INSTEAD, I STAYED HUDDLED IN MY CORNER OF the cell, as far away from Arow and the others as I could manage. I used a strip of cloth ripped from my cloak to bind my wrist as well as I could. At the very least, it kept me from moving it and hurting myself even more. Wiggling my fingers hurt, but I was satisfied to know that I could move them if I had to. I continuously moved them throughout the night to make sure I still could. Arow and the others talked amongst themselves for a while before going to sleep, at which point I finally calmed down.

Moonlight shone through the small, barred window set high into the wall. It lit up a patch of the stone floor by my feet, and for a long time I stared at it as it slowly crept across the cell. I didn't want to look around the cell. A quick glance earlier had shown me letters scratched into the walls, none of which I could read, but I understood them well enough. People wrote their names to leave some sort of record of themselves.

Maybe they had the right idea. I picked up a small stone and used it to carefully scratch the four letters Tannix had shown me into the stone at my feet. It felt like it had been days since I'd watched him write them out with his fancy quill. I drew each letter carefully and as accurately as I could. It might not have been correct, but I felt better having done it.

I shivered and tucked my cloak a little closer around my body. I drew my knees up and tried to get comfortable. Although I didn't want to sleep, I could feel my eyelids getting heavier and my thoughts wandering in strange ways, so I knew it was only a matter of time.

"THIEF, GET UP."

I flinched away from the bars, suddenly awake. The first thing I saw was Arow and the other two standing over in their corner, and I realized that he hadn't been the one who kicked the bars I was leaning against. I knew who had spoken. I avoided looking at the bars as I got to my feet, not wanting to seem too familiar with him.

"I didn't say move away from the bars, did I?" Tannix asked dryly.

"I'm sorry, sir," I said timidly, moving a bit closer but still refusing to look up.

"Look at me."

I glanced up quickly. He had his arms slipped through the bars and his hands clasped together on my side. He'd come down in full regalia, the deep blue cloak draped over a light tunic and dark pants. Sword and dagger both strapped to his belt, rings glinting on his fingers. I wondered whom he was trying to impress. Or intimidate.

"Who are you?" he asked.

"Finagale, sir," I replied. "I'm a ..."

"Thief, I know," Tannix said. He motioned for me to come closer, and once I was within reach, he grabbed my shoulder and pulled me even closer. "Are you hurt?" he whispered.

"No more than I was last time you saw me."

"Good." He let go of me and I quickly moved away, pretending to be scared. "So tell me, Finagale, why would a thief just happen to show up at the same time as two assassins?"

"Bad timing, sir," I said.

"It certainly seems like it," Tannix said with a nod. He stepped away from the bars and crossed his arms. "Guards, I'd like him taken to a solitary cell so I can ask him more questions."

They were the same two guards from the night before, and they instantly moved to obey Tannix's instructions. They stormed into the cell, and while one grabbed me, the other yanked my hands behind my back to shackle them together. I tried to not put up too much of a fuss, but Tannix must have noticed me wince when my right hand was grabbed.

"Careful with the broken wrist," he added sternly.

"My apologies, my lord," the guard mumbled. He still pulled back my arm and clamped the manacle shut around it, but at least he tried to be gentle. Together they dragged me from the cell, though one of them would have been more than enough. They brought me to stand in front of Tannix. I kept my head down, and purposefully made my breathing a little staggered to make myself look scared.

"I'll take him from here." He reached out for me. Just as his hand closed around my shoulder, a loud clang echoed down the stone hallway and I pulled away from him, startled. At the end of the hallway, a door had just been slammed shut. Three men were purposefully walking towards us. The one in the lead looked vaguely familiar, and was dressed up much like Tannix without the cloak. The two men who flanked him were clearly guards.

Tannix followed my gaze, glancing over his shoulder and then fully turning around. "Director?"

Suddenly I knew why I recognized the man. He'd been the one climbing after me as I'd fled back to Tannix's room. I jerked against the guards involuntarily. "Tan… Lord Tandrix…" I stammered.

Tannix waved his hand at me dismissively, but I was sure he understood the reason for my panic. "My lord, what brings you here?"

"The thief you arrested," the director replied, his gaze sweeping past Tannix to land on me. He kept walking, forcing Tannix to step out of his way. "I will be conducting his interrogation."

"My lord, he's my prisoner," Tannix protested. "I plan to question him myself."

"You are shaken up by your ordeal." The director slipped his hand under my chin and forced me to look up at him. I glanced quickly at Tannix.

"I've been trained to deal with such events," Tannix said. "When I'm in the army I'll have to handle interrogations after even more taxing ordeals. I need practice."

"You will get your practice. We'll give you another prisoner."

"Would it not be better if I practice on one I arrested myself?"

The director let go of me. He spun to face Tannix, getting close in an attempt to intimidate him. "Are you arguing with me, Lord Tandrix?"

Tannix hardly batted an eyelash. "Yes, I am, my lord," he replied steadily. He had really grown into his power over the last four years, and it didn't hurt that he was a little taller than the director. "I arrested him, he's my prisoner." He glanced over at me. As much as I was grateful, I knew that if he got himself in trouble there would be no chance of him getting me out. I shook my head, hoping he'd understand.

"That said, my lord," Tannix continued slowly, looking a little confused at my reaction. "Maybe I am a little shaken up by the attack. I might make a mistake." He took a small step back. "I apologize for my behaviour, my lord."

The director didn't look entirely pleased, but he seemed satisfied as he turned to me again. "Guards, we'll take him to a private cell. I doubt this will take long."

"My lord," Tannix said again. "May I observe the interrogation?"

The director shook his head. "Not this time. You need to rest. In time, killing will become easier for you, but those two were your first and it is never easy." He clapped his hand on Tannix's shoulder in a paternal gesture. "Come speak with me later."

Tannix nodded. "Yes sir."

The director motioned to his two guards, who took me away from the others. They followed him as he started walking down the hall, half dragging and half carrying me between them. Almost every movement jolted the manacles around my wrist and shot pain up my right arm, but I did my best to not react or give them any signal to show that I was hurt. I didn't want to remind them.

I tried to keep track of where we were going, but the jail was confusing. We walked down numerous hallways, most of which were lined with cells. Some were empty, but most had one or two occupants, occasionally more. The other prisoners shouted insults and curses, some muttered prayers to themselves, and others were silent. It was unnerving and I couldn't help but imagine being in a cell as long as they had been. The thought terrified me.

When we finally stopped in front of a cell, it was different. The hallway was almost perfectly silent. There were other cells, but they all looked strange. Instead of a wall of bars, there was only one solid metal door with a small barred window in it. Beyond, the room was pitch black. The director unlocked the door with a large key from a ring on his belt, and pushed it open. It seemed to take some force; the door was heavy.

He picked up a torch burning beside the door and walked into the cell. He used it to light two torches within the room before the guards pulled me in. There was a wooden chair in the centre of the room, with old leather straps on the armrests and two front legs. My terror was overwhelming and I couldn't even struggle to protect myself as the guards led me to the chair and briskly strapped me in. They then retreated to stand by the door. The director stood in front of me. The three torches caused his shadow to flicker oddly on the wall behind him, on which various weapons were hung. I closed my eyes, trying not to look at or think about the tools.

The director chuckled. "Calm down, boy. I do not intend to use any of those on you unless you drive me to it, but I think you want to cooperate. I know you left that letter in my office. All I want to know is what you know about this assassination attempt. Unfortunately, the letter does not provide enough information for me to take any action." I could tell that he was slowly circling me as he talked. "But you will give me everything I need, yes?"

"I don't know anything," I said quietly.

He hit the back of my head, but it was surprisingly light given that he was probably going to kill me later. "Maybe looking at the interrogation implements for a few hours will help you remember something." I heard him walk away. The door swung shut, thudding heavily against the stone frame. The unmistakable sound of a lock clicking followed, and then only silence.

CHAPTER
Nineteen

The silence was broken by harsh screams. They echoed in from another cell, somehow piercing through the thick metal door to mine. I did my best to ignore them, just as I had been doing my best not to think about the weapons on the wall in front of me. I had opened my eyes only once since the director had left, to glance quickly around for any possible means of escape that I hadn't seen the first time. There was nothing.

However, despite the screaming and the probably unavoidable torture, I felt calm, almost resigned to what was going to happen. I'd come up with a simple plan: tell the director everything I could without putting Tannix under any suspicion. If he was going to get me out, he needed people to trust him.

The amount of trust I was piling on Tannix was frightening. I couldn't remember the last time I'd relied so much on another person. This was the first time I'd been in a situation where there was no hope of me getting out without help, and all I could do was try to survive long enough for help to come.

I wasn't sure how much time passed before my door unlocked. I opened my eyes to see what was happening, managing not to look at the weapons.

Two guards walked in, one carrying a small table and one a chair, both of which were placed in front of me. The two guards returned to the door as the director walked in. He was carrying a pile of paper, which he put on the table before taking a seat on the chair. The door was shut, and the room went silent as we looked at each other.

Finally, he picked up a piece of paper from the top of the little pile and cleared his throat before he read aloud. "Lord West Draulin's son, Tandrix, seems to have picked up a companion. I suppose it was only a matter of time, given his position, before he would draw the lesser nobles towards him. There is something about this boy, however, which I find suspicious. First and foremost, I do not recognize him. Granted, I have only been with these boys for two weeks, and I have yet to get to know all of them. It is entirely possible that I simply did not notice him before he joined Tandrix. I will look into it further."

The calmness I'd been feeling seemed to break apart piece by piece with every word. I managed to hold back the panic when I realized what the director was reading. He paused to look up at me, his expression confident, as if he knew I would quickly crumble away. He remained like that for a moment, giving me a chance to speak. When I didn't, he turned back to his piece of paper.

"I overheard Lord Tandrix and the boy speaking today, and the boy referred to himself as Finn. I will look into my records for any sign of him." The director paused to flip the page over. "I had the boys practice climbing walls today, and I have realized what it is that unnerves me about this Finn. His partly Native appearance can easily be attributed to a Native mother, which is common among the lesser lords. However, I spoke to him after observing him climb to a roof with no hesitation along the way. He speaks with a distinct Native accent, and particularly he sounds like a Native from the city. During the noon meal I heard him say "Telt," which is a term used mostly by lower class Natives, rarely by upper class Natives, and never by Teltans."

I noticed that I was biting my lip only when I tasted blood. Malte had figured me out so much earlier than I'd thought, but aside from that, I knew the account was condemning. I had been hoping to claim to be an exploring thief who accidentally came across a fight. There was no way the director would believe that now. My mind raced, trying to figure out a way to explain it all away.

"I am planning to take Lord Tandrix and Finn on a trip to the lower city today, to gauge the boy's reaction and mannerisms. I have concluded that he snuck into our headquarters and somehow managed to blend in without anybody noticing. This can be partially explained by his friendship with Tandrix, since many of us, myself included, are hesitant to upset the young lord. I do not believe Tandrix has any idea that his friend does not belong in the Order. The only thing my theory does not explain is the boy's Order ring." The director paused and glanced up to look at my hands. I was grateful that I'd given the ring to Tannix. "While in the lower city today," he continued, "I noticed that Finn seemed unusually comfortable with the surroundings. Most young lords are confused and mildly disgusted when they see firsthand the way the Natives live. He told me that his name is Finagale, and that he is from a farming villa near Kitsi. It is possible, but unlikely."

The director put down the piece of paper to pick up a second one. "I attempted to conduct an interview with Finagale today. He kept to his story of being from near Kitsi, and claimed to have a Native mother, which he used to explain away his name, accent, and physical appearance. I was interrupted by my friend and colleague Lord Nata Co, who I had been expecting for days. He reported to me that he believed a young thief on the Zianna streets had taken his Order ring weeks before, during his last trip to the capital. I called the alarm instantly, but unfortunately, after a search of the ground, it was clear that the thief had escaped."

The director put down the piece of paper. He leaned forward in his chair and rested his forearms on his knees. I avoided his gaze, and since I didn't want to look at the weapons, that meant I had to stare at the ground. The silence drew out until he shifted and his chair creaked. I glanced up involuntarily.

"Tell me, boy. What is your name?"

There was no point in lying. "Finagale."

"Ah." The director leaned back in his chair. "So, four years ago you managed to get into the headquarters and remain there for a few weeks. You befriended Lord Tandrix. Now, more recently, you left a note hinting to an attempt on the king's life in my office. Then, during an attack on the same Lord Tandrix, he arrested you. Did he decide that he didn't want any part of the assassination?"

"No," I replied sharply, my desire to protect Tannix completely overruling the need to protect myself.

"No? So tell me what happened."

"I… I want food," I replied. "Then I'll tell you." I hoped the delay would give me enough time to put together a story.

The director chuckled. "You are in no position to bargain. I could just as easily torture the information out of you."

"Of course." I was glad to notice that the tremor had left my voice. "Of course you *could*, sir. But certainly you know that under torture, I'll just tell you what I think you want to hear so you'll stop hurting me. And that information might not be accurate. However, sir, if you would consent to have food brought, I will be more than willing to tell you what you want to know."

"Lord Malte warned me that you are an adept speaker when cornered." The director was smiling, as if I amused him. I couldn't decide whether that was good for me or not. After a moment's consideration, he looked to the guards by the door. "One of you get some food and water. You," he added, turning to me, "are going to start your story."

I knew I couldn't push for more time, and I hadn't been expecting the food at all, so I nodded. "Yes sir, of course." I hesitated though, until one of the guards had left the room. As soon as the door closed, I launched into my story before the director could get annoyed. "Yes, I stole Lord Co's ring, but I took it because I'm a poor thief. I needed it for money. I had no idea it was important. I climbed over the wall completely by accident while trying to escape from some guards. I arrived during some sort of wrestling practice, where Lord Tandrix attacked me. I was wearing the ring at the time; he saw it and assumed I was part of the Order. I made up lies to protect myself, and I fully intended to run the first chance I got, but I had to go into the building with him not to arouse suspicion. I decided to wait out the night and leave the next morning, but then I heard about a breakfast. Sir, when someone grows up on the streets, money and food became very important. I decided to risk being caught to get some food. I found Lord Tandrix and stayed with him because I knew who he was."

As if summoned by my mention of food, the guards returned carrying a tray. I stopped speaking, my eyes drawn towards him. Upon the tray was a jug of water and some pieces of bread. Not in any way a fulfilling meal, but I'd long ago learned not to be choosy. It was placed on my lap, and the director reached towards me to undo the strap on my left wrist. I grabbed the bread and ate quickly before they could decide to take the food away. I then picked up the jug and drank half of it before it was taken from my hand.

"Keep talking," the director said, placing the jug on the table beside him.

"So yes, we became friends, but he never knew who I was. When Lord Malte discovered who I was, I realized that the food was no longer worth the risk and I ran. Last week, I stole the letter from some men in the upper city. I can't read, but judging from the look of the letter, I believed it to be important. I decided to give it to someone who would know what to do with it, if it did turn out to be useful. I knew I could get in and out of the Order's grounds, seeing as I'd done it before, so I decided to leave it with you. I knew where your office was because Tandrix pointed out the window four years ago, and I have a good memory for locations."

He handed the jug back to me. This time I took my time drinking, trying to buy myself some more time before I had to explain the arrest. I finished it sooner than I hoped, and reluctantly passed it over. He took it and looked at me expectantly.

"Yesterday, I was desperate to get some food, and I decided to try to sneak back into the Order's building. I climbed up the wall out of sight of the guards, like I had before, but this time I noticed Lord Tandrix standing there. Well, I believed it to be him, so I moved a bit closer to get a better look. That was when he was attacked. One man fell over the edge, and then he stabbed the other one. He noticed me, and he attacked me before realizing I had no weapons. He did something to my wrist, but aside from that, I wasn't hurt. I don't think he recognized me."

"So it was all a coincidence?" the director asked.

I nodded. "Yes, sir. A very unfortunate coincidence."

"Well, that is a huge relief," he said thoughtfully. "I would hate to think that Lord Tandrix was involved in any sort of assassination attempt."

"He isn't, sir," I agreed, starting to feel more at ease.

"Good, good." The director motioned to one of his guards, and got to his feet. One of the large men walked over. I was still watching the director, so I didn't realize what was happening until the guard had grabbed my left arm and strapped it back to the chair. Alarm suddenly replaced the relief. The director looked down at me. "I truly am glad to know that Lord Tandrix is not involved. Although I find it odd that you are so certain of that fact, when you have not spoken to him in four years. If I am to take you at your word, the only way you could know he is not involved is if you know who *is*." He paused, probably to let my mind process what he was saying. "And you will tell me."

I shook my head, but could think of nothing to say. He smiled at me, and I knew that it was not a good thing that he found me amusing. He clasped his hands behind his back and strolled over to the wall of weapons. My eyes followed, although I didn't want to watch. The guards were working together to move something into the room. I looked over at them and regretted it. It was a brazier, a metal pot on legs, which was filled with coals. They placed it near the wall and used a torch to light the coals.

"I believe you are a smart boy," said the director, drawing my attention away from the brazier. He had picked up an iron rod, the end of which twisted into a shape I couldn't make out. He turned it in his fingers and he walked slowly towards the brazier. "You know what this is, correct?"

I nodded slowly.

"Good." The branding iron clanged against the metal as he shoved it into the fire. "Unfortunately, that will take some time to be ready for use. I think for now I might settle for a knife." He wandered back over to the wall, moving slowly to heighten my terror. He lightly ran his hand over a few of the knives' handles before picking one no longer than his hand. "This is one of my favourites," he said. He returned to his chair, but moved it a little closer to me before sitting down. "Let me see, which wrist was it that Lord Tandrix injured?"

He slid the blade of the knife up under my left sleeve. I flinched at the touch of the cold metal, but tried not to give him any more of a reaction. He used the blade to cut up through the fabric, exposing almost my forearm. My foreigner bracelet came into view, and the director thoughtfully ran his finger over it. "What is this?"

"I don't know where it came from," I said quickly. "Someone was selling it in the market and I stole it. I'm just a thief, sir, I don't know anything about the letter…"

The director cut me off by pressing the blade against my skin, though not quite hard enough to draw blood. Then he reached over to my other wrist and started the same process of cutting back my sleeve. He prodded at my right wrist with his fingers and when I flinched, he smiled. "This is the one. It feels broken. It must hurt to have it strapped to the chair."

"No," I lied, shaking my head slightly. "It's fine now."

He smirked. "Of course it is." He looked over at the two guards. "Is it ready?" Without looking over, I could tell that the guards had nodded because his smile grew. Turning his attention back to my left arm, he ran his knife up under the sleeve up to my shoulder to give himself an easy target for the iron.

As he walked over to the brazier, I closed my eyes again and tried to collect myself. I tried to slow my panicked breathing. At least my story was almost entirely true, it would be easier to remember than if I had made the whole thing up. I ran it over in my head quickly, especially the last part about the letter. That was the part he would ask about. I would keep insisting that I knew nothing about it, and maybe he would believe me, but in the back of my mind, I knew he was unlikely to stop until I'd told him exactly what he wanted to hear, even if it was far from the truth.

I was so concentrated on calming myself that the sensation of heat on my shoulder caught me off guard. I tensed and tried to shy away from it, but the chair kept me still. The iron was not yet touching my skin but it was very, very close. The chair in front of me creaked.

"What do you know about this letter?"

I had to pause before answering, to once again rein in my thoughts. Deliberately, I replied, "Nothing." I kept my eyes closed, knowing that he would love to see the terror in them. With them closed, I could at least keep myself under some control.

"So you do not know what the letter said?"

I shook my head. "No, sir. Aside from what you've said about an assassination attempt, which I didn't even know before you told me." I hoped I sounding convincing.

"So you did not read it before delivering it to me?"

"I cannot read," I said it slowly, to stress the fact. Then I couldn't help myself. "Please get that away from my arm."

The director waved his hand, but instead of taking away the iron liked I'd hoped, the guard moved it so that I could feel the heat against my cheek. Alarmed, I turned my head away, but a strong hand forced me to face forward again. The brand was so close I felt like my skin must have been burning even without direct contact. I was afraid to move my head in case I accidentally touched it.

"Do you wish you revise your statement?" the director asked.

My hesitation was for an entirely new reason. "I don't know what that means." He sighed. "Revise. Change. Correct. So?"

"My statement is as correct as it can be, sir. There's nothing to change."

"Open your eyes."

I did what I was told only because I was worried about the iron touching my face. The director had picked up one of the papers he had been reading earlier, which he held up in front of my face. I could recognize a few of the shapes. In a couple places, I thought I could see my name, and maybe Tannix's, but the rest was complete nonsense. I shook my head slightly.

The director lowered the parchment. "Messengers often cannot read," he said, putting it back on the little table. "The information they are carrying is sometimes too valuable to risk a messenger reading it." He gestured to his guard, and to my relief the brand was moved back slightly. It was still dangerously close, but at least my cheek didn't feel like it would start to melt off. "So," he continued. "Who gave you the letter?"

"I stole it."

"From whom?"

"I don't know," I said. "It was two men in the upper city. They looked wealthy so I decided to check their pockets."

"Do you go to the upper city often?"

I almost shrugged. "I guess so. More than other thieves."

"Why is that?"

"There isn't much to take in the lower city," I said. "And there are many thieves looking to take things. It's worth the risk."

"I am not surprised a thief would get drawn into this." The director sounded disappointed. "If the result is getting rid of the king and starting a civil war that might allow your people to regain control, being a messenger must be worth the risk."

"No," I said. "The king is mine as much as he is yours. I'm as loyal to him as I can be. I don't hate every Telt on principle, you know."

The director glanced at the guard. The brand was taken away from my cheek, but before I even had a chance to feel better, I felt pain burst through my shoulder. I instinctively tried to jerk away from it, at the same time clenching my jaw so that I wouldn't make any noise. I knew better than to put on a show. When the brand was drawn away, my whole arm felt like it was on fire. My shoulder was almost numb, but pain radiated away from it like flickering flames. I could almost imagine the flames running down my arm and across my shoulder to my neck. Jarring my right wrist against the bonds hadn't helped either, and pain was shooting up that arm as well.

It took me a moment to realize that the director was talking to me. Nothing seemed to exist but the pain. His words finally started to cut through the fuzziness. I tried to listen to him, but it was hard to fit any of the words together into sentences that made sense. It all seemed jumbled, but after some concentration, I made out one statement that grabbed my attention.

"Leave him. He needs some time to himself to think about how much he would like to avoid being branded a second time."

As he walked towards the door, I began to lose control over the fuzziness that was fighting against my thoughts, then the fuzziness turned to blackness and took over.

CHAPTER
Twenty

I woke up slowly. The first time I opened my eyes, I was still alone in the cell. I couldn't tell if my arms still hurt or not. It was hardly a second before my eyes drifted closed again. The next time, the guards were back, but the director was nowhere in sight. Confused as I was, I didn't understand that one of them was undoing the straps that held me to the chair. I was pulled to my feet and held up by one guard while the other tied my wrists together with a rough rope. This time I stayed awake, though things seemed slow and blurry. I was dragged from the cell and down numerous hallways that I instinctively tried to remember.

The sight of a courtyard ahead cleared my mind. I did nothing, letting the guards think I was partially unconscious. I didn't expect to be able to escape, but I didn't want to hurt my chances if the opportunity came. The courtyard was small, bordered by the prison's walls. It wasn't the main courtyard that led out of the prison; this one was private and secluded. The faint flicker of hope I'd built up from seeing daylight faded and I knew there was no way I could get away. A thick wooden pole stood in the centre of the courtyard. About halfway up it, hammered into the wood, was a metal hook. I knew what I was looking at.

The two guards pulled me over to the post. They stopped nearby, each holding an arm as if one of them wouldn't be strong enough to hold me. We were facing a wooden door opposite the one we had walked though. It had been closed, but just as we stopped, it swung open. The director walked in first, and I winced when he looked at me. He turned around to greet the men who were following him. Of course, interrogations and executions often drew crowds. Usually they were held in the market square. I'd been present for quite a few of them but I never watched—it was easy to sneak amongst the distracted shoppers and merchants. My execution seemed like it would be a more private event.

A handful of men walked into the courtyard, one of whom I recognized. Malte arrived, looking exactly as he had four years ago. He didn't even look at me as he went to join the other men. A flicker of blue over by the door caught my attention, and I instantly felt better. Whether he could do anything or not, I felt better just seeing him.

The director didn't bother officially greeting Tannix. Instead, they exchanged a quick nod before approaching the rest of us. They joined the group and the director began to explain what exactly was going on. Tannix was staring at me. I could tell when he noticed the brand, because his eyes widened and his hand, which was resting on his sword pommel, tightened. He glared at the director so hatefully I was almost afraid he'd pull out his sword and cut off the man's head right there. I'm sure he was imagining it.

My two guards started moving, and I was pulled over to the wooden post. One guard lifted my arms so that the rope binding my wrists could be slung over the hook. It left me standing on the tips of my toes, facing the pole. Pain flared through my left shoulder, radiating out from the brand and reminding me that it was there. At the same time, my broken wrist was throbbing and I tried to adjust so that most of my weight was on my left wrist. If it wasn't for the broken wrist and brand, I might have been able to use the hook to climb up the pole. The guards then completely cut away my cloak and tunic, leaving no protection between the skin of my back and the whip.

The director unhooked the whip from his belt dramatically as he approached me. I stared at Tannix, and despite everything, I felt comforted that he was meeting my gaze.

The director appeared at my side. "Is there anything you want to tell me?"

"There's nothing else to tell," I replied steadily.

"We shall see." He sounded quite confident in himself. I almost wished there was something I knew, something I could tell him so that he wouldn't hurt me. But I knew that even if I had some bit of information, he would always believe that there was more. He flicked the whip at his side, resulting in a loud crack that filled the courtyard. The sound shattered my resolve. I started shaking, and no amount of concentration could stop it.

The courtyard was silent. I could hear the director's footsteps as he backed away from me. He flicked the whip once more for show. I tried to prepare myself for the coming blow, but the first lash still took me by surprise. I managed not to make any sound as the whip slashed my back, though I tensed and jerked against my bound wrists at the pain it caused. The second strike also took me by surprise, as I was trying to recover from the first. I yelped, which faded into whimpering. By the third strike, I'd resorted to pleading, to no avail. By the fourth everything was starting to black out again.

A HAND ON MY CHEEK WOKE ME UP. I WAS LYING FACE DOWN ON A STONE floor, and I tried to move my arms so that I could sit up. Before I could, the hand moved to rest on my forearm and Tannix's voice broke the silence.

"Don't move."

I listened to him. "How many?" I asked. My back felt like it had been mauled by a wild beast, and I'm sure it also looked that way. It hurt enough that I almost forgot about the broken wrist and the brand.

"Ten," Tannix replied. "You passed out around the fifth and there was no fun to be had in beating you after that, but he kept at it."

"Did I..." I hesitated, because I'd unconsciously shifted a little and the pain flared up. I grit my teeth and once the pain had faded, I finished my question. "Did I say anything about you?" I opened my eyes for the first time so I could watch his reaction.

Tannix shook his head. "No. You begged him to stop for a while. You insisted that you couldn't read a few times, and you mumbled Zianesa's name. I have some salve for your back. I had to bribe my way down here, and you're not supposed to be treated, but if you let me, I'll apply it. It might hurt."

I nodded gratefully and closed my eyes, finding it easier to ignore the pain that way. "Yes, please."

"Try to be quiet," Tannix told me. His hand left my forearm and I heard him unscrewing a lid. I felt the cold touch of his hand on my back and winced, but stayed quiet as he'd instructed. It took him a few minutes to rub the salve gently over my whole back. I could feel it numbing my skin and the pain cooling away. Afterwards, he carefully dabbed some onto the brand. By the time I heard him closing his container, I had relaxed considerably. He then moved his attention to my wrist. I felt him pick up my right arm and start wrapping something around it.

"What is it?"

"What is what?" Tannix asked.

"The brand. I haven't been able to look at it."

Tannix sighed. "It's the letter T, it stands for thief," he told me. After he'd finished with my wrist, he continued. "At this point, I'm fairly certain the director believes that you don't know anything else, but he probably intends to kill you because you know too much. If I give you a key, could you get out?"

"No," I said. "I can hardly move, let alone climb walls with this wrist."

He was silent for a moment. "Does anything else hurt?" He was touching my head again. "When they unhooked you from the pole they dropped you, and you hit your head. I can't feel any bumps though."

"No." I opened my eyes again to look up at him. "Don't let him kill me."

"I won't," Tannix promised. "You have some time." He picked up a thin blanket from nearby and rolled it up into a bundle, which he gently placed beneath my head. He took a key from his pocket and pushed it into the centre of my new pillow. "Rest. Tomorrow, when the guard changes at noon, you'll have to try to get out. You're in the main part of the prison now. There's a window just down the hall that you'll be able to fit through. I'll have people waiting on the other side to help you."

"Who?" I asked.

"I'm not sure yet. Get some sleep."

The order was pointless, because I was tired enough that I had fallen asleep before he even left my cell.

WHEN THE GUARD WALKED AWAY, I HAD TO TAKE MY CHANCE. DESPITE the pain movement caused my back, I knew I had no choice. I waited until his footsteps faded and gingerly got to my feet. The key was in my hand already. I reached through the bars and felt for the lock before sliding the key into it and turning. The click as it unlocked sounded loud in the silent corridor. I froze, listening for any sounds of the guard coming back. When none came, I pushed the cell door open and slipped out, grabbing the key as I did so. I didn't want them to know someone had given it to me.

Following Tannix's directions, I walked down the hallway towards a square of daylight. Subconsciously, I was moving the fingers of my right hand, testing their mobility. The bandage he had put on my wrist the day before had worked wonders. I could move my fingers with hardly any pain, and as long as I didn't try to rotate my wrist, it felt fine. I wasn't sure how it would hold up to climbing. My back stung furiously. I knew that every movement tugged against and ripped the scabs that had formed over night, but I did my best to ignore it. It wasn't so bad that I couldn't walk, as long as I was careful.

The window was higher on the wall than I'd hoped. It would have been no problem if I was uninjured, or even if I'd been taller. I looked up at it thoughtfully. The bars were wide enough apart that I could probably squeeze through them, if I could only get up. Cautiously, I reached up with my right hand and grabbed at a rock. The feelings that shot down my arm convinced me that I couldn't make the climb. I glanced around for something to step on, maybe a stool or bench.

A clinking sound echoed down the hall, like parts of armour clicking together. I started running without thinking it through, away from the sound that was almost certainly a guard. I didn't want to duck into another cell and trap myself, so I turned into a dark doorway that led to a set of steep, curved stairs. There was no light in the staircase, but I could see the flickering of a torch around the corner. I slowed as I crept down them, hoping both that the guard hadn't noticed me and that there would be no one in the room below me.

The room was large and damp, with only one torch sitting in a bracket near the stairs. The flickering light didn't quite reach the corners of the room, but I could see a little. It was part of the sewage system that led to and from the palace. The water was clear and clean. At the sight of it, my stomach jumped. Water made me uneasy, although it was a tiny stream and the fear quickly disappeared. I crouched next to it, scooped some water into my hands, and took a drink. It tasted a little odd and was cold—clearly from one of the underground streams. I drank some more and splashed a handful of water onto my brand before I heard cries coming from above me. They knew I was out of my cell.

I realized that there was only one doorway into the room. The only other ways out were the tunnels on either side of the stream. It was gushing out of a hole to my right, which was far too small for me, but it ran through a larger tunnel to my left. The grate was too narrow for me to crawl through, but without any other options I had to try something.

I stepped into the stream, which came up to just under my knees. I hurried to inspect the grate. The lower half looked rusted. Without a second thought I kicked it, and my foot broke through as if Zianesa herself was helping me. I kicked it again to widen the hole, but then I was out of time. Taking a deep breath, I ducked under the water to drag myself through the hole.

It was a tight fit. I took my time easing my shoulders through, to avoid my brand scraping against the metal. I was less cautious with my hips. Once I'd wiggled through, I popped my head up to gasp for air before moving further back in the tunnel so that the light from the torch couldn't reach me. I could hear footsteps in the room and two voices, but neither of them seemed to think of looking down the tunnel. I started walking down it, slowly so that I wouldn't splash the water. I couldn't see any light ahead, but it was the only way to go.

It didn't take long for me to reach a slight bend in the tunnel, and when I turned around, I was looking at almost complete darkness. Some light bounced off the damp walls, but not much. I kept walking. Darkness didn't bother me, it never had, but my mind started to wander. I imagined walking down under the city and falling into a huge freezing lake. I imagined the tunnel getting smaller and smaller until I could no longer keep going. I thought of the stream suddenly swelling and filling the tunnel completely. I had to stop, with a hand on each of the damp walls, and force myself to think of something else. It took me a moment to gather my thoughts and focus them on the warm city I was trying to get to and the people there. Mostly I thought of Tannix, or Baisan, Kassia, and the other thieves. I wondered if they knew I had been arrested or if they thought I'd just left them. As more time passed, I found my mind wandering to my mother. I hadn't thought of her much these past few years, and it came as a bit of a shock when I realized what I was remembering.

The distraction did its job well, and while remembering one of the happier times with my mother, I saw a prick of light in the distance. By then I was shivering from the cold of the stream, and I longed to get out and into the sun. The light got bigger and bigger until finally, I found myself at the end of the tunnel. It was covered by a grate, but it was in worse condition than the other one had been. A single kick managed to break it loose and I pushed the whole thing off. Once out in the open, I pressed myself against the wall and took in my surroundings. The stream poured out of the tunnel and into a hole in the ground, where it disappeared from sight. Having just thought about my mother jolted a memory of the place. It was of her holding a bucket under the falling water and using it to give me a bath. It was an obscure corner of the lower city. Relief flooded through me as I realized that I'd made it.

CHAPTER
Twenty-one

"**D**on't wake him up."

"He'll be fine." The voices crept into my dreams, and a hand shook my right shoulder. Annoyed, I threw my arm over my face and hoped that whoever was bothering me would go away. The clearer of the two voices had been Kassia's, and I assumed it was Baisan poking at me. I'd met them both the day before after stumbling my way towards our home. They'd helped me back, and in light of my condition, Baisan hadn't even found it necessary to lecture me about being late.

I was shaken again, and this time I groaned. "Go away."

"Get up."

"No," I argued weakly. "Leave me alone."

"Finagale."

My eyes flew open and I shot up into a sitting position. My back screamed out in protest, but I couldn't help it. "What are you doing here?" I asked Tannix, sounding more panicked than I'd intended. He looked so out of place, sitting cross-legged on the ground near my little makeshift bed. Kassia was crouched next to him; Baisan and Castin were off near the other side of the room. Castin was standing without any apparent trouble from his cut. Everyone else was gone.

"I came to see if you had made it out," Tannix replied.

"You can't be here," I said. "You can't see this. Go away."

"I've already seen it," he said.

"You..." I hesitated, trying to figure out how best to put my feelings into words. "You're too good for this world."

Tannix smiled and shook his head slightly. "Don't be ridiculous, Finn. Let me see your back." He pulled a little jar from a pocket under his cloak. "I've brought the salve."

"We already have some," Kassia said.

"This will be better," Tannix said.

"Fine." Kassia slipped the jar from his hand and moved out of his reach. She unscrewed the lid and dipped a finger into the cream. "Why would you use up expensive salve on a Native?" she asked.

"I got it for him," Tannix said. Kassia still looked doubtful, so he added, "I told you where to find him, didn't I? Why would I help him escape just to hurt him?"

"He wasn't where you told us he'd be," Baisan said. "You said he'd be near the window."

"I couldn't make it through the window," I said. "Kassia, don't worry. He's already used that on me. It was fine."

Kassia hung back, looking at Tannix warily. After a moment, she returned to my side. This time, she gently pulled the loose tunic I'd struggled into the night before over my head. She scooped up some of the salve with her fingers. "I'm sorry if I hurt you," she said quietly, before beginning to rub it onto my back. I flinched, but she was gentle and her touch didn't hurt.

Tannix watched her for a moment before his gaze dropped to my bound wrist. "How does it feel?"

"Better since you wrapped it up. How did you get here?"

"Same way I did two days ago. I came down and stayed around the main gate until someone tried to pickpocket me. I grabbed his arm and asked about you, and when he nodded I insisted he bring me to your home."

"Who was it?" I asked. Tannix shrugged, so I glanced over his shoulder at Baisan.

"Leker."

"I hope you didn't scare him too badly, Tannix," I said. Kassia finished with my back and moved on to the brand. The pain almost entirely disappeared, and I relaxed a bit.

"No, I don't think so. He brought me to meet Baisan, but he didn't bring me here, and I explained how I had given you the key and told Baisan where the window was. This time, I stood near the gate again until I saw the same boy, and then I caught him and made him bring me back here." He reached under his cloak again and took out my dagger and the chain with my Order ring, both of which he held out to me. "I thought you might want these back."

"Thank you." I took them gratefully. I put the dagger on the ground, but I held the ring to fiddle with while I glanced back up at Tannix. "Thank you for getting me out."

"I wish I could have done it sooner," he said. He was close enough that he could reach out and touch my shoulder, near the brand. "I should have stopped this."

I shrugged. "I don't know if you could have. At least now I have something to show for being the greatest thief in Zianna. How many thieves do you think get branded and manage to escape?" My attempt to lighten the mood didn't work. Tannix dropped his hand and Kassia silently finished up with the salve.

"I didn't tell you the truth back in the cell," Tannix said. "You did say something while he was whipping you. Nothing about me, but right before you passed out you mumbled Malte's name. He was arrested on the spot."

"Why?"

"The director must have thought you were saying that Malte is the "M" mentioned in the letter. I'm sure he'll be found innocent, unless of course he is guilty."

"I didn't mean to," I protested. "Can't you tell…" but I trailed off, knowing that he couldn't say anything. "Will he be hurt?"

"Potentially, but he has some rank to protect himself with. He might be able to avoid torture for a while." Tannix glanced around the room quickly. "Do you think you could take a walk?"

"Yes." I started to get to my feet, but Baisan motioned for me to sit down.

"Last time he went anywhere with you, he got arrested and tortured. You're not taking him anywhere."

Tannix sighed and stood up. Though he wasn't trying to look menacing, Baisan took a nervous step backwards. When Tannix reached under his cloak, I could see Castin grip his knife, ready to jump to Baisan's aid if need be. Instead of a knife, Tannix pulled out a bulging pouch, which he placed in Baisan's hands. Baisan stared down at it with wide eyes before slowly nodding.

Kassia helped me stand up. "Did you just buy me?" I asked, slightly distressed at the thought.

"No, I just bribed your guard," Tannix said. "Let's go."

TANNIX WAS WEARING ONE OF THE SAND COLOURED CLOAKS FROM THE Order, but it didn't help him blend in. It was the way he held himself, and the way he acted. Luckily, there weren't many people around to see us. We stayed off the main roads and walked slowly to accommodate my injuries. At first we didn't speak, just enjoying each other's company—and in my case, enjoying freedom.

Tannix broke the silence. "That girl, she seems to like you."

"Kassia?" As much as I appreciated not having to think about what had happened for a moment, his comment surprised me.

He nodded. "I think so. She was pretty protective; she didn't want me waking you up."

"I didn't want you to wake me up, either," I said.

"She likes you."

"Well, maybe." I shrugged uncomfortably. "So, what am I supposed to do?"

"Why would I know?"

"You're the son of West Draulin," I said. "You must know how to deal with girls."

Tannix laughed and shook his head. "Hardly. I'm engaged."

I stopped walking suddenly, and he took another step before noticing. The information had taken me off guard. I was shocked it hadn't come up before.

He turned around to look at me. "What?"

"You're engaged?"

"Yes, technically. It's a political arrangement." He started walking again, and I followed. "The Lord of East Draulin only has one child, a daughter. My father has a plan to have my family in control of both sides of the Straights of Draulin. Tandrin will take West Draulin, as he should, but I will marry Lady Mayah and inherit the east. We've been engaged as long as I can remember, although I don't know her all that well. She is a year or two younger than me, and very attractive." He shrugged. "I've just never had to think about girls before, and even if I did, getting involved with someone would be shameful for both of our families. Not to mention that if I ruined his plan, my father would be tempted to disown me."

"Can he disown you?"

"Yes, but he wouldn't. I was joking. We're close, compared to other high class families."

"Are most not close?" I persisting in questioning him. Since our reunion, I'd answered countless questions about my life. It was nice to have a chance to question him for once, and he didn't seem to mind.

"It depends on the family," Tannix replied. "Some are distant, and the children are raised by servants and never really get a chance to interact with their parents. Mine weren't like that. My father would ride or practice fighting with Tandrin and me. My mother taught my younger sister how to be diplomatic, and how to hold her own in a world ruled by men."

"What's her name?" I asked. "How do girl names work?"

"Work?"

"Telts give their children similar names. Natives don't do that."

"Oh, right." He nodded. "Her name is Tairia. It's my mother's name, Clairia, combined with the first letter of my father's name. Lord Tandrael."

"Do the names ever get confusing?"

"Rarely, and not within our family. Sometimes other families can be confusing," Tannix said. "But I had to learn the names of all the major nobility, and much of the lesser. Well, the lesser on New Teltar, at least."

"You have to know everyone by name?"

He shrugged. "To an extent. I need to know the people I'll be interacting with, and I need to know the people who are more important than I am."

"Who is more important than you?"

Tannix hesitated, for once seeming a little uncomfortable. "Truthfully, not many people. There's the royal family, as well as my father, brother, and mother. Some of the more higher-up generals and ministers…"

"That's it?"

He nodded after another thoughtful pause. "Yes."

For a moment, I couldn't think of what to tell him. How was it possible that we had become friends when we were so far apart? I couldn't wrap it around my head. "You know that you're as close to the king as I am to the lowest person in the city?"

"That's not true."

"No, you're right. I'm probably closer. Can you get any lower than being a wanted criminal?" I asked, once again trying to lighten the mood.

Tannix looked away. "I suppose not."

He was clearly uncomfortable with the topic, so I changed it. "Is there anything we can do about Malte?"

"I'm not sure yet, but I'm trying to think of something. There's only so much I can do without incriminating myself, and you need to stay out of the upper city entirely until this blows over. If it ever does."

I nodded—no argument there. It would take some time before I would be able to go back there, let alone feel comfortable doing it. "Will you come meet me then?"

"How often do you think I can get away from the Order without people being suspicious?" Tannix asked. "I've managed it twice now, but it won't be a frequent thing. Most people don't question me, but the guards might report it if I'm leaving every week. Or even every second week."

"Then you need to become better at climbing over walls," I said.

"I don't think that will work." He sighed. "I haven't done it for years."

"Why would you stop? You were good."

"Hardly."

"You were," I repeated. "For someone who hadn't been doing it since they were young."

Tannix reached over to give me a very gentle shove. By then, we were heading back towards the old brothel. I was guiding us, and since Lothian Dusk would be falling soon, I assumed he would want to go home. As we walked, I eyed him again.

"You really don't blend in down here."

"I know," he admitted. "You're better at blending in, even with that hair. I really should have known you weren't a Teltan."

I quickly ran my hand through my hair. "Yes, probably," I agreed. I stepped into the entrance to my home. We could hear voices up ahead; Baisan, Castin and Kassia were talking. When we reached the little room, I saw that the other four had returned. They were all sitting around a small fire, sharing some meat and bread that was probably bought with Tannix's money. They all looked up when we entered.

The younger four were obviously startled to see Tannix. Baisan got to his feet and approached us. "Glad to see you still alive, Finn."

"We just walked around." I brushed by him and approached the fire. Kassia offered me a piece of bread, which I gratefully took. I turned around to see that Tannix and Baisan were warily looking at each other. I groaned and walked back over to them. "Tannix, I think you make Baisan nervous," I said. He glared at me, and I grinned innocently.

"I understand," Tannix replied.

"Do you need help finding the gate?" I asked him.

"No," Baisan said. "You're hurt, Finn. You're staying here. Cast?"

Castin shoved a chunk of meat in his mouth and got to his feet. "I'm injured too."

"You're better off than Finn."

"Maybe if he learned how to hold a knife he would be able to avoid getting arrested," Castin said, coming to join us.

"That's a lost cause," Tannix said.

"No," I protested, but it was too late. They had found something to agree on, I could tell in the way they had quickly glanced at each other. I shook my head and went back to the fire, where I sat down beside Kassia before the two could start to tease me. Still, as they walked out together, I could hear them talking about how impossible it was to teach me anything about fighting.

Kassia smiled as she slipped some more food into my hands. "Good walk?"

I nodded, too busy eating to reply verbally.

She started picking at her own food. "You seem close for being so different."

I swallowed. "I know."

"Isn't it strange?"

"A bit, maybe, but we met when we were young, when he didn't know who I was. Are you going to finish that?"

Kassia looked down at the bit of meat in her hand. It was some sort of bird, chicken or duck, I thought. She handed it over with a smile. Our hands brushed together and she gripped my fingers lightly for a moment. "Do you want more salve?"

I nodded.

She pulled it out from her pocket. "I'll let you finish eating first."

I ate the rest of my food and carefully pulled off my tunic.

CHAPTER
Twenty-two

*I*t was raining; a miserable, cold rain that made us want to do nothing but huddle inside under a blanket. So huddle we did. Baisan and Castin were quietly talking in one corner, the girls in another. Orrun and Leker had dozed off. I was bored. I sat by the fire, cross-legged, just staring at it. It had been a few weeks since my escape from jail. My brand still hurt sometimes when I moved my shoulder oddly, but it had healed into a dark, shiny scar. My wrist was still useless for climbing. My back had entirely healed, but Kassia said there were a couple scars that would probably take some time to fade. I poked at the fire absentmindedly and added another few pieces of wood. Our pile was getting low, and if it weren't for the rain, I would have volunteered to go try to find some more. It was always easy to find pieces of wood from broken furniture, or I could steal a chair, if Baisan ever let me out on the streets again.

"Finn, come here."

Baisan's voice shook me from my bored daze. I went over to join them. He and Castin had the chest, which used to be mine, open in front of them. There were some copper siyas, and a single brass. I eyed it, wondering briefly how we managed to burn through Tannix's money so quickly. "What do you want?"

"If I give you ten siyas, would it be worth it to go to the tavern?" Baisan asked. There was just a slight sense of hopefulness in his voice that he was clearly trying to hide from me. He didn't like that I was the only one who could turn a profit at the tavern.

"You're letting me out?"

Baisan nodded. "You're healed enough for this, aren't you?"

"Suppose so. How much do you want?"

"As close to a hundred siyas as you can manage."

"A hundred?" I asked, louder than I intended. The girls glanced across the room at us. "Are you joking, Baisan? None of the poorer men will play with me once I've won around fifty siyas, and the bigger games refuse to let me in regardless of how much money I have. I've tried."

"So supplement your winnings a bit," Baisan said with a shrug. "You've done it before."

"And I almost got stabbed in the back."

"Take Castin."

"So *he* can get stabbed in the back? All right."

Castin swore under his breath. "Do you think I like being your bodyguard?"

"When my money buys us dinner? I think that makes guarding me worth it."

Baisan closed the chest and locked it. The action drew my attention and I stopped arguing with Castin. "Right. I promise you fifty siyas. I'll see what I can do beyond that."

Baisan smiled as he handed me the brass siya. "Take my cloak for the rain. You were bored anyway."

"That's the only reason I'm agreeing to go. Come on, Castin."

THE TAVERN WAS NEAR THE MAIN GATE. IT WAS BUSY, PROBABLY IN PART because of the heavy rain. Castin and I slipped through a side door and pushed back our wet hoods. Like everything in the lower city, it was an old building, but large. It was targeted towards the sailors and merchants who came to the city, and Natives rarely used it. There were smaller taverns and bars scattered around for our use.

Castin and I weren't there for the ale, though. We shouldered our way between the crowded tables. As promised, I grabbed a few things along the way from men too drunk to notice me, and Castin did the same. Near the back of the wide room, we found the tables we were looking for.

They looked just like any other tables, except that as well as tankards of ale, the men sitting at them held cards. In the middle of the tables were small piles of money, as well as piles in front of some of the men. The higher stakes game was the furthest back, and I forced myself to ignore them. As I'd told Baisan, they wouldn't let me in even if I could afford it. Instead, I walked up to the closest table. Castin hung back, leaning against one of the wooden pillars holding up the roof.

I tossed my brass siya onto the table. "I want in."

The man with the most coins, which he'd neatly piled into a little tower, glanced up at me hungrily. I crossed my arms but submitted to the gaze. He would think I was a desperate boy from the streets who didn't know what I was getting into. He probably hoped I had a bit more money on me that he could take. He smiled widely. "Of course, lad. Join in."

I sat down in one of the empty chairs and took my five cards from the pile in the middle. For a while, not much happened besides us passing around cards when it was our turn. The winning man was still winning; he kept collecting money from the centre to add to his pile. I had a strategy, though. While he gathered his money bit by bit, I was going for a complete win. A few of the other men tossed down their cards with groans, giving up, until it was just me, the winning man, and two others.

Finally, I was given the correct card to complete my set. I dropped my cards to the table casually, letting it seem like I'd given up for a moment before I said, "Stampede."

The men all stared at me, then my cards, then me again. The winning man threw down his cards and pushed his money into the centre in disgust.

The man beside him chuckled. "Didn't expect that from you, boy."

I leaned across the table to gather all of my coins and shrugged. "A fluke, probably. Care to play again?"

The four men exchanged glances. "I'm in," the winning man finally said. He put another ten siyas into the middle, and I added ten from my new pile of money. Grudgingly, the other men did the same.

The second game went more quickly. Just as I'd expected, the men refused to play a third game against me. As Castin came to help me collect the winnings of the two games, the man who had been playing so well got to his feet.

"You cheated." He glared at me across the table, a knife suddenly in his hand.

I slipped the money pouch under my cloak and took a step back. "No, I'm just good." I tried my best to sound apologetic.

He didn't believe me. He moved so quickly that I didn't have a chance to back out of the way. I suddenly found myself held against the pillar, with the man's hand tight around my neck. In vain I grabbed his wrist as if I could pull his hand away.

One of the other men yanked him back. His hand slipped from my neck but clenched the front of my tunic, tearing it as he pulled me forward. The other man was speaking, but my attacker's gaze had snapped to my exposed shoulder.

His eyes narrowed in realization and he pushed away the other man. "You're that thief. There's a price on your he-"

There was the sound of glass shattering and he fell to his knees. I scrambled backwards and pulled Baisan's cloak back over my shoulder. The man swore and stood, rounding on Castin, who held the remains of a broken bottle in one hand and his little knife in the other. There was a reason other thieves avoided fighting Castin. The man was nearly twice his size, but he hesitated at the sight of the weapons.

I took my chance and kicked the back of the man's knee, causing him to stumble forward. Castin leapt out of the way. We glanced at each other quickly before both running in opposite directions. The man was just getting back to his feet when I slipped through the front door. I ran down the street and ducked into a side alley. The noises from the tavern got louder for a moment as someone opened the door, but the rain made it impossible to hear footsteps so I wasn't sure if the man was following me.

I nearly yelped when a hand grabbed my shoulder, but it was just Castin, tugging me further down the alley. I followed, and we ran, zig-zagging through the streets until we knew we were far enough away to be safe. Only then did we slow and start to head back home. I pulled up my hood in a useless attempt to keep my already soaking hair dry.

"Thank you."

I knew he'd heard me, but he didn't speak until we'd turned onto another street. "You're going to have to be more careful now that you've got that brand."

I scratched my shoulder absentmindedly. "I know."

"So… how much did you get?"

I allowed myself a small smile. "Hundred siyas, as well as whatever we grabbed when we were in there."

"I thought you said a hundred siyas was impossible to get."

"I took the risk, went for a slighter higher game. Usually I play in the ones where people only bet a few siyas each, not ten." I glanced sideways at him quickly. "I wouldn't have done it without you there to back me up. The poorest men don't tend to threaten me when I win. The more money at stake, the more likely someone is to try to hurt me."

"Thank Zianesa I didn't have to actually fight him. That man was huge."

"Just having the knife was enough to surprise him," I pointed out. "So like I said, thank you."

Castin smiled. "Anytime, brother. Now… do you cheat?"

"No! How could you suggest that? I'm just good at the game."

"If you say so." He smirked. "Baisan'll be happy either way."

"At least there's that."

THE WEATHER CLEARED UP LATER IN THE DAY. BAISAN AND CASTIN WENT out to buy some food with my money, leaving me in charge of watching over the others. I ended up sitting in front of the fire once again, fiddling with my Order ring distractedly. I was so deep in thought, wondering when Tannix would visit again, that at first I didn't notice Kassia sit beside me.

"How's your wrist doing?"

It took me a moment to register that she'd spoken. "Oh, fine. As long as I don't try anything with it."

"Let me look." She gently picked up my wrist and pulled it over to rest on her knee. She unwound the binding, then starting prodding me. I tried to pull away but she held my arm firmly. "Stop it. I'm just trying to feel if anything has healed."

"How could you tell?"

"By the way it feels," she replied unhelpfully. "So you're good at gambling? Why?"

I knew she was trying to distract me from the poking, and I tried to let it work. "Because I…" I flinched and hesitated. "Because there are three ways to get money when you live on the streets: thievery, prostitution, and gambling. I couldn't survive just off stealing things, and the second option was entirely out of the question, so I taught myself how to play Stampede. And Sailor's Dice. And Commandeer. And all the typical games the sailors play when they come into the city."

Kassia glanced up from my wrist. "You're very smart, aren't you?"

"I don't know about that."

"I do, but I think you try to hide it."

I stared at the fire again, a little uncomfortable with the way she was looking at me. "I'm not trying to hide anything."

"Not hide, then, but downplay."

"I… I don't…"

"Don't worry, Finn. I won't let anybody onto your secret." I looked up to see that she was smiling at me, as if the other girls, Leker, and Orrun hadn't heard our whole conversation. She started to wrap my wrist back up carefully. "I think it's healing well."

"Oh. Good."

She'd just finished when Baisan and Castin returned. Baisan was carrying a loaf of bread, and Castin had a large, unplucked pigeon.

I rotated my wrist experimentally and stood up. "Did you really waste money on that bird?"

"Castin caught it," Baisan said. He handed me the bread, while Castin went off to hand the bird and his knife to Stria.

I was actually impressed, but disguised it in a taunt. "He can't skin it himself?"

"Do you want to skin it, Finn?" Castin asked.

"No, does Stria?"

"I don't mind," Stria said. "Last time any of you tried to cook something you ruined it anyway." She settled down beside the fire and got to work.

I sat down opposite her and started to slice up the loaf into eight pieces. All in all, once Stria had cooked the pigeon, it was a fairly good meal. We drank rainwater, which had collected in buckets left outside for that purpose, and we each got a thick slice of bread and a few pieces of pigeon. As far as wild meat went, pigeon wasn't bad. We'd tried rat once a few years ago when we were desperate, and decided to avoid it from then on if we could. Fresh birds really were the best, if we could manage to catch them.

We spent a few hours lounging around the fire, making up stories to pass the time. The girls braided each other's hair in the classical Native style while we lay around on the floor, gnawing on bones to get the last pieces of meat off before tossing them into the fire. It was nice to relax for once.

CHAPTER
Twenty-three

I t was another few weeks before Tannix managed to return to the lower city. Since going to the tavern, Baisan had started to let me out more, convinced I was healed enough to manage normal duties. He always sent Castin or Kassia with me, or came with me himself. Although I knew that he was just doing it because he was worried about me, it still annoyed me. More than once, I managed to lose my escort, which always resulted in a lecture.

I was sitting through one of these lectures when Tannix appeared in the doorway. I was cross-legged on the floor, picking at the bricks with my knife absentmindedly, not really listening to anything Baisan was saying. Everyone else was gone, it was just the two of us. I noticed movement in the doorway and glanced up. Baisan had his back to the door, so he carried on chastising me without noticing that my attention had shifted.

"What did you do?"

Baisan flinched and spun around, startled by the sound of Tannix's voice. I grinned. "Oh, nothing. He's mad at me for running off earlier today."

"You ran off?"

"Yes, well…" I trailed off and shrugged. Tannix was wearing one of his blue cloaks and had his sword strapped to his side. He hadn't bothered to hide who he was this time. "Gave up on blending in?"

"I decided there was no point." He crossed his arms and leaned against the doorframe. "If someone tries to pickpocket me, I'll just arrest them."

I winced. "Please don't."

"Not one of your group," Tannix said.

"No one," I insisted. "You can just scare them away, there's no need to send anyone to jail. If anyone tries, it'll probably be a starving child, anyway. You wouldn't arrest a child, right?"

"No." He shook his head. "I wouldn't."

"Good." I got to my feet and walked over to him, ignoring Baisan's glance in my direction. "Are they still looking for me?"

"Not actively. You're to be arrested on sight, but no one is specifically looking out for you anymore. How are you doing?"

"Better."

"I'd like someone to look at your wrist, to make sure it's healing properly."

"Won't that cost money?"

Tannix raised an eyebrow. "And since when has money been a concern?"

"Sometimes I forget that you're rich enough to throw hundreds of siyas into the ocean without worry," I said.

"I don't think you forget." Tannix looked over me at Baisan. "Do you mind?"

Baisan sighed. "I guess not. He's getting restless anyway. Maybe when you bring him back he'll be more willing to sit around and heal."

"I doubt it," Tannix and I replied, almost in unison.

"So do I," Baisan said.

Tannix handed me a blue bundle that I hadn't noticed him holding. "Here, put this on. I told the guards at the gate that I was coming down here to retrieve one of my servants."

"They need to ask?" I shook out the bundle, which opened into a blue cloak. It was duller than Tannix's, but still beautiful. I turned it around in my hands, inspecting it before pulling it on.

"Getting away from the Order was one thing," he replied. "Getting into the lower city was another. Yes, they needed to know why Lord Tandrix would be entering alone, and I needed to give them a reason that would explain me leaving with somebody."

"We can't just climb?"

"Can you climb?"

"No," I admitted grumpily. "Not yet."

"Exactly. Now, we can't have anybody knowing who you are, so keep your hood up and head down, and don't make eye contact with anybody." He reached over to pull up my hood for me. "Try to act like a servant."

"IT DOESN'T MAKE ANY SENSE TO HAVE YOU LEAD," I COMPLAINED, TRAIL-ing after Tannix through the narrow streets. It was interesting to see how people reacted to him. Most ducked out of his way, but I saw a few people eye him curiously—the way I would have if I hadn't been with him. I wondered how much of the behaviour Tannix actually noticed, or if it all went unseen because he was so used to being respected and feared.

"The master always leads," he replied.

"Yes, but the master's lost," I said.

Tannix turned around, looking concerned, and I started laughing. I kept laughing as he looked at the buildings surrounding us, and then down the road. "The gate is just down there, isn't it?"

I nodded and managed to stop laughing. "Yes."

"Then what do you mean, I'm lost?"

"I lied," I replied with an innocent grin. "I wanted to see what you'd do. It's interesting watching you down here."

"Is it?" He continued down the street.

I caught up with him quickly. "Yes, it is. Have you noticed that people either are scared of you or are considering robbing you?"

"How many people are considering robbing me?"

"About every third person we pass, I'm sure. Most of them aren't seriously considering it; I've only seen a couple people who I thought might jump on you."

"And you didn't say anything? Or tell them to leave me alone? You did that when we were here with Malte, didn't you?"

I smiled and pulled down the front of my hood to cover my face. "You think I want people to know that I'm with you? I'm Zianna's greatest thief; I can't go making friends with royalty."

"I'm not royalty," Tannix said.

"As good as, as far as we're all concerned." I gestured at the people on the street, including myself with them.

"You certainly look like royalty to me," a voice purred. I instantly knew what was going on, but Tannix seemed confused by the girl who was practically hanging off his left arm. She was wearing some sort of dress, which did not cover her nearly as much as it should have, and a ruby necklace I vaguely recognized. Her eyes were scanning Tannix, taking in his rich looking clothing and figuring out how much she could earn from a night with him.

"My lord," I said pointedly, pulling Tannix's attention away from her. "We should be going, should we not?" They both looked at me as I spoke, so I ducked my head to hide my face. If the necklace was one I'd stolen, I didn't want the girl to see me. Chances are she'd recognize me, even if she didn't know my name.

"Why leave now?" the girl cooed, and I looked up to see that her attention was fully on Tannix again. She was slowly running a hand down his chest. "Surely you want to stay. We've only just met…"

"No, he's right." Tannix pushed her away, although I was pleased to see that the push was gentle. She just wanted money; I could relate to that.

The girl looked upset and grabbed at his hand. "Oh, please."

I stepped up beside Tannix. "My lord has urgent business," I told the girl, still keeping my head down so that the hood covered most of my face. I pulled a little blue pouch from under my cloak and from that removed a few copper siyas, which I subtly slipped into her hand. Flashing money around would only get us more attention. She glanced at her hand, then eyed me suspiciously before disappearing into the crowd.

"When did you take that?" Tannix grabbed the pouch and slipped it into a pocket.

"When she was touching you." I poked him in the chest. "Were you tempted?"

"Confused."

"Your betrothed will not be happy to hear about this." I smirked and turned around, this time making him have to catch up with me.

"I said confused, not tempted," Tannix said.

"Of course."

I didn't lead for long, because we soon reached the front gate and I stepped back to let Tannix take over. Although I knew the guards would let him through, I still found it oddly unexpected. For my whole life, the exception being when I was with Malte and a few times with my mother, I'd never walked through the gates. The guards had rarely even given me a second glance when I was nearby. Now, as I followed Tannix through, I knew they were looking at me, and it was a little unsettling.

One of the guards on the other side was holding the reins to a large brown horse, which Tannix walked right up to. Nervous, I followed, but didn't get close.

"Thank you," Tannix said, taking the reins.

"I see you found your servant, sir," the guard said.

"Yes." Tannix started adjusting the saddle. After a moment, he put a foot in one of the stirrups and pulled himself onto the horse's back. "Come here," he told me, with a tone I wasn't used to hearing from him.

Reluctantly, I approached the horse on the side opposite the guard. "I've never ridden," I whispered once I got close enough.

"You told me you had."

"Back when you thought I was a lord," I said.

Tannix sighed. "Not now. Get up here." He held out his hand.

I grabbed his hand and he pulled me up. I settled onto the horse's back behind him and tried to act calm, though it was taking all of my willpower to not cling to him. That wouldn't be considered proper behaviour from a servant, after all. The horse began to walk up the main walkway. I looked around curiously the whole way up. We were mostly ignored, but occasionally a guard would nod or salute to Tannix. We stopped at a large gate similar to the last one, and only had to wait a moment before it was pulled open for us. Then we rode into the upper city.

The gate led almost directly into the marketplace so that traders wouldn't have to travel far. It was busier than the walkway had been and much more crowded. From the horse's back, the crowd almost looked like water. The way people split apart in front of the horse made me think of water splitting when I ran my finger through it. I was entranced, so much so that when the horse jerked a little, I almost lost my balance and grabbed Tannix for support.

"Finn!"

"Sorry," I muttered. I loosened my grip but didn't let go entirely, in case the horse did it again. It seemed likely, given the crowd. A moment later, the horse stopped walking and Tannix motioned for me to hop off its back. I did and he followed me.

"I can't have you clinging to me like that in public," he said. He wrapped the horse's reins around his wrist. "So we walk. Are you hungry?"

"Do you even need to ask?"

He smiled. "No, I guess not."

Though we were no longer riding, the fact that the horse was following us still made it easier to walk through the crowds. The bright blue of Tannix's cloak also helped. We walked into the marketplace and passed a few stalls before we saw one with food. I rushed ahead of Tannix, worming my way through the crowd like I was used to doing. The stall was covered in baskets of different kinds of dried food. Some of it was meat and some of it was fruit or vegetables. It was clearly foreign, that was the only reason for drying food. It was easier to transport. I scooped up a handful of some sort of wrinkly orange fruit. I was about to stick one in my mouth when the merchant noticed me.

"Thief," he growled, reaching for a dagger.

Tannix appeared just in time to stop the merchant from coming at me. "What did I tell you about waiting?" he asked me, sounding exasperated. "I apologize for my servant," he said to merchant.

The merchant looked confused about Tannix's arrival, but then the confusion turned to awe. "Oh no, my lord. My apologies. I should have known he was with you by the colour of his cloak."

Tannix looked at what I was holding, and then at the basket they had come from. There was a card tied to it with the number ten written on it. He handed me the horse's reins and pulled out his coin pouch. Though the merchant protested, Tannix paid him anyway before pulling both me and the horse away from the booth.

"Really?" he asked once we were lost within the crowd again.

"What? I wasn't stealing, I was waiting for you. I thought you were closer to me than that. Besides, money is no concern, right?" I looked at him innocently.

"Right. Let's go get your wrist looked at."

LUCKILY, THE APOTHECARY HE TOOK ME TO WAS NOT THE ONE KASSIA and I had stolen the salve from weeks earlier. The man looked over my wrist, and after poking and prodding at it for a few minutes, he decided that it was healing well on its own. Tannix was told to make sure I rested it, and we left.

On the way back, we passed by the marketplace again. It was even more crowded than before, but people weren't moving around. It didn't take long to figure out why. There was a platform in the middle of the marketplace usually used for executions. Now, it was surrounded by guards.

"What's happening?" I stopped walking, forcing Tannix to stop with me.

He didn't have to answer, because as soon as I'd finished speaking, the king walked up onto the platform, followed by his two daughters. I was intrigued. The king was dressed in a gold robe, and the crown on his head was so rich and expensive I'd have killed to get my hands on it. His daughters were both wearing pale dresses made of a creamy yellow coloured cloth. Both princesses were covered in jewellery, as well as the simple crowns sitting on their blond hair.

"Are we staying?" I asked, glancing at Tannix. He was lightly leaning against the horse's side, arms crossed. He nodded and I moved back to stand next to him. "The speech will probably be boring, so are we staying because you want to stare at the princesses? How will your betrothed feel about that?"

"I doubt she'd be pleased," Tannix replied, without taking his eyes away from the royal family. "But that's not why we're staying. Believe it or not, I take an interest in our country's politics."

"Of course you do," I said with a sigh. "Someone might die and put you next in line for the throne after all."

"More than one person would have to die for that to happen."

I nudged his side. "Sure you're not just attracted to the princesses?"

"I thought everyone was attracted to the princesses," Tannix replied.

I shrugged. "They're too perfect for my taste."

"I thought you liked perfect things."

"I love perfect things. I like perfect people. The problem is that I'm a thief from the lower city, and I can't get perfect. Those princesses would never even give me a second look if I did try to earn their affections. So why would I try? I'm used to having very little. I could see them enjoying your company, though."

"But if you did have a chance, which one would you rather marry?" Tannix asked.

"Marry?" I laughed. "If I was to be involved with either of them, it would be as their slave, but even that's unlikely."

"Which one?" Tannix repeated.

"Megara, I think," I replied after a pause. The king was talking, but neither of us was listening to him. "Esmeranda will be queen, after all, and needs to marry someone who would make a good king. Like you."

"I would not."

"You would," I said. "You have training and talent and money and the right kind of personality, the people would love you as king. Not to mention that you look like a prince."

Tannix glanced down at his clothing. "I do not. I look ..."

"Very rich."

"Yes, well. I am very rich, but that's the only true thing you said." Tannix glanced at me and ruffled my hair affectionately. "But thank you."

"It's all true, don't lie to yourself." I pushed him away, trying to act unimpressed. I was distracted by a thought. "Megara's full name is Esmegara, isn't it?"

Tannix nodded. "Yes, why?"

"I just remembered something my mother once told me," I said. "We were walking home from the house of a man who…" I trailed off uncomfortably.

"And?" Tannix prompted gently.

"We were in the upper city, and the guards didn't bother us because they knew she had been working and we were going back to our proper place. She used to have to take me with her, when I was younger, because the others didn't want to have to watch me. We were walking right here when the king stepped out to make a speech. The queen was alive then, and she was with him, holding the hand of Princess Megara. Princess Esmeranda was standing on her mother's other side. I remember asking my mother who they were. She explained to me that they were the rulers of our city, and she told me their names. Then she said, "Finn, do you remember what I once told you about our people's lost language?" I said that I did, the story of the lost language used to fascinate me. My mother said, "The Princesses' names hold a piece of that language. Esm. It means that they are royal girls." I asked my mother why the princesses had stolen some of our language. She laughed and answered, "The princesses did not steal it. Many years ago, their family stole it." I didn't understand, I thought she was saying that the royal family were thieves. But that was what I was learning to become, and I knew I was nothing like the royal family, or any of the high class Telts. My mother said that they weren't like me. "They are the kind who steal peoples' homes and their languages and their gods. They are the worst kind of thieves." We left then, to go back to the brothel in the lower city. I've always remembered her words, though."

Although the marketplace was as loud as ever, it seemed quiet as silence fell between Tannix and me. He looked thoughtful and I was drifting back into more memories about my mother. He took me by surprise when he spoke a few minutes later.

"I'm beginning to see why you dislike us."

"I dislike Telts because I'm supposed to. But I don't dislike you because you're not like the rest of them." I shrugged. "There's nothing we can do about it now. The language is gone and all we have left is a few commonplace words."

"Lord Tandrix?" The voice took us both by surprise, but this time it was Tannix who caught on faster. I pulled the front of my hood down a bit to hide my face and watched out of the corner of my eye as he shook hands with one of the two men who had approached us. They were both older than he was, but from the way they were treating him, it was clear that he was higher ranking.

"Good afternoon," Tannix replied warmly. He nodded in the direction of the king. "Have you been listening?"

The two men exchanged a glance. "Not really," one said. "We've just arrived; we're here to talk to Lord Meyat. Your father hoped we would see you." He reached into a bag he had draped over one shoulder and pulled out a folded piece of paper, which he handed to Tannix. "Have you really not been back to New Teltar in four years?"

Tannix slipped the note under his cloak. "I decided that I might as well wait until I'm out of training," he replied.

The men nodded appreciatively. "You're very dedicated," the talkative one said.

"It's a good trait," the second added.

Tannix smiled. "Yes, thank you. I hope your meeting with the director goes well."

"Thank you, my lord," the second man said. The three of them shook hands again before the two men walked off.

I watched them go, so distracted that it took me a moment to realize that Tannix was saying my name. I turned to face him. "The director's name is Meyat?"

Tannix nodded.

"Meyat begins with an M, does it not?"

CHAPTER

Twenty-four

"It makes sense, doesn't it?" I asked, excited. "He's so high ranking that no one would ever suspect him of anything, and he has the means to help with the attempt. What did the letter say, that M would give information?"

Tannix shrugged. "Finn, it's ridiculous. He's been the director for so long now, if he'd wanted to kill the king, he could have done it sooner."

I had managed to keep quiet until Tannix had escorted me back to my home. Now, I paced back and forth across the small room while he leaned against the wall near the door, arms crossed over his chest and eyes watching me. The three girls were there, across the room from us. Kassia was showing the two younger ones how to mend clothing, and they weren't paying attention to us. As soon as we'd walked in, I'd started talking. I couldn't hold in my suspicions any longer.

"But he isn't in charge," I pointed out. "He's just the asso…"

"Associate."

"Right, that."

"Yes," Tannix sighed. "That's what the letter said, but that doesn't mean anything. For instance, he tortured you for information." He noticed me flinch, but kept talking anyway. "Why would he torture you to get information about something he was already involved with?"

The question stumped me. I sat down in the middle of the room to think about it. When it was clear to Tannix that I wasn't going to talk, he pulled out the letter the men had given him. I watched him as he read. His eyes flickered across the page so quickly I couldn't understand how he was taking in anything. He groaned suddenly and refolded the paper.

"What is it?" I asked, distracted from my theory.

"My brother and father are coming to Zianna to watch my ceremony next week, but I was expecting my mother and sister to come as well."

"Why? What ceremony?" I asked. "And why are you disappointed?"

"The ceremony is to name me as a full member of the Order, which means that I'll no longer be in training. I was expecting my whole family to come, because that is the tradition, and they should have arrived over the next few days. However, Tairia developed some sort of sickness and my mother and father are delaying the trip to stay with her longer. Tandrin is still arriving on schedule, and my father will be here in time for the ceremony, but I shouldn't expect Tairia or my mother."

I tried my best to follow what he was saying. "So you're disappointed because she's sick?"

"Yes. That and the fact that since this is a formal ceremony, I'm expected to have a woman with me," Tannix muttered. "I was going to take my sister."

I laughed. "Is that allowed? Shouldn't your betrothed be accompanying you?"

"You would think so, but she isn't coming. So Tairia was my best option," he said. "And to be honest, I would prefer her over Lady Mayah."

"Why?"

"Because I don't know Lady Mayah," he replied. "And when I do finally get the chance to get to know her, I would prefer it to not be so formal."

"Oh, well, you could take Ninavi," I suggested as seriously as I could manage.

"What?" Ninavi looked over at the sound of her name. "What did you just say?"

"That I should escort you to a very important ceremony next week," Tannix told her. "You would fit in quite nicely, I believe."

Ninavi blushed and dropped her gaze. Stria and Kassia laughed at her. "I can't believe you'd suggest that, Finn!" She practically squeaked the words out. "I'm not nearly good enough to go to something like that, sir," she told Tannix apologetically. Then her voice took on a lighter tone. "But maybe you should make Finn dress up as a woman and take him."

I sent her a quick glare, and when I looked up at Tannix, I could tell he was holding back laughter. "Stop it."

He smirked. "I don't know, Finn. It seems like a perfectly good plan to me." The girls were obviously delighted that he would join in on the joke, because they started laughing even louder.

"I hate Telts."

"Oh, no you don't," Tannix replied. "At least not all of us."

"No, but I do hate the director." Suddenly something occurred to me. "What if he was torturing me because he was worried that if I knew about the plot, someone else might as well? Maybe he wanted to make sure that I hadn't told anybody about him. You said yourself that he was just going to kill me; wouldn't it make sense that he was doing it to protect himself?"

"I don't know."

"And those men who attacked us!" I continued, as suddenly everything made sense to me. "The director must have hired them to look out for me in case I came back. They must have seen me that night and followed me, but they didn't expect to attack someone who could fight, so that's why you beat them."

"The director would have told them to not attack anyone else if they were after you," Tannix said. "There are so many important people on the grounds; it would be risky to just let them attack whomever they wanted."

"He's involved in a plot to kill the king. I highly doubt he cares about killing some lords who get in the way," I replied. I could tell I was getting to him.

"I was hardly in the way."

"You were between them and me," I said. "Tannix, please, at least consider the possibility. You don't like the director any more than I do."

He was avoiding looking at me. "I hate him because of what he did to you, but I still respect him. I have to. I don't believe he could be part of this."

"You must agree that it's possible."

"It's possible," he said. "But unlikely." He stood up straight. "I have to go back. Is there anything I should bring next time I come?"

"Yes, money and food," I said. I couldn't help but be a little sulky at his response to what I thought was a perfect theory.

He crouched in front of me, startling me a little with his closeness. "Finn, I'll look into it, all right? If the director does anything even mildly suspicious, I'll make note of it. If, well, if we get more information, and if it seems valid, I'll go to the king myself."

I smiled. "And risk having to explain where you got your information?"

"I'll tell him all about you and your role in saving his life, and he'll consider you a hero and knight you, and then you'll be as rich and important as me." Tannix pressed a few coins into my hand. "Until then, you'll have to make do with this." He ran his hand up my left arm and pushed back my sleeve to look at the brand. "It's healing well."

"I'm glad you know so much about brands."

"I know about burns," Tannix said. He looked at it a little longer before getting to his feet. "I'll be back as soon as possible." The girls' attention had been drawn to us as soon as the money showed up, and Tannix nodded at them. "Ladies, it was a pleasure to see you again." All three of them giggled, and I rolled my eyes. As he walked to the entrance, Orrun and Leker walked in. He nodded at them as well, and then left, leaving the younger boys staring after him.

"It isn't leaving my hand until Baisan arrives," I announced into the silence that followed. I knew that the girls would want to see the money, but mostly I was trying to get rid of the slight tension that always built up when Tannix was around. I looked over at Orrun and Leker. "How did you do?"

Orrun shrugged. "Not too well."

"Speak for yourself." Leker nudged his brother. "Orrun's upset because he almost got caught stealing some fish."

"You didn't have to tell them," Orrun said.

"It happens to the best of us," I said. "I got caught, after all."

He looked a little bit happier, but not much. Without a word, he and Leker went to join the girls. They started talking to the two younger girls, as Kassia got up and came over to me. She sat down and for a moment, we looked at each other. She examined at my brand, and gently looked at my newly bandaged wrist.

"I think the director is involved." She spoke quietly and moved her hands so that she was holding my hand instead of my wrist. She let her fingers twine with mine, and looked up to meet my gaze. "I think your reasons all make perfect sense. I'm sure Lord Tandrix will believe you once he's had time to think about it. I guess I just mean…" She paused. "For what it's worth, I believe you."

"Thank you," I replied. I dropped my gaze to the coins in my hand and wondered what kind of evidence Tannix would find, if any.

Part Three

THE ASSOCIATE

CHAPTER
Twenty-five

"Finn, wake up." Baisan shook my shoulder and I lazily waved at him to try to ward him off. It didn't work, and he shook me again. "Get up."

I groaned and opened my eyes to glare at him. "What?"

"I need you to go out with Ninavi."

"Why me?"

"Kassia and Stria left earlier. I'm taking out the boys, and Castin's staying here to guard. That leaves you." He poked me. "So? You were complaining about not being let out."

"I wasn't asleep when I was complaining," I muttered, but I sat up anyway and stretched. After a moment, I rotated my wrist experimentally. It was feeling better, probably due to Baisan making sure I didn't do anything with it. "You know, I think I might be able to climb soon."

"And if you try, you'll fall to your death," he said. He walked away and returned with a piece of bread, which he held out to me. It was from the night before. It was so unusual for us to have extra food that I rarely ever ate in the morning, so I dug in eagerly.

"If Tannix's money is lasting so long, why do we even need to go out?" I asked through a mouthful of bread.

"What else are you going to do with your time? Besides, you don't want to get out of practice, do you? Someone else might become the best thief in Zianna."

"Unlikely." I got to my feet. "No other thief brings in as much money as I do."

"You don't steal it, it's given to you," Baisan said.

"But stealing led to me becoming friends with Tannix which led to the money."

He pointed towards the door. "Go."

I laughed and did what I was told. Outside, I ripped another piece off the bread and looked around. "Ninavi?"

Ninavi landed lightly beside me. I glanced up to see where she'd come from. There was a boarded up window just above me, but the sill left more than enough room for climbing. She grinned at me. "I've been practicing. I'll never be as good as you, but," she shrugged, "I'm much better at being cute."

"I stand no chance at beating you there," I agreed.

"And really, I'm more a beggar than a thief." Ninavi started walking ahead of me, and I followed her, still eating my bread. "Finn?"

"Hmm?"

"Do you think Lord Tandrix..."

"I'm sure he wouldn't mind if you called him Tannix."

Ninavi walked backwards a few steps just so that she could give me an annoyed look. "Do you think Lord Tandrix meant what he said about me fitting in at his ceremony?"

I regarded her carefully, wondering what kind of answer she was looking for. "I think you could easily fit in, given the right clothing."

She spun around, so I caught up with her. We walked in silence for a while, weaving through the streets we knew so well to reach one of the busier ones. As usual, the bigger streets were crowded with people and merchant carts. I glanced up and down the road, taking in the different stalls and what they were selling.

Ninavi broke into my planning. "Why are you and I better at blending in than the others?"

I sighed. "Ninavi, you know why."

"But Castin was born in a brothel too," she said.

"Maybe his father was a Native," I replied with a shrug. I went back to trying to plan which stalls to go for. "Or a foreigner. Or maybe he was a Telt and Castin just doesn't look like him."

"Do you ever wonder about your father?"

Annoyed, I almost snapped at her until I saw the look on her face. "Oh, Ninavi. No, I don't wonder about him. Why should I?" I took her hand and drew her back into a little alley, where we were out of the way of the moving crowds.

She brushed tears away from her eyes. "Because... because I want to know who mine is. Stria and Kassia knew their fathers."

I pulled her into a hug and she clung to me, burying her face in my tunic. Her next words were muffled. "Do you ever wonder if he was one of them?"

"One of who?"

"Like Lord Tandrix. Rich and powerful."

"Well, he was a Telt, so at the very least he was richer than a Native ever could be," I said.

"If the world was fair, you and I would be rich." Ninavi pulled away from me.

"If the world was fair, you and I would never have been born," I pointed out. "Because our mothers wouldn't have had to work in a brothel. I don't know about you, but I'm quite happy that I was born. Even given where we live and what we have to do to survive, don't the good moments make up for the bad?" I smiled, hoping to coax one from her.

It worked, and she tentatively smiled at me. "I guess so."

"Besides, you and I are good at having fun." I put an arm over her shoulder and drew her to my side so that I could whisper conspiratorially. "See that man over there? He's far too rich to be in the lower city. We have to help him fit in, don't we?"

Ninavi's smile grew into a mischievous grin. "Maybe you should go talk to him, and then I can help him."

"A wonderful idea. On my signal."

She nodded.

"NINAVI IS TURNING INTO QUITE THE THIEF," I ANNOUNCED PROUDLY AS we walked back into our ruined building. Castin was idly throwing pebbles across the room, but he was the only one still there.

"Are you letting him ruin you, Ninavi?" he asked.

"Ruin, hardly!" I sat next to Castin, and Ninavi placed herself in front of him. "If I'm the king of thieves, you must be the princess."

"Princess of thieves. I like that." The pouch she pulled from under her cloak caught Castin's eye instantly, but she didn't hand it over to him. "So what does that make Castin?"

"The bodyguard." I nudged him. "Isn't that right?" Without giving him a chance to reply, I continued speaking. "See, Ninavi? Who needs a rich Telt father when you're the royal family of all thieves?"

"I'm sure your father was the lowliest of all Telts," Castin said. "So low, in fact, that the other Telts refuse to acknowledge him as one of them."

"And your father was banished from his home country for being so annoying that they couldn't stand his presence anymore," I replied with a grin.

"But at least he had fun doing it."

"I'm sure he did."

"Well, I win then," Ninavi said. "Because my father was a rich lord, which means that I'm a lordess."

"That's not a word," Castin said, shaking his head. "I guess that makes you a lady, though."

"Lady Ninavi, Princess of Thieves," I declared dramatically.

Ninavi laughed and Castin groaned. "Did you let him into a tavern?" he whispered to her, just loud enough for me to hear.

"He ran away from me," she said. "What was I supposed to do?"

"Liar. Don't believe a thing she says, Cast."

"If I'm a lady, maybe you *should* tell Lord Tandrix to take me to that ceremony," Ninavi said, laughing.

"I'll tell him the next time I see him," I promised. A thought occurred to me. "Castin, where's Baisan?"

"He won't let you go. You're not healed enough."

"I'm fine," I said. "Besides, you don't know what I want to ask him."

"I think I have a pretty good idea."

"You don't know what he'll say."

Castin raised an eyebrow. "I think I have a pretty good idea."

IT TOOK LESS BEGGING THAN I EXPECTED FOR BAISAN TO AGREE TO LET me go to the upper city. All I had to do was point out that I had been there countless times, and I knew my way around. He reluctantly agreed to let me go, as long as I didn't draw any attention to myself. No stealing, no climbing around the rooftops, and of course, no being arrested—all of which I agreed to heartily.

Tannix had left behind the blue cloak, by accident or on purpose, I couldn't tell. I was more than happy to wear it again. As I pulled it on, I noticed the red crystals on my bracelet and quickly came up with an idea. Slipping the bracelet over my hand, I crouched in front of Ninavi and held it out to her. She'd been tentative to take it, but I'd insisted that a lady needed some nice jewellery.

Besides, I had a feeling I'd be wearing blue for a while.

Getting into the upper city was easy. I was careful with my wrist while climbing, using my right hand more to steady myself than putting any force on it. The blue cloak fit well enough not to get in my way. As always, going up was easier than going down, but when I finally hopped to the ground, it was much sooner than I'd expected. My wrist and shoulder were sore, but my back felt fine. I hadn't had a chance to look at it, but Kassia said there was hardly any scarring. Soon, the brand would be the only easily noticeable proof of my time in jail.

I brushed off any dust from the cloak and pulled up my hood before heading out onto the wide upper city street. I regretted the promise I'd made to Baisan about not stealing. With the blue cloak, it would be much easier to go unnoticed. It looked new, and if not expensive, at least it made it look like I worked for someone rich.

I wandered openly down streets I used to sneak through, only bothering to avoid getting too close to guards. They were unlikely to recognize me, but I was still cautious. I passed by the marketplace, which was bustling with people. Part of me wanted to go walk through it, but I knew the temptation to take something would be too great. Instead, I walked past it, heading for the Order.

The walls soon came into view. I did not intend to climb over them; I knew it would be too risky. I still wanted to look at them. My thoughts wandered and I remembered the first time I'd climbed over them, to escape the guards who had been chasing Baisan. So much depended on that single moment, and I wondered what my life would be like if I had hidden instead of climbed. Baisan probably would have been caught and arrested, and Castin would have had to take over the group. I probably would have never joined them. And, of course, I would have never met Tannix.

Meeting him had resulted in both good and bad. He was easily the closest friend I'd ever had, in spite of the difference in status. He'd given me food and his money had fed the rest of the thieves. I'd been arrested and tortured because of him, but if my theory was correct, the men were after me all along, and he was the only reason they hadn't killed me. But without him, I would have never gotten involved in the first place.

"Boy! What are you doing?"

Shaken from my thoughts, I looked over at who had spoken to me. It was one of the guards standing near the Order's front gates. While thinking, I'd gotten a lot closer to the gates than I'd intended. I started to mumble an apology when I suddenly had an idea. "My master sent me to deliver a message to Lord Tandrix of West Draulin."

The guard glanced at his companion. The two of them were wearing the usual yellow uniforms and light armor. They had swords hanging from their sides and spears in their hands. The one who had spoken looked back at me. "We will pass on your message."

"I was told to deliver it directly to the lord, sir," I said, shaking my head apologetically.

The guard turned to the gate and rapped against it with his spear. A moment later, a younger guard walked up to the other side. "What is it?"

He gestured at me. "A messenger for Lord Tandrix. Go get him."

"*Get* Lord Tandrix?" the other guard asked. "What if he refuses to come?"

I waved my hand tentatively to get their attention. "Tell him Sir Baisan sends the message. I'm sure he'll come."

The second guard looked at me in disbelief. "Lord Tandrix. Of West Draulin."

I shrugged. "They're good friends. I don't think the lord will mind."

"No lord enjoys being summoned." The guard sighed. "Particularly not the ones who are rich enough to buy a kingdom." He continued mumbling as he walked off.

I smirked at his comments, but hid my face so the remaining guards wouldn't notice. I spent the next fifteen or so minutes trying to avoid eye contact without acting too suspicious. I clasped my hands behind my back, and mostly stared at the ground until movement near the gate drew my attention.

"Of course Sir Baisan would send you," Tannix said for the sake of the guards. But there was a touch of warning in his voice meant solely for me.

"I'm the fastest messenger, my lord," I replied politely.

"I know." Tannix motioned for the gates to be opened. Instead of inviting me in like I expected, he walked out past the guards. "Luckily, I was already on my way out to the city. Come, we'll talk along the way."

I followed him, letting some distance come between us and the guards before speaking again. "Where are you going?"

"To see my brother," he replied. "What are you doing here? If I didn't know any better, I would say that you wanted to be killed."

"If I wanted to be killed I wouldn't have run away from jail," I said. "I came to the upper city to practice climbing again. I wandered closer to the Order than I meant to and the guards noticed me. I had to tell them something."

"Sir Baisan?"

"I had to pick a name you would recognize. I almost said Lord Finagale but thought better of it."

"Thank the goddess you think sometimes."

"I always think," I said. "Besides, I like the sound of Lord Finagale. Especially when you say it."

Tannix smiled. "What about me saying it makes it better?"

"It sounds almost real coming from you."

He said nothing but smirked like I amused him. We walked down a street I'd rarely been to, which was bordered by large buildings that looked like houses. It wasn't where most people in the upper city lived, and I realized that they must be the richer versions of the inns we had in the lower city. There were guards scattered around, and some other rich looking people walking in and out of the buildings. Tannix led me to one of the larger ones and knocked on the wooden door. While waiting for a response, he turned to me.

"Well, Lord Finagale, ready to meet someone who outranks me?"

CHAPTER

Twenty-six

The door was answered by a girl wearing a simple green dress. She was holding the edge of a tray with her right hand; the other edge was balanced against her hip. It had a plate and bowl laden with food, as well a tall mug of some sort of drink. She looked a little flustered as her eyes trailed over Tannix, trying to figure out who he was. She completely ignored me, but I'd put on the good servant act so it didn't bother me.

"That's for Lord Tandrin." Tannix said it more like a statement than a question.

The girl nodded. "Yes, my lord, I was just on my way to bring it up to him. He's been waiting for you. Please follow me." She led us into a spacious front room. A hall led farther into the building towards what were probably the kitchen, dining room, and servants' quarters. A huge white staircase curled up towards the second floor, and then carried on even higher. We followed her up the stairs, passing by the second floor and stopping at the third. The walls were decorated with paintings, statues stood in corners, and there were plants sitting on little tables or shelves.

I nudged Tannix and whispered, "The Order doesn't look half as nice as this."

"The Order aims for functionality more than luxury," he replied. "If you think this is nice, you should see our rooms in West Draulin."

My witty reply was cut short when the girl stopped in front of an ornate wooden door. She knocked on it lightly and shifted the way she was holding her tray.

When there was no reply, she reached up to knock again, but Tannix gently caught her hand. "Let me." He reached past her and banged his fist against the door once. "Tandrin! Stop being so lazy and come get your lunch."

The door swung open less than a second later. "Calm down, little brother!" The young man pulled Tannix into a warm hug. The girl slipped past them into the room and returned a moment later without her tray. She left without a word. I stood there quietly and watched the two brothers. Tandrin looked so similar to Tannix that it took me a little by surprise. He was a bit taller, and his hair was bright blond instead of light brown like Tannix's, but they had the same blue eyes and the same smile. Tandrin was wearing a loose blue tunic with black pants, and I couldn't help but wonder if blue was the only colour their family owned.

They broke the hug and walked into the room. Although Tannix didn't say anything to me, I walked in after them and closed the door behind me. Then I stayed near it nervously while the brothers continued greeting each other.

Tandrin smacked his brother's shoulder playfully. "Why are you so dressed up, little brother? You're meeting me, not a council."

"I have an image to maintain," Tannix said. "People in Zianna actually know who I am now."

Tandrin grinned and plopped himself down on a red armchair. He crossed his hands behind his head and put his feet up on the little table in front of him. "Right. Because you enjoy showing off who you are *so* much."

"I've gotten used to it," Tannix replied.

"Of course you have. And look at you! You've grown."

"You haven't seen me in four years."

"Which is why you've grown," Tandrin said.

Tannix took off his cloak and quite unceremoniously tossed it onto the nearby desk. Then he removed his sword and gently placed it on the table in front of the chairs. He sat down on the armchair facing his brother's. "Where's your guard? Father will be furious at you for not having them around."

Tandrin shrugged. "Out exploring the city. You're one to lecture me on having my guard nearby. Where's yours?" He pretended to think. "Oh, I believe they were left behind in West Draulin. Great help they'll be when you're attacked."

"I don't need them following me around here. Acen has them training constantly, so they're not bored. I'm usually within the Order, in any case. And I can defend myself."

"I suppose you did get rid of those two assassins. Father was delighted. Really, you should have heard him when he got the news. I swear he reminded me of it every day. "Tandrin, your brother killed two assassins. What have you done recently?" As if it's my fault I'm the eldest and had to stay back in West Draulin while you got to run off to Zianna and learn useful skills. Would you like to know what I had to go through yesterday? A council meeting with all the higher lords of New Teltar. Do you have any idea how boring that is? I'm a good twenty years younger than any of them, and... Why are you smirking at me?"

Tannix laughed. "I would much rather take on two assassins than a council of lords."

"Exactly my point. You get to be a general and do exciting things with your life. I promise I'll force you to accompany me to as many meetings as I possibly can."

"As much as I appreciate the effort, don't go out of your way. I'm sure you can handle the politics on your own."

Tandrin groaned good naturedly. "My only hope at this point is that by the time I take over, I might be old enough not to find meetings boring. Until then, I'll just have to sit through them and stare blindly at the maids... and drink lots of wine."

"Is that all you do at the meetings? How about paying attention?"

"Staring at the maids is much more fun. Have you ever tried?"

"There are no maids in the Order."

"You're missing out."

"Doubt it." Suddenly, Tannix seemed to remember my presence and he glanced over at me. "Come here."

I walked over nervously, unsure of how exactly I was supposed to be acting. I stepped up next to Tannix's chair and dropped my gaze to the floor. I tried to wrap my head around the fact that I was standing in the same room as the heir to West Draulin, but it seemed impossible. I thought I'd gotten used to being around Telts, but I was clearly wrong.

Tannix lightly touched my arm to get my attention. "Finn, Tandrin hardly counts as someone we need to be careful around."

"H-he doesn't?" I asked, surprised at how shaky I sounded.

"Finn?" Tandrin spoke up. "Oh, this is the thief you told me about in your letters."

"Yes. See, Finn, I already told him everything."

"Why wouldn't you tell me that?" I said.

Tannix made an attempt at an innocent smile, but I saw right through it. "I wanted to see how you'd act around him. You're always going on about how much I'm like royalty. Well," he paused to gesture at his brother, "he's even closer. He's actually inheriting something."

"Inheriting the right to sit through meetings." Tandrin sighed dramatically. "Truthfully, Finn … Finagale, right? Anyway, truthfully, I couldn't care less whom my little brother decides to befriend. The very fact that he actually has a friend is so amazing that I'm happy for him regardless. He was never good at making friends." I made up my mind then, at the sound of my full name, that I liked Tannix's brother.

"What Tandrin means," Tannix said, "is that because I'm not nearly as cocky as him, I never saw the need to have hoards of children flocking around me when we were young."

Tandrin grinned. "What can I say? They loved me. Whereas Tannix's best friends were his guard."

"I spent most of my time with them, training," Tannix said.

"I know, I know." Tandrin glanced at me. "Despite what you probably think, I didn't come to Zianna just to annoy my little brother. So, Tannix. Your ceremony."

"Tell me about Tairia first," Tannix replied. He paused to look at me and gestured to the wooden chair in front of the desk. "Pull it over, Finn. You don't have to stand."

"Bring over my lunch while you're at it," Tandrin added.

"He's not a servant," Tannix said sharply.

I paused halfway to the chair. "I'll do it if you let me have some," I said, this time surprising myself with my boldness.

Tandrin looked at me and for a moment, I thought I'd gone too far, then he started laughing warmly. "I like him, Tannix. You can have the salad."

I nodded gratefully. After moving the desk chair beside Tannix, I retrieved the tray of food for Tandrin. I put it on his lap, took the bowl, and retreated to my chair, where I started picking at the food with my hands. Tannix sighed but didn't bother correcting me.

"Tandrin, tell me about Tairia." He leaned forward in his chair and rested his forearms on his knees. "Is she getting any better?"

His brother was busy sawing through the thick piece of meat on his plate. After a moment, he held up a bite-sized piece. "No, but she hasn't gotten any worse and the physicians think it's just a fever. They even said that if your ceremony was a few days later, she would be healthy enough to attend." He stuck the piece of meat in his mouth and chewed it slowly. "It's a shame you can't delay it."

"Why can't you?" I spoke up curiously. It seemed to me that the lords of West Draulin should have been able to change the date of a ceremony quite easily.

"It's symbolic," Tannix replied. "It makes the end of my fourth year in the Order."

"Oh." I turned my attention back to the salad. It had been a while since I'd eaten anything remotely salad-like, and I was enjoying it thoroughly. Tannix watched me for a moment before his attention went back to his brother.

"My ceremony begins at noon. You and Father have seats near the front. He needs to make a speech, but you don't have to do anything but watch," Tannix explained. "I don't need to remind you that we're representing West Draulin."

Tandrin shook his head. "No, sir, you don't," he replied with a grin. He stabbed another piece of meat with his fork. "Carry on."

"The king and most of the higher advisors will be there. Before you ask, the princesses will not be. Not to mention all of the available lords who are members of the Order. Lord Macad is attending."

"Without his daughter? Odd."

"I'm under the impression that he wants to inspect me a little more before he lets Lady Mayah and me spend time together."

"You're engaged. You have been since you were two. Even if you were the ugliest, laziest lord in the kingdom, he'd have a hard time backing out of that agreement. That said, there's nothing about you that he can dislike. You're successful, you're talented." Tandrin sat up and put his tray on the table, suddenly serious. "Tannix, I know you're nervous about being in front of so many important people, but believe me when I say you'll do spectacularly. And not because you were born into power, but because you're smart and you're charismatic and people like you."

That's exactly what I'd been talking about when I said that Tannix would make a good king, but the rest of it was new. It hadn't occurred to me that he might be uncomfortable around other lords. When we first met, I remembered him being a little uneasy about his power, but recently he seemed so confident.

Tannix ran a hand through his hair, ruining its usual perfect styling. "I've gotten used to it," he admitted. "I know where I stand and I have learned how and when to use it. But…"

"It's a lot of people," Tandrin said gently. "I understand."

"I just don't want to disappoint anyone."

"Look at it this way, little brother. How many people at the ceremony do you actually need to impress?"

Tannix shrugged. "I don't know. You, Father, the king. Maybe the director. Lord Macad."

"Father and I are nothing to worry about. The director and the king are already impressed with you for killing those assassins, and Lord Macad won't be able to find fault with you even if he tried. As for the rest of the lords and advisors, you're from West Draulin. You're already more important than most of them."

Tannix smiled ruefully. "Well that solves all of my problems, doesn't it?"

"I'm simply trying to point out that there will be no one at the ceremony that you need to worry about. If you stop worrying about impressing people, you'll do fine. Trust me, I've been learning how to stand up in front of groups of lords my entire life." Tandrin rolled his eyes. "And it's terribly boring, but that's beside the point."

"Are you sure people don't like me just because I'm important and they're supposed to?"

Before Tandrin could answer, I cautiously reached out and touched Tannix's shoulder. "I don't like you because you're important and I'm supposed to," I pointed out. "Really, I should hate you for being a Telt, but I don't. And it's not because you give me food and money, it's because of what your brother said. About being charismatic. That's why Baisan and the others like you. They wouldn't otherwise. You know we're all taught to hate Telts."

"I thought Baisan disliked me."

"You make him nervous, but I think he likes you as much as he can. He trusts you, in any case, and it takes a lot to get a thief to trust somebody."

Tandrin glanced between us, obviously confused. "How many thieves are you friends with?"

This time Tannix's smile was genuine. "Only Finn, really, but he lives with a group of seven others that I've gotten to know a bit."

"Right. So, feeling better about yourself?"

"Well…" Tannix paused. "If you two are convinced that Lord Macad and Baisan both like me, then I suppose the rest of the lords shouldn't be a problem."

"There you go." Tandrin punched Tannix's arm playfully. "Would it make you feel even better if Finn went?"

"Went to what, the ceremony?"

Tandrin nodded. "Of course. You are allowed to invite friends."

"Yes, but Finn's…" Tannix trailed off.

"In that cloak he looks like a normal servant to me," Tandrin said. "I'll bring him."

"You can't bring him into the Order. He'll be arrested." Tannix sounded more alarmed. "Finn, don't get any…" He cut himself off with a groan and buried his face in his hands.

I was already nodding.

CHAPTER
Twenty-seven

A few days later, I was back in the upper city, trying to not draw attention to myself as I walked through the crowds. I was wearing the blue cloak again, and my wrist was freshly bound by Kassia. My knife was attached to my belt, and I had even tied my hair back.

Baisan hadn't been happy when I told him what I would be doing, but he didn't try to stop me. He must have realized that it would be next to useless; I was going to Tannix's ceremony either way. I was curious, both to see what the ceremony was like and to see all the lords. They were rich, and they intrigued me. On top of that, I knew I'd be safe. I trusted Tannix's brother because Tannix trusted him.

I saw them before they saw me, which wasn't surprising. They were standing by a building near the Order's gates, where we had planned to meet. Tandrin was leaning against the wall and Tannix was pacing. Their clothing was almost identical. Deep blue cloaks with gold embroidery around the neckline, dark pants and boots, light tunics. Each wore multiple rings and Tandrin had a thin gold chain around his neck, which was visibly hanging over his shirt. If they had been in the lower city, they would be surrounded by thieves.

I walked up while Tannix's back was turned and waited for him to notice me. He was complaining about something, but he stopped as soon as he saw me standing there. His eyes looked over me thoughtfully. A little uncomfortable by the attention, I crossed my arms and did the same to him. I wondered for the umpteenth time whether he realized how much like a prince he looked, of if he was too used to it to notice. It wasn't just the clothes or the rings or the sword, but the way he held himself, moved, and looked. Eyes, hair, face… Everything.

"You look good," he said after a moment. "You should have no problem blending in."

Tandrin stood up and moved closer to us. "Blue suits you. No bias, of course."

"Of course," Tannix said. "I need to go in before they start looking for me. Tandrin?"

"Hmm?"

"Take care of him."

"I will," Tandrin replied with a grin.

"I'm being serious," Tannix said. "Take care of him. Don't let him out of your sight, don't let him near any guards, and don't let anybody talk to him. The only way I'm letting him go in there is if you agree."

Tandrin regarded his brother for a moment, and then nodded solemnly. "Nothing will happen to him."

Tannix looked at me. "Don't leave Tandrin's side."

"I have no intention of leaving his side," I said. "I'm not out to get myself killed, remember? Stop worrying about me; you have a ceremony to worry about."

Tannix sighed. "I know. I'll be glad when it's over." He turned and walked briskly towards the doors, as if waiting any longer would make it harder. Tandrin motioned for me to follow and we started walking at a much more leisurely pace. It felt strange being alone with him.

"I have four guards with me," he said. "Have you noticed any of them yet?"

"Two," I admitted, wondering why he would ask. "There's a man across the street who was watching you both, and the other was around the corner."

Tandrin nodded. "I thought you might notice them. You're well aware of your surroundings."

"I have to be," I said. "I have to know whether it's safe to approach somebody or not. I wouldn't have gone near you or Tannix; it wouldn't be worth the risk. I'd have been tempted, though. Where are the other two?"

Tandrin shrugged and smiled. "On break. I never said they were with me at the moment." He stopped talking when we reached the Order's gates. He didn't have to say anything to the guards in front of it; they opened it up without question, allowing us, and his two personal guards, to walk in.

As soon as we walked past the gates, I noticed the courtyard. It was filled with chairs, all facing a raised wooden platform across from us, near the main building. There seemed to be twice as many guards as usual, and servants milled about; some carrying drinks, some moving chairs, and some leading lords and ladies. The nobility caught my attention, though I forced myself to not stare at them in awe. They were all dressed up like Tannix and Tandrin were, but there were many different colours—reds, greens, purples, a few other blues. I noticed that no one was wearing gold or yellow, those being the king's colours. Almost everyone we passed wore rings, and the ladies all had elaborate and expensive looking bracelets, necklaces and pins. I was overwhelmed by the concentration of wealth and quickly realized I had to distract myself before I unconsciously reached out to take a lady's jewellery. I turned to Tandrin.

"Tannix has a personal guard too?"

The young lord nodded distractedly. I hadn't noticed, but many of the people we passed were trying to greet him, and he was greeting them in turn. He knew many of their names. "Six of the best men in our army. Father chose them for him when he was ten. There were various tests and competitions they had to go through. It was the same with my guard."

"Why did he leave them behind?"

"There's no place for them at the Order—good afternoon, Lord Laynon— and there are so many guards here already that it seemed unnecessary. But they aren't really a guard so much as an elite fighting group, of which Tannix is a part. He's as much a soldier as they are, whereas I get to be a politician." Tandrin smiled at woman who called his name and stopped walking. "Lady

Tilana, it's a pleasure to see you again." He took her gloved hand and lifted it to his lips, kissing the back of it and causing the lady to giggle.

"Ever the charmer, Lord Tandrin," she said, smiling. "Where is your brother?"

"I'm sure he's somewhere hidden from sight, being told exactly what to do during the ceremony. You'll be able to talk to him afterwards."

"It will hardly do him any good if I wish him luck afterwards," she replied lightly. She pulled her hand away and looked at something over his shoulder. "My husband is calling. I'll have to find Tandrix later." She walked off, the crowd swallowing her up.

"Who was that?" I asked, staring after her. She'd been wearing a silver bracelet with purple crystals of some sort, and I couldn't help but watch her walk away with it.

"Our cousin," Tandrin replied. "Married to one of the lesser lords on New Teltar. Do you bother Tannix with this many questions?"

I hesitated before replying, trying to decide whether he sounded annoyed with me or not. I decided on not. "I probably ask him more."

Tandrin laughed, and we continued our walk through the crowd. The next time he stopped, it was quite sudden. He motioned with his hand and suddenly one of the guards I had noticed earlier was standing at his side. He'd changed, though. He had been wearing a grey cloak in the city, probably to blend in. Now the cloak was gone, showing off a dark blue uniform and a large sword hanging from his belt. I noticed for the first time that Tandrin didn't carry a sword of his own like Tannix always did.

"My lord?"

"Do we know where my father is?" Tandrin asked.

The man was taller than Tandrin, and he used that to his advantage as he looked over the crowd. "I believe he's near the stage. Lord Tandrix isn't with him."

"No, I didn't expect him to be. Thank you." Tandrin changed course, heading through the chair-filled courtyard instead of around it in order to get to his father sooner. I followed him and the guard fell back again.

"So he was chosen for you when you were ten?" I asked.

"Sir Eppson? Yes. He's the captain of my guard, younger son of a lesser lord. That's where they usually come from. They aren't going to inherit so they join the army. I believe Tannix's captain has a similar background."

"Why don't you have a sword?"

"I'm a politician," Tandrin said. "But that is exactly the reason I must find my father. He and I wear ceremonial swords to important events, and he has mine. Father!" He waved his hand to get the attention of a man not far from us.

I hung back, letting Tandrin approach his father without me around. I wasn't sure if their father was supposed to know about me. I could see the similarities in the two men as they greeted each other. Their father was the same height as Tandrin, and had the typical Teltish blond hair streaked with grey. Despite being older, he looked fit and strong, and the sword at his side looked more practical than decorative, more than I'd expected from a ceremonial sword. His clothes were much the same as his sons', with a little more gold embroidery.

As I watched, he took a sword from a nearby guard and handed it to Tandrin. It too looked more useful than I'd have thought. It made sense; they wouldn't bother carrying swords they couldn't use. The weapons were a little fancier than the one Tannix had, the gold hilts and sheaths adorned with blue jewels. I moved a little closer to them, mostly because I wanted to get a better look. Tandrin took the sword and pulled the belt around his waist while saying something to his father. I moved a little closer.

"He'll be fine. He's nervous, but who can blame him? He's been taught to stand at the head of an army and taunt death, not stand in front of a group of lords who just want to praise him." Tandrin grinned. "Maybe I should take his place. I quite enjoy praise."

"I know you do," his father said. His voice was a little gruff, but sounded kind, and he was smiling. "That's a good line, 'taunt death.' I might need to use it in my speech."

"By all means, but give me credit," Tandrin said. "Actually don't. I don't want him knowing I'm jealous."

"He already knows," his father replied, sighing as if the fact was tragic. "I suppose I should go find him and give him some words of encouragement."

He grasped Tandrin's shoulder briefly. "Don't forget your sword next time." He smiled before walking away.

Tandrin watched him go and I walked over to join him. "When you said ceremonial, I thought you meant it would be skinny and shiny." I reached out my hand tentatively, touching the hilt of the sword.

"I *can* fight," Tandrin said. "I've been trained, just not nearly to the same extent as Tannix. So it's ceremonial, but also useful. Just in case. When you're in power, you always have to be a little concerned about someone trying to kill you. Hence my personal guard." He gestured towards the two men, who were still following us but never getting too close.

"So you're concerned while surrounded by all these lords and the other guards?"

Tandrin shrugged. "Formality." His eyes wandered over the crowd and suddenly he started walking again. I caught up quickly, unsure of where we were going. I soon understood when he waved down a servant who was carrying a large tray. On it were a few open bottles of what was probably wine, as well as metal chalices. Tandrin grabbed a chalice and a bottle, which he handed to me. "I've got to have some reason for keeping you near me, and here it is. You're to make sure my glass is never empty."

"So you want to be drunk during your brother's ceremony?"

"I have a little more self-control than that," he said. We returned to the area we had been standing in before. Tandrin glanced over the seats in the front row, looking thoughtful. He picked the one right in the middle of the row, and sat down. "One would think I deserve a better chair than this," he muttered under his breath, but I got the impression he didn't really mind. He held his glass out to me. "Sit down for now, but once the ceremony starts you'll have to move off to the side of the courtyard."

I poured some of the dark red liquid into it before sitting down on the chair beside his. They were nice chairs, and had padding on both the seat and the back. It was something I wasn't used to. The temporary stage was right in front of us. On it there was a row of chairs facing us, where I assumed the people most important to the ceremony would sit. In the centre of the stage stood a wooden podium.

"How many people are going to be speaking?"

Tandrin took a sip of his wine. "Oh, I don't know. Father, the king, the director... What?"

I had flinched involuntarily at the mention of the director, and shook my head, trying to play it off as nothing. Tandrin kept looking at me quizzically.

"Oh, of course. He's the one who tortured you, isn't he? Tannix told me all about it. You know, we're not all like that. I'll admit I never particularly cared about Natives, but I never disliked them. People like Tannix and I just don't think about it much. We're not exposed to you. There aren't many Natives on New Teltar."

"I know that," I mumbled.

"You do?" he sounded surprised.

I sighed. "You and Tannix are always so shocked when I know something. Of course there aren't many Natives on New Teltar. That's where the gods live. Lived. Before you came." I paused for a moment to collect my thoughts and started over. "Before the Telts came the island was called Jandor. We believed that our gods and goddesses lived on it, where they were safe and could watch over us. Then the Telts came and you "discovered" it and called it New Teltar. The gods either left then or were never there in the first place. We don't think you're gods," I added, as if it hadn't already been clarified.

Tandrin nodded slowly. "So you don't think Tannix and I look like gods?"

"No. Well, maybe, but looking like one and being one are not the same thing."

"Of course not," he said. "I find that interesting, though. I knew you were polytheistic, but I didn't know the island had anything to do with it."

"We're what?"

"Polytheistic. You worship more than one god. Some Teltans find it terrible, an insult to the goddess." He shrugged. "I don't know. I find it all fascinating. And who's to say we're the ones who are right?" Tandrin shrugged again, but this time it was more of a nervous gesture. "I could get in trouble for saying that, but I can't help but be curious."

I gazed at him in wonder. "You think like that?"

"I suppose it comes from having Native blood. My mother's mother was a Native. Disregarding your beliefs would mean disregarding hers, which would be disrespecting some of my ancestors."

"You and Tannix are strange," I said after a moment of silence had passed. "You're supposed to hate me because of who I am and you're supposed to think you're better than everyone else in the entire kingdom. You're supposed to show off your wealth and power, and scoff at everyone who has less than you do. But neither of you are like that."

"You're meant to hate Teltans because of who we are. You should be greedy and take everything you see even if you don't need it. You should be sneaky yet unintelligent enough that the guards often catch you. You're supposed to be dangerous and violent when trying to take something. Luckily, you aren't like that."

"Some of us are," I said, thinking of Arow.

"And some of us are corrupt, but not all of us. You were lucky to meet Tannix instead of one of the other young lords."

"I know." I noticed that his glass was almost empty, and reached out my hand to touch his lightly, steadying the chalice. Though I wouldn't normally have touched him, I didn't want to risk spilling wine all over his legs.

"You're much more comfortable around me than I would have expected."

This time I shrugged. "I guess I got used to Tannix, and the two of you are fairly similar."

"I suppose so." He raised the glass to his lips and took a drink, but by the way he was still looking at me, I suspected there was more to it.

IT TOOK SOME TIME FOR ALL OF THE LORDS AND LADIES TO GET SETTLED. Tandrin had slowed down with the wine, and was lazily swirling it around in his glass, taking the occasional sip. Once the seats around us started to fill, he sent me to stand at the edge of crowd. I ended up beside his enormous bodyguard, who cast me a quick glance before his gaze went back to his lord.

It was boring standing there, but I distracted myself by watching the wealthy people around me. Movement on the stage caught my eye, and I looked up to see that people were walking out onto it and taking the chairs. I recognized Tannix's father, and the director, but the others were unknown to me.

The director – Lord Meyat, I reminded myself - moved up to the podium just as a gong was rung somewhere in the courtyard. The lords and ladies fell silent. He looked out at the crowd for a moment before gesturing to the side of the stage. "His Majesty King Edarius III!" he announced with a flourish. The lords and ladies applauded as the king walked onto the stage, flanked by two guards. He had a long gold cloak draped over his shoulders and his crown glinted in the sunlight. I really wanted to touch it.

Even though my suspicions weren't exactly proven, I didn't like seeing the king so close to the director. At least the Order was filled with guards. The kind himself was flanked by guards, and then there were countless personal guards for the lords and ladies, as well as the usual guards for the Order. It didn't seem like anything could possibly happen here.

The king sat down and his guards stood behind his chair. I tore my attention away from them to look at the director, who once again pointed off stage. "Lord Tandrix of West Draulin," he said, with less enthusiasm. The crowd applauded again. Tannix walked out, his eyes roaming across the crowd. He noticed his brother first, then glanced over at me quickly a smiled. He took the last empty seat, between the king and his father. He crossed his arms and looked a little uncomfortable, but he hid it well.

On stage, the director cleared his throat. "I welcome Lord Tandrael West Draulin to speak." He stepped back from the podium and Tannix's father stood.

He paused dramatically, looking over the crowd before starting to speak. "I have always known that my sons would be powerful and respected. Four years ago, I sent Tandrix here so that he could excel. He was already talented back then, an excellent swordsman who could even, on occasion, get the better of me in a duel. I knew that at the Order he would only improve, so it came as no surprise to me when I received his reports.

"As we all know, this Order is one of the oldest organizations in the kingdom. It was created by King Edarius I, our first king, to give the younger sons of his subjects a purpose. In Teltar, sons would often get into fights, even small wars, over who would inherit the family land. King Edarius I solved this problem. In fact, the Order is such a respected organization that many of us older sons are jealous of our brothers. I was certainly jealous of my two younger brothers when they came here, while I had to trail after my father and learn about how to run West Draulin. I know my son Tandrin feels the same."

Tandrin waved dismissively, to both acknowledge his father's words and, I thought, to grab the crowd's attention. There were a few chuckles, likely other lords who also knew the feeling of being jealous of their brothers.

Lord Tandrael smiled. "Yes, it often seems like our brothers come to Zianna to learn the exciting things; how to fight, how to control an army, how to be a spy. There was never any doubt in my mind that Tandrix would go into the army and become a high-ranking official. The recent events have only proved this further. He single-handedly killed two assassins who attacked him while he was on guard. The news shocked and worried me at first, but I realized then that my son is more than capable of protecting himself.

"When he leads armies and taunts death, I will worry for him as a father always will. However, I know that he is prepared for the task at hand, and I will be confident in his ability to achieve victory."

Beside me, Tandrin stood up and cheered. I was surprised, having thought that the elite were more formal. Other men started cheering, and turning around, I saw that a good number of the lords had stood up and were clapping or cheering. It was mostly the younger ones. They settled down when Lord Tandrael motioned at Tannix, who got up to join his father at the podium. Once again, I could see Tannix's gaze dart in my direction. He took a deep breath.

"Father, unless 'on occasion' means 'more often than not,' I believe we are remembering our duels very differently. That said, talent can only get a person so far. Coming to the Order is what taught me how to use my skills, and I owe much of my future to this place and the lords who instructed me over the past four years.

"People often assume that when one is born into power, he will receive high rankings for solely that reason. I am proud to be considered capable. Whatever I achieve in the future, be it captain or general, I have proven that I have the skills needed. My title will not be an empty one. I will serve our kingdom to the best of my abilities, I will serve King Edarius, and I will serve the people of Zianna, be them Native Zian or Teltan."

There were more cheers, instigated once again by Tandrin. More people than last time joined in. I did too. The line about serving the people got to me. Tannix had stared at me as he said it. The people. He was acknowledging that the Natives existed, that we were people of the kingdom.

Tannix stepped aside then because the king had gotten to his feet and approached the podium. The crowd went silent once again. King Edarius placed his hand on Tannix's shoulder.

"Truthfully, one of my favourite duties is that of welcoming young men into the Order. Of course, Lord Tandrix, you have been a valued member for four years now. Valued enough that I, too, have been receiving your progress reports, which is a very rare thing." He smiled at Tannix. "I have been keeping an eye on you since your first year, your instructors noticed your potential. I am pleased now to greet you as a full member of the Order, the group to which I owe so much gratitude for the loyalty they have always shown myself and my ancestors, and their willingness to serve our kingdom. You said it well yourself."

King Edarius paused. He turned slightly so that he was facing Tannix, who did the same. The king took his hand from Tannix's shoulder and held it out towards him. After a brief pause, Tannix took it. The king clasped Tannix's hand with both of his, while Tannix dropped to one knee.

"Lord Tandrix of West Draulin," King Edarius said. "Do you pledge to dedicate your life to the wellbeing of this kingdom, its lands, and its people?"

Tannix nodded solemnly. "I do."

"Do you pledge to live by the Order's tenets: solidarity with your brotherhood, secrecy in the tasks you carry out, and sacrifice should it be necessary?"

"I do."

"Then, in this, the 422nd year since King Edarius I came to this land, I name you as a full member of the Order." The king let go of Tannix's hand. "Within the week, we shall have a position opened for you in the army."

Tannix stood up. "Thank you, Your Majesty."

With those words, the lords and ladies stood up and clapped again. Tandrin got to his feet, climbed onto the stage and pulled a shocked Tannix into a hug. Their father joined them a moment later. When the hug broke up, the other lords who had been sitting on the platform all moved forward to shake Tannix's hand. I realized then that they must be the various teachers he had. The director also approached him for a handshake, and I thought I detected a hint of reluctance in Tannix before they grasped each other's hands.

People were moving around again. Not wanting to be separated from them, and remembering Tannix's order to stay near Tandrin, I got up and moved closer to the stage. Tannix noticed me and waved me over. I looked for the director, but he had moved away and seemed to be talking to a servant girl who was wearing a veil. Reluctantly, I hopped up onto the stage.

"Should I be here?"

"No one is going to notice," he said. "They're all too busy getting ready for the celebration."

"There's going to be a celebration?"

"Of course. Not to mention the meetings that will happen tomorrow, most of which are not related to me, but since the lords and ladies are all in the city anyway, it's the perfect opportunity."

"Oh. What was all that about sacrifice?"

"Solidarity, secrecy, sacrifice," Tannix said, holding up his hand to draw my attention to his Order ring. "It's the Order's motto. Says so on the rin—"

"What did I tell you, little brother?" Tandrin was suddenly there, an arm draped over Tannix's shoulders. "You did wonderfully, and that was a nice little speech. Well done teasing Father like that. Did you know that the 'taunting death' line was mine?"

Tannix eyed his brother. "How much did you give him to drink, Finn?"

I held up the bottle, which was still half full.

"I'm not drunk, Tannix. I'm excited for you," Tandrin said, rolling his eyes. "Try to have some fun sometimes. Now, before this celebration starts, I think I'm going to find a maid and ..."

"I really don't care," Tannix said. "You need to help me with Finn."

"What's going on with Finn?" Tandrin glanced at me.

"We need to get him out of here."

I shrugged. "You two can't just vanish. I don't mind following you around for a little longer."

"Well, all right, but stay close," Tannix said. "Tandrin, go find your maid."

Tandrin grinned. "I can wait, unlike some people." He jerked his head towards the other side of the courtyard. It took me a moment to see what he'd noticed: the director walking with the servant girl. I stared after him suspiciously while Tandrin continued speaking. "Besides, little brother, Lady Tilana was looking for you. I'm sure there are countless other lords and ladies who want to talk to such a hero. You'll need my support."

"Probably," Tannix agreed with a sigh.

"Good. Finn, hand off the wine to one of the servants. I don't need it anymore." Keeping his arm over Tannix's shoulders, Tandrin led him over to the stairs at the edge of the stage. I followed them.

CHAPTER
Twenty-eight

We ended up staying at the celebration for hours. Neither Tannix nor Tandrin could leave long enough to get me out of the Order's walls, and with all the guards around, there wasn't a chance of me risking it by myself. I followed them as they made their way through the crowds, talking to almost every lord and lady we passed. They had casual conversations with the ones they already knew, and lengthy introductions with those they didn't.

I didn't mind following them. It was interesting to hear about the nobility, their names and where they came from. When the servants started carrying around food, I was even more glad to have stayed. Though I couldn't take any from them myself, Tannix often took food that was offered to him and handed it back to me. I'd never seen such fancy foods. There were little pieces of bread with various toppings. There were different types of meat and fancy foreign fruit. Everything was delicious and I more than ate my fill.

By the time I got back into the lower city, Lothian dusk had come and gone, and real night was settling over the city. As I neared our old brothel, I could hear voices. Castin and Stria were sitting outside, talking quietly. They looked up when I passed, and Castin nodded at me, but aside from that, we didn't interact. I walked into the brothel, pulling off my cloak.

"Baisan! I'm back," I called while still in the hallway.

"Thank Zianesa," he said, appearing in the doorway ahead of me. "What happened?"

I shrugged and brushed past him. "Tannix is a full member of the Order. He's going to be joining the army." I tossed my cloak into my corner of the room, and suddenly felt a pang of sadness. If he was going into the army, that meant he'd be leaving Zianna. I had to force myself to ignore the thought, and I turned back to Baisan, reaching into my pocket.

His eyes widened when he saw the little pile in my hand. Three rings, two bracelets, and a pin. I couldn't help myself. "They'll sell well."

Baisan picked up one of the bracelets to inspect it. "I'm going to assume he didn't realize you were doing this?"

"He would've been furious." I took off my belt and knife and dropped them on top of my cloak. "But you should have seen these people. They were so rich, they'll just buy more and not be any poorer for it. But us? If we sell these we'll be able to feed ourselves for months."

Baisan nodded. "They're definitely more useful to us." He took the rest of the jewellery from my hand and slipped it into a pocket. "We'll go out tomorrow and look for customers."

"Check the brothels first."

"Yes, I know." He paused. "Did Kassia find you?"

"What do you mean?"

"Right after you left, she went after you. She wanted to tell you something."

I shrugged. "No." I started to walk over to my corner, and then froze as something occurred to me. It was so obvious I was surprised that I hadn't realized it before. Things fit together in my head: things she had said, things Tannix and I had mentioned around her, the way she'd acted—the girl we'd seen with the director.

"Finn? What's wrong?" Baisan asked warily.

"It's her," I muttered. Then I turned and ran.

GETTING TO TANNIX WOULD BE IMPOSSIBLE. THE ORDER WAS STILL FILLED with the nobility, and there were many more guards than usual. I didn't even know if I could make the climb. My trip over the dividing wall had been hasty, and I'd already wrenched my wrist a bit. I made up my mind quickly.

Guards still patrolled the streets, but it was dark and I was wearing black pants and a black tunic. The cloak had been left behind in my rush, but I realized that was a good thing as I ducked into a shadow, hiding from yet another pair of guards. When their footsteps faded, I carefully looked around the corner. They were far enough down the street that I didn't think they'd notice me. Carefully, I stepped out onto the cobbles and walked up the street.

It was oddly dark, I realized. There were no visible stars; clouds must have covered the whole sky. A warm wind blew down the streets, making me think that a storm might be on its way. Storms were rare, but they happened. Voices broke into my thoughts and I once again slipped into an alleyway. My trip continued like that, running along the street and hiding for a moment before running again. By the time I reached the building, I was exhausted.

I had a good memory for locations. I could tell which window was Tandrin's even though I hadn't seen it from the outside. I glanced around furtively before approaching the wall. Three floors up. I pulled myself up on the first windowsill and grabbed at a brick above my head.

Strong arms suddenly wrapped around my waist and pulled me down. I struggled against them, trying to hit whomever was holding me, to no avail. My hands were roughly bound behind my back and a hand clamped over my mouth and there was nothing I could do about it. My wrist ached furiously.

"Tiny for an assassin," a voice muttered.

"They usually are. Brute force isn't an assassin trait," the man holding me replied. I realized that I recognized the voice.

I jerked my head to the side quickly, dislodging the hand. "Eppson," I yelped. "Your name's Eppson."

He turned me around sharply, but didn't let go of me. He seemed bigger than he had earlier in the day. His grip so strong that his hand might as well been a metal cuff. I almost felt like I was shrinking under his gaze. "How do you know that?"

"L… Lord Tandrin told me," I stammered. "I was the servant with him today, you saw me. Please, sir, I need to speak with him."

"Why is a servant trying to sneak in?"

My mind raced but I couldn't think of a good reason. "I'm not a servant," I said. "But please let me talk to him. He knows who I am, and he'll want to see me. Please."

Sir Eppson stared at me for longer than I thought we could spare, but there was nothing I could do about it and I stood still. Finally, he nodded at the other guard. Without saying anything, Sir Eppson dragged me to the stairs leading up to the door. We walked in and up the staircase I'd found so pretty last time. There was a slight glow from the multiple candles, which were burning along the halls. I hardly noticed them, distracted by worry and the pain in my wrist.

There was another guard standing outside Tandrin's door, and I couldn't help but flinch when he looked me over. "What's this?"

"He wants to talk to Tandrin," Sir Eppson said, giving me a shake. "Says he knows him and I think I recognize him from the ceremony. But we'll see what our lord says."

The door guard hesitated. He opened Tandrin's door and walked in, while Sir Eppson, the other guard, and I waited outside. Irrationally, I started wondering what the guards would do to me if Tandrin said he didn't know who I was.

I needn't have worried; Tandrin appeared in the doorway a moment later, looking tired but fairly alert. "What are you doing, Eppson? Let him go. What's going on, Finn?"

"I need to talk to Tannix," I told him, while the huge guard untied my wrists. "But I couldn't get to him so I came here." Once free, I rubbed my right wrist gently, hoping the pain would fade.

"And it can't wait?"

"No."

Tandrin nodded at the guard who had been outside with us. "Go get my brother. Tell him to be quick, Finn…" He cut himself off and glanced at me.

"Baisan. I've used the name before. He'll understand."

"Tell him that Baisan is here," Tandrin told the guard, who immediately jogged off. Tandrin gently pulled me into the room and closed the door, leaving his other guards outside. "Are you going to tell me what's going on?"

"Do you know about the letter?" I asked cautiously.

"What letter?"

After a moment of internal debate, I decided to tell him. I explained everything that had happened since I had first found the letter. Some of it Tannix had already told him, but with less detail. He was particularly surprised when I told him that I had killed one of the two assassins. I explained my theory about the director, and finally my thoughts about Kassia.

Tannix's timing was perfect. He burst in right at that moment, but froze when he saw me. I was startled by his appearance. He looked like he'd run the whole way from the Order, and he wasn't wearing his usual cloak or his sword. On top of that, he looked panicked, and it scared me a little.

I suddenly found myself wrapped in arms again, but this time it was a hug. I was confused but once again there was nothing I could do about it. He might not have been as strong as Sir Eppson, but he was still stronger than me. I could feel his heart racing.

"Tannix, what's wrong?"

He broke our hug but didn't let me go, holding me at arms' length. "Why did you do that to me?"

"Do what?" I asked, so confused that I couldn't even begin to understand what he was talking about.

"Say it was Baisan. Why would Baisan need to see me urgently? I thought he was going to tell me that you hadn't made it home. Or that you'd been arrested. Or hurt somehow. Or killed."

"Sorry," I said, still puzzled. "But why would Baisan come to Tandrin?"

"Maybe you told him to. I don't know, Finn! I wasn't thinking rationally!" He let go of me and ran a hand through his hair. He took a couple slow breaths. "What is so urgent?"

"Kassia," I said. "Kassia's the assassin."

"What?"

"Well…" Faced with him, I started second-guessing myself. "Think about it. She was around a lot when we were talking about the whole thing, and she was interested in it. She even said she believed me when I said the director was the associate."

"We don't know if that's even true."

"Just assume it is for a moment. When I got back, Baisan told me that Kassia had followed me earlier. But I never saw her. She's gone to him."

"If it was her, why wouldn't she have gone to him earlier?" Tannix asked.

"Because she never got the letter," I said. "She knew where she was supposed to go but she didn't know who she was supposed to go to. Then she heard us talking about the letter and she must have realized that we would figure something out." Tannix still looked doubtful, so I pulled out the last of my evidence. "I didn't realize it at first because I wasn't paying attention, but we saw the director with a girl earlier. It was her." I gave him a moment to think about it, and I could tell when he finally believed me.

"We need to go talk to him." The calm and powerful Tannix I was used to came back instantly. "Finn and Eppson, with me. Cail, your sword." The door guard handed his sword over wordlessly. Tannix took it and started turning his wrist, testing the weight of the weapon.

"I'm coming too," Tandrin said.

"No, you're not."

"You can hardly stop me," Tandrin said. He'd picked up his ceremonial sword and was attaching it to his belt. "When you need a speaker, you'll be glad I'm with you. Just because I never killed an assassin—one, mind you... Finn told me the truth—doesn't mean I can't use a sword." He strode past his brother towards the door. "Shall we?"

Tannix muttered something under his breath. While slipping his sword under his belt, he followed his brother. "You'll do what I tell you."

"Of course, little brother."

Tannix waved at Sir Eppson and me. We both started following him, though the knight kept back a bit and I made sure to keep pace with Tannix. He walked quickly, keeping his left hand on the sword pommel to steady it. Without a sheath, he could probably hurt himself by accident.

"What're we going to do?" I asked.

"Figure out what's going on," he said. "If I have to arrest the director, I will. I have the authority now."

It was different walking through the streets with Tannix and Tandrin. I didn't have to hide from any of the guards, though multiple times I almost tried to instinctively. I stayed up beside him the whole time. Tandrin was just behind us, and Sir Eppson was behind him, where he could keep an eye on all of us. I was grateful for his presence, though my wrist still ached from when he grabbed me.

Tandrin's building was not far from the Order. When we reached the gate, it was opened instantly. The guards were clearly confused, but they weren't about to argue with both of the young West Draulin lords.

Within the walls, things looked different. Already the chairs and the temporary stage had been removed, leaving the courtyard empty. There were only a few people still out, mostly guards or servants. We ignored them and they ignored us. We entered the main building through the front doors, something I hadn't done in four years. It looked the same as it had then, the black stone just as shiny and strange.

We went up a staircase I had never used before. I thought I remembered the director's office being on the fifth floor, and I was right. One staircase led to a hallway, which led to another staircase. We walked down a plain, thin hallway, and then Tannix stopped in front of a large wooden door.

He looked at me. "Don't speak to him."

I nodded. Talking to the director was not something I ever wanted to do again.

Tannix took a deep breath. "I can't decide whether I hope you're right so that this won't be a huge embarrassment, or if I hope you're wrong." His grip on the sword tightened, and he pushed open the door.

CHAPTER
Twenty-nine

The director was sitting at his desk. He looked up at us as we walked in, putting down the piece of paper he was reading. A candelabra stood beside him with five flickering candles, but besides that there was no light in the room. A slight breeze came through the open window, causing the flames to jump and make odd shadows on the walls.

"Lord Tandrix," he said calmly. He slipped the paper into a drawer, then interlocked his fingers and rested his arms on the desk. "And Lord Tandrin. To what do I owe the pleasure?" He looked at me then, and his eyes narrowed. "Did you arrest him again?"

"No." Tannix approached the desk. He put down his right hand and leaned on it, his left still clenched around the sword handle. I hung back with Tandrin and Sir Eppson, who had closed the door behind us and stood facing it as if an enemy was about to burst in.

"In fact," Tannix said, "he brought something to my attention regarding a letter. Tell me, my lord, why would you torture him for information you already had?"

The director shook his head slowly. "I'm afraid I have no idea what you are talking about, Tandrix."

The tension in the room jumped up a notch at that. Even I knew that dropping Tannix's title without permission was extremely offensive. Tannix's reply was calm and steady. "You're denying knowledge about the letter?"

The director ignored him and looked at me. "You told me that Lord Tandrix had nothing to do with this. I can't say that I'm surprised that you lied to me, but it's quite a shock to find that the lords of West Draulin are out to kill the king."

"They're not," I said, forgetting my promise to Tannix in my desire to defend him. "You are."

The director laughed. "You believe that *I'm* part of this? No doubt they helped you escape so that you could carry out your plans. I knew there was something suspicious about you getting out."

Tannix slapped his palm on the table, drawing the director's attention. "Whether you are involved or not, you know something about the plot. Tell me. I have the authority to follow up on it myself, and I fully intend to."

While the director was distracted by Tannix, I approached them. I was curious about the paper he had hidden from us.

"Had you found the letter, you could claim rights to information regarding it," the director replied. "As it is, you cannot."

I crept around the side of the desk. The director must have noticed me, but not realized yet what I was trying to do. He didn't react until I reached for the drawer. I grabbed the handle and suddenly he lunged at me.

It happened too quickly for me to follow. One moment he was coming at me with a knife and I was sure he was going to stab me and that would be the end of it. The next, Tannix had vaulted across the desk and jumped right into him, slamming him against the wall. Tannix drew his sword, and with his left hand tightly held the front of the director's tunic.

"Carry on, Finn."

I hesitated, eyeing the director warily in case he tried to get around Tannix and attack me again. Out of the corner of my eye, I saw that Tandrin and Sir Eppson had also pulled out their swords, and I decided I was safe. I reached for the drawer once more, ignoring the furious look from the director, and pulled out the first few pieces of paper.

The one on top was the letter. I recognized the wax seal. The second piece was a diagram. At first, I was confused, but then I turned it to the side and recognized it with a gasp. Tandrin, who had walked up behind me to look over my shoulder, figured it out at the same time.

"It's a drawing of the castle. That's the king's chamber." He pointed to a room with a splat of red ink on it.

I noticed then that the ink near where I was holding the diagram was smudged. The tips of both my thumbs were black. "It's still wet," I said. "Tannix? If he drew this for Kassia, she must have just left."

"He's right," Tandrin said, taking the paper from my hands. "Odd that he'd mark the king's chamber. He has hours of meetings to go through tonight, and he'll be in the throne room for most of it." He looked up from the paper, across the room.

"So we alert the guard," Tannix said, meeting his gaze. He pulled the director from the wall. "I place you under arrest, Lord Meyat. Sir Eppson, escort him to prison. Tandrin and Finn, come with me."

Everyone started moving, but I stood still, staring at the open window. Sir Eppson collected the director, and Tannix and Tandrin headed towards the door. I walked towards the window, not exactly sure why the idea had come to me. By the time Tannix noticed me, I was already crouched on the windowsill, one hand still inside, steadying myself.

"Finn, no."

I turned my head, glancing back into the office. "I can catch up with her."

"No."

"I know her. Maybe I can stop her."

"No, Finagale." He started towards the window, probably intent on grabbing me, and I pulled myself off the windowsill. He wouldn't come after me, there wasn't time. I climbed quickly, ignoring him when he yelled my name a few times. The wind had picked up, blowing my hair into my eyes. I was glad I didn't have the cloak. It would have been billowing out behind me like a flag, potentially pulling me from the wall.

When I dropped to the ground, I knew that Tannix had given up on calling after me, and instead went for the guards. Honestly, I doubted I could stop Kassia, but I hoped to at least to delay her. I had a better chance of catching up than Tannix and the guards did. I got to my feet and ran around the building.

I'd never paid attention to how close the Order was to the castle. Part of its wall joined up with the one protecting the castle. Kassia would have gone that way. There would probably be less security, since an enemy was not likely to try to go through the Order.

The section of wall I ran to was taller than rest by about a storey. I rotated my right wrist while planning a route. The ache was getting worse, running along almost my entire forearm. I could make the wall, I was sure of that, but if I had to do much climbing afterwards, I ran the risk of my arm giving out. I wasn't scared of heights, I never had been, but falling was a different story altogether.

Planning my path only took a few seconds. I rolled my shoulders and started up, using my left arm almost exclusively and again trying to use my right only to balance myself. Sometimes it wasn't avoidable, and I had to put weight on it. I made the wall in good time, all things considered, and crouched on top to plan out the next part.

I had never seen the castle grounds before. They looked larger than I had imagined. The Cliffs of Loth loomed to my right, and the wall curved away from the stone before joining the southern wall. In front of me was a wide green yard, dotted with trees and flowerbeds. The colour green was rare in Zianna because the city was so dense that there was almost no room for things to grow. It looked strange to me. A portion of the field was fenced off, and through the darkness, I could see large shapes that could only be horses. Next to that was a wooden barn. A wide paved road led from it to a large gate to my right, which was flanked by two guardhouses. In the middle stood the castle.

It was tall and looked to be made of the same odd black stone as the buildings in the Order. It had quite a few turrets, but the two front ones were the tallest and were topped by pointed roofs. I knew there would be guards along the tops of the turrets and battlements, as well as by every door. I could see two entrances from where I was, one main one blocked by a large portcullis, and a smaller one blocked only by a gate. I knew that was my best chance, and it would be Kassia's as well.

Aside from near the gates, the grounds themselves looked deserted. I began to climb down the wall, confident that in the darkness no one would see me. As I climbed, I considered my options. Running across the grass wouldn't be hard, and it was unlikely that anyone would notice me. There really was no other option.

When I got close enough, I hopped off the wall, landing lightly on my feet just as thunder boomed overhead. I flinched, taken off guard by its loudness. Rain was uncommon in Zianna, thunderstorms even more so. I took off running across the field, grateful that I no longer had to use my right hand for anything.

I made sure not to go anywhere near the smaller gate, and so reached the castle along the walls. I pressed myself against it and closed my eyes, catching my breath. I waited before moving on, making sure that I hadn't been seen. There was nothing—no sounds of men calling to each other or alarms being rung. By the time my heart rate had slowed, I felt as safe as a thief could be in the castle grounds.

I walked along the wall, letting one hand run against the stone to prevent myself from straying too far away from it. The closer I was to the wall, the harder it would be to see me from above. A guard would actually have to lean over to look down at me, which was unlikely. As I neared the door, I slowed down, suddenly realizing that I had no way of getting through the gate if there were guards in the way. Oddly, it hadn't occurred to me before; I'd been too concentrated on actually making it to the castle.

When I saw the dip in the wall ahead of me that indicated the gateway, I stopped walking and crouched. I watched the door for as long as I thought I could, but nothing happened. I couldn't see any movement or hear the sounds of anyone shuffling around. Cautiously, I moved forward, keeping low to the ground. When I got right up to the edge, I peeked around the corner.

The gate was almost close enough to reach, but there was no guard standing in front of it. Looking down the tunnel, I could see no guards behind the gate, only a few dark piles that looked like bags of some sort. I stood up straighter and walked closer, still being cautious. I had been expecting to pick the lock, but upon closer inspection, I realized that the gate wasn't locked. It had been, but now it hung open, as if someone had pushed it closed a little too gently and it hadn't quite caught.

I slowly pushed on it and as soon as there was room for me, I squeezed through. The only way to explain the gate was if Kassia had already been through before me. The tunnel was almost pitch black. I could see light up ahead of me, and some faint light shone in front outside, but it was only getting darker outside. I was nearing the bags when my eyes adjusted. I gasped and took a step back.

Bags didn't wear the black and gold uniforms of the city guards. They didn't have arms or legs. I closed my eyes and touched the wall with my left hand, taking a moment to steady my nerves. Despite where I lived, despite the risks involved with my life, I rarely came across death.

I started to panic. If Kassia had done this, and there was no reason to think otherwise, then I didn't know if she'd listen to me. Why would she? If everything she'd told me had been a lie, it was just as likely that the feelings she'd been showing for me were too.

I opened my eyes. I couldn't explain why, but I felt the need to see this through. I found the letter and, although inadvertently, it was my fault Kassia knew who she was supposed to speak to. If the king was killed, I would blame myself. I stood there just a little longer, collecting myself, and then took a deep breath and walked past the two bodies.

The tunnel opened into a little courtyard. I thought back to the diagram Tandrin had taken from me, and could almost see it in my head perfectly. The king's chamber had been a few floors up, but the throne room, if I was thinking of the right place, was on the main floor, close to where I was.

Seeing that there was no one around, I stepped out into the little courtyard and ran across it to the next doorway. The corridor ahead was dark, but I walked in without hesitation. On my way towards the throne room, I had to take multiple corridors. A few times, I had to duck into a side passage to hide from some guards, but it was much easier than I would have expected to get through the castle.

Then I saw the doorway that led into the throne room. It was large and wooden, with two guards standing on either side of it. I hung back in the shadows while I tried to figure out my next obstacle. The doorway was at the end of a large atrium. There were a few other guards scattered around, most of them talking quietly amongst themselves. The two at the door were perfectly still, as if they had been carved from stone.

Many corridors opened into the atrium. There were a few servants walking around, carrying trays or large baskets. The guards paid them no attention. The servants, I realized, were all woman, some young, and some old. Some of them were Natives but most of them were Telts. Without meaning to, I thought back to when Ninavi had told Tannix to dress me as a woman. It might be possible to put on a disguise, if I had time.

I didn't have long to contemplate it because a line of servants walked by, distracting me. They were each carrying trays of food, and they walked in an orderly line towards the doors. One of the guards grabbed a handle and pulled his half of the double doors open. I got a glimpse of a long table covered with a red cloth, and many men and women sitting around it. I looked back to the servants, and there she was.

I had to do a double take, looking back at the servant, making sure I was right. She was in the middle of the line, by then walking into the throne room with her back to me. She was wearing the same simple white dress as the rest of the servants, but I recognized the hair. It was her.

Without giving myself a chance to change my mind, I ran towards the door. My eyes locked on Kassia. I heard guards shout but they sounded strange and distant. The line of servants turned around towards the noise, and she looked at me. Her eyes widened in disbelief. One of the door guards tried to grab me and I dove at the floor, rolling under his arms before gracefully getting back to my feet. I threw myself at Kassia, knocking the tray from her hand and sending us both crashing into the floor.

CHAPTER
Thirty

Guards pulled me off her almost instantly. I'd been expecting that. Two of them grabbed me, each holding an arm tightly. Kassia, on the other hand, was gently helped to her feet. I was pleased to see that the guard kept a grip on her arm. She dusted off her dress and looked at me, her eyes so full of anger that I almost thought I'd drop dead just from looking at them like in some old legend.

Everyone in the room was standing. Some chairs had even been knocked over in the nobles' haste to get to their feet. The king, at the far end of the table, looked particularly confused. He left his space and walked around the table towards us, the clicking of his boots on the stone floor the only sound in the room. He ignored Kassia, instead coming to a stop in front of me.

I was so overwhelmed, it wasn't until one of my guards pushed my head down that I even remembered that one was supposed to bow in the king's presence. I ended up staring at his boots, which I noticed were shiny and likely very expensive.

"What is the meaning of this?" he asked. His voice boomed out in the almost perfect silence, causing me to flinch.

I hesitated, then steadily, without looking up at him, replied, "The girl is an assassin."

"This girl?" he asked. It didn't sound like he believed me, but at the same time he seemed a little wary. He couldn't risk not believing me. He walked away, and only then did I raise my head. He was standing in front of Kassia. The guard beside her let go of her arm and took a step back. "Who are you?" the king asked.

Kassia stared at the ground. Her hands were clasped and she was wringing a bit of her dress between them. She started to murmur out a reply.

"Louder, girl," he ordered.

Kassia gulped and looked close to tears. "M-my name is Kianna. I've been working in the castle as a maid for as long as I can remember." Her voice was still quiet and tiny. She didn't look anywhere but the floor at her feet, and her hands kept fiddling with the bit of dress. I would have believed her if I didn't know her.

"She's lying," I said.

King Edarius spun around and the guard on my left twisted my arm back painfully. I bit my lip and ducked my head again, not wanting to make things worse by looking at the king. He had just begun to approach me when the door behind us was flung open. Startled, I looked towards the door just as everyone else did.

Tannix didn't look at me, and I didn't expect him to. I didn't know if I'd ever been happier to see him. He walked into the room calmly, Tandrin and about a dozen guards behind him. "Your majesty, there's an assassin in the castle."

The king showed no reaction to Tannix's news. "We've already caught him."

"Him?" Tannix glanced at me, emotionless. "We're looking for a woman. A girl, really."

I couldn't help myself. "She's right..." But then I stopped, because she was gone.

Everyone turned to look at where Kassia had been standing. The guard there looked sheepish. "You're majesty, I..."

"Silence," the king ordered. He reached up, rubbing his beard with his hand. "Lord Tandrix, what is going on?"

Motion across the room caught my eye. Behind a pillar, I saw the swish of a white dress. I wrenched myself from the guards' hands, taking them by surprise with the suddenness of my movement. They yelled at me—everyone was yelling—but I ignored them all as I bolted across the room. Kassia had already started climbing up a bookshelf. She was heading for one of the tiny windows up near the ceiling. Guards and lords tried to grab me. Luckily, I was fast, and they were all shocked enough that no one really got close to me.

The bookshelf was as easy to climb as a ladder. My wrist started aching again, but I pushed it to the back on my mind and concentrated on speed. The wall above the bookshelf was smooth, and I was forced to slow down. So was Kassia, though she was almost all the way up the wall by then. She slipped through the window well ahead of me and I tried to quicken my pace. There were a few large paintings hanging up, and their frames were wide and thick. Usually I wouldn't risk it, seeing as they were attached to the wall by only a few nails and could easily fall under my weight. This time, without thinking about it, I grabbed a picture frame.

Suddenly an arrow thudded into the painting next to my left hand. I almost recoiled, only just managing to stop myself. I risked a quick glance down. People were moving around the room, confused at what they should be doing. Tandrin was talking to the king. There was one archer over by the door, and Tannix was holding the top of the bow. I realized that he must have grabbed it just in time to make the archer miss. Once again, I owed him my life. He looked up briefly, meeting my gaze, and nodded.

Understanding his meaning, I turned back to the wall and climbed up the last little bit. I easily fit through the window. The storm had finally broken, and the rain was so heavy it soaked me instantly. Kassia hadn't gained much distance. Through the pounding rain, I could see her drop over the edge of the roof. I pulled myself up quickly, running after her. When I reached the edge, I could see her again. She was heading back down, jumping from one bit of roof to the next, getting lower and lower with each hop. I went after her. Everything was slippery and wet, and I quickly prayed to Zianesa that I wouldn't fall and break my neck.

I didn't get any closer to Kassia, but neither did I fall behind. We finally reached the ground floor in one of the passages that would eventually lead around to the main courtyard. I lost sight of her when she turned a corner up ahead of me. A moment later, I reached the corner myself, and expected to see her still running up ahead. She wasn't there and I was brought to a sudden stop. Confused, I glanced around, trying to figure out where she could have gone. The rain wasn't helping anything. I reached up to brush my soaked hair away from my face, and just at that moment, I felt hands tug me to the side.

She had me up against the wall with a knife at my neck before I understood what was happening. I silently cursed at myself for falling into her trap. Briefly, I considered trying to fight back, but she touched the knife to my skin and changed my mind.

"Finn," she cooed gently. "Don't even think about it." Her voice sounded slightly different, and I suddenly understood that she'd been putting on a Native accent before. A good one. The memory of her speaking Deoran the day we'd nearly been caught stealing flashed through my mind.

"Why?" I wasn't asking about her words, and she understood.

"I was hired," she said. With her free hand, she reached up to stroke my cheek. "I never meant to get caught up with you, but I was acquainting myself with your lovely city when I saw that man attacking Castin, and I'm not out to let little boys get hurt." She smiled briefly, and her hand drifted up to my hair. "I *do* like you, but unfortunately I have to run, and I don't think you can keep up. At least this works out in my interest. The guards already think you're involved, so now they might just forget about me."

She leaned forward suddenly and our lips met. Taken by surprise, I didn't know how to react. She shifted to wrap her right arm around my neck, and she lay the flat side of her knife's blade against my cheek, probably to remind me that it was there. It wasn't until I heard a quiet click that I knew what she had done.

I jerked away from her and met her gaze. Without looking down, I gave my right wrist an experimental tug, but the cuff she had placed around it felt strong and my wrist was already sore. I panicked, but tried my best not to show it and glanced down at my arm. The cuff was attached by a short chain to a ring in the wall.

"Shh, Finn." Kassia's hand cupped my chin and she moved my head so that I had to look at her. She almost looked like she regretted what she'd just done. "They'll arrest you, but I'll get away." We both flinched suddenly when something clattered against the wall near us. In unison, we looked towards the sound to see an arrow falling to the ground.

Kassia's eyes widened and she looked quickly in the direction the arrow had come from. She met my gaze again before turning and running. My left hand flew to the cuff around my wrist. I tried to slip it over my hand, but it wouldn't go. In vain, I kept trying, desperately hoping that if I could just move my thumb in the right way, the cuff would come off.

Tannix's arrival startled me. He was holding a bow in one hand and had a quiver hastily slung over one shoulder. He glanced at me, then up the passage, obviously contemplating chasing after Kassia. Then he looked back at me and he noticed the cuff.

"You missed," I said dryly.

He shouldered the bow and walked over to me. "I'm not an archer. Stop that." He gently pushed my left hand away from the cuff. His eyes followed the chain back to the wall. Without explanation, he pulled out his dagger and stuck the blade into one of the chain links. He sharply jerked the dagger to the side and the link snapped, freeing me from the wall.

I wanted to go after Kassia, so I started forward, only to be stopped when Tannix grabbed the front of my tunic and pushed me up against the wall again. I understood why a moment later, when we heard footsteps running along the battlement above us. We were perfectly still for a moment, letting the wall hide us from sight, until the footsteps disappeared into the rain. When I believed they were gone, I tried to move, expecting Tannix to let go of me as I did. Instead, he only tightened his grip on my tunic and pulled me closer.

I hadn't been expecting his kiss any more than I had the one from Kassia, but this time I responded. The whole situation flew from my mind as suddenly feelings and thoughts from the past weeks made sense. I understood why I had wanted to see him so often. I understood why, despite me never making good friends, I'd felt so close to him. It all came together. It felt like both forever and hardly a second before Tannix broke away from the kiss and his grip on my tunic loosened.

"Tannix…"

"Lord Tandrix!" The call came from down the passage, and we both turned to look for the speaker. A small group of guards had just turned a corner and could see us clearly. Tannix let go of me, but it was too late by then. They'd seen me and it would reflect badly on him if he let me go.

"Tannix, arrest me."

He tore his gaze from the approaching guards to look at me. "I… I can't. Not again."

"You have to." My mind was racing, trying to come up with a plan. Any other plan, but nothing came to me. "I can survive prison, I did last time. The only way I'll get out is with your help, and you can't help me if you lose credibility for letting me go in the first place." At this point, the guards were close enough that I wouldn't be able to get away from them either way.

Tannix sighed, frustrated. "I'll get you out," he said.

I nodded, hoping I didn't look as terrified as I felt.

He gripped my tunic again, but this time he used it to pull me away from the wall. The other guards reached us then and one of them pulled me away from him. My hands were held behind my back while someone roughly tied them together.

"Well done, my lord." The captain of the unit bowed his head slightly in respect to Tannix.

"Thank you," Tannix replied coolly.

"The king would like to speak to you," the captain said. "We'll allow you to inform him that the assassin has been caught."

"Thank you," Tannix repeated. He didn't correct the captain. I hoped he'd be able to explain everything to the king. He brushed past the captain to approach me. "I'm allowed to take a prize, am I not?"

"Of course, my lord. He is your prisoner."

Tannix reached up to my neck. He slipped a finger under my chain, pulling it out from beneath my tunic. The Order ring was still hanging on it, but he clasped his hand around it before any of the other guards could see, and he slipped the chain over my head.

"I doubt he has anything else of value," Tannix said, his voice laced with contempt. "He is just a common thief, after all. I'm done with him."

The guard holding me started to pull me away, but a wave from the captain stopped him. "My lord, are you not going to tell him his sentence?"

Of course, I hadn't expected a trial. They thought I was in on the attempt; there was only one punishment for treason.

Tannix turned back to me. "You'll be imprisoned for a year and a day," he told me sharply. He then paused, which probably looked dramatic to the others, but I understood that he was struggling with the thought himself. "And then you'll be executed."